TOTAL IMMERSION

"ONIONSKIN": After a decade of asking questions of rabbis, missionaries, professors, and lovers, Sharon suddenly walks out of a class on Augustine in Honolulu, cleans out her checking account, and heads for the hills of Jerusalem. . . .

"VARIANT TEXT": Cecil Birnbaum studies Shaw and doesn't believe in God. But Cecil insists on praying only in the most traditional manner—and on wearing an Abortion Rights button to synagogue. . . .

"FAIT' ": Ginnie's sister is getting married. Ginnie's Berkeley boyfriend (he woke up only to watch the bloody parts of *Ran*) is coming for a visit. And Ginnie keeps hearing the sound of a drowning person. . . .

"TOTAL IMMERSION": Caroline wears diamonds and can't hide her New England accent. Alan is learning not to wear a suit to work. And Sandra wants only to teach her students French. Bound by the Jewish heritage they share, they're all making a new start in Hawaii. . . .

And 7 Other Superb Stories

Total Immersion

Allegra Goodman

DELTA
Trade Paperbacks

A Delta Book
Published by
Dell Publishing
a division of
Bantam Doubleday Dell Publishing Group, Inc.
1540 Broadway
New York, New York 10036

The author gratefully acknowledges The New Yorker, where "Onionskin" and "The Closet" first appeared, and Commentary, where "Variant Text," "Wish List," "Young People," "The Succession," and "Total Immersion" first appeared.

Library of Congress Cataloging in Publication Data
Goodman, Allegra.
    Total immersion / Allegra Goodman.
      p.   cm.
    ISBN: 0-385-33299-8
    Contents: Onionskin — Variant text — Young people
Wish list — The succession — Retrospective — And also much cattle
Further ceremony — Fait' — Total immersion — The closet.
    I. Title.
PS3557.05829T68   1998
813'.54—dc21   97-53050
                                                                CIP

Reprinted by arrangement with the author.

Book design by Ellen Cipriano

Manufactured in the United States of America
Published simultaneously in Canada

September 1998

10   9   8   7   6   5   4   3   2

BVG

To my parents,
Lenn and Madeleine Goodman,
and my sister,
Paula

Contents

1. Onionskin 1

2. Variant Text 20

3. Young People 52

4. Wish List 79

5. The Succession 117

6. Retrospective 143

7. And Also Much Cattle 161

8. Further Ceremony 196

9. Fait' 220

10. Total Immersion 238

11. The Closet 269

Onionskin

Dr. Friedell,

This is to apologize if I offended you in class a few weeks ago, though I realize you probably forgot the whole thing by now. I was the one who stood up and said "Fuck Augustine." What I meant was I didn't take the class to read him, I took it to learn about religion—God, prayer, ritual, the Madonna mother-goddess figure, forgiveness, miracles, sin, abortion, death, the big moral concepts. Because obviously I am not eighteen and I work, so school is not an academic exercise for me, and not just me, as I'm sure you'd realize if you looked around the room one of these days and saw there are thirty- and forty-year-olds and some a lot older than you are in the class—the point is, when you've been through marriage, kids, jobs, welfare, and the whole gamut and you come back to school you're ready for the real thing, and as far as I'm concerned Augustine's Conception of the Soul or whatever is not it. What is "it"? you're asking—well, that's what I came to find out, so you tell me. Obviously what you are paid for is to deal with the big religious issues and you are not dealing with them, which is what I was trying to point out when I made that remark in class, which I apologize for tone-wise but not for my feelings behind it.

My feelings still are that basically as a "mature student" I was supposed to feel grateful that the University of Hawaii let me in or gave me a second chance on life or whatever, like I am the lowly unwashed and I should come in the gates to be blessed by the big phallus. Or I am a housewife coming "back" to "school" driving my white Isuzu and eating my curds and whey. Look, I didn't come to salivate at your office door. You like to make distinctions, so you should make distinctions between you the employee and me the customer. You're the guy behind the counter.

Can I take a guess at what you're thinking?— "Another crazed woman in my class anti the educational system." But I'm not, I'm putting everything I've got on the line for religion.

Because the thing is that after I walked out on your class I sat down by the sausage trees near Moore Hall and I started watching the undergrads walking by in their Bermuda shorts going to lunch without a thought in their heads. I felt bad because for some reason I sort of believed in the universe part of university, that it was all about Life and Time and God, and Freedom, and when I got back in it was just so male and linear and there wasn't any magic in the religion classes, it was all a construct—

the angels were symbols and the miracles were just things in nature. So I got up and took all my books to the bookstore and sold them back (for less than half what I paid for them) and I went home—a room in a termite palace. As I was saying before, I felt really bad because I think you might have the wrong idea about me—you probably don't know how into school I really was. I originally dropped out of Simmons in 1974 for a lot of reasons, my father died for one thing, but basically because I didn't see myself in school at that time in my life. The only thing I could really see myself doing was folk dancing—I was in the original core Israeli folk-dancing group at MIT, which you probably have never even heard of, but it's actually nationally famous—it's almost like the model for all the other clubs in the country. I spent those "college" years living in Brighton and dancing. When I say dancing I'm talking about a way of life—I knew over two hundred dances and I also did Balkan. We would get over to MIT and dance straight from 8:30 to 11 P.M., steaming into Walker Gym straight from the snow to sweat like you would not believe. We stripped down every night from coats, sweaters, and boots to tank tops, gauze skirts, bare feet, and cutoffs, and when we left we were so hot we carried our parkas under our arms. I actually knew a lot of the key people in the folk scene and performed in New York at some of the big festivals. So that was kind of my "school-ing." I was a secretary—actually for two years I temped, we were all menial slaves in the folk club, with a few graduate students and programmers sprinkled in. At the time I was in a relationship with one of them, which is how I ended up going to Hawaii—he had an upgrade deal. After a week he freaked out and took off for Fiji, and I was stranded at a fleabag joint in Waikiki with about twenty-two dollars to my name and the room bill.

When he took off I sold my return ticket and got a job busing tables at Zippy's, then I worked in the kitchen doing prep, then I worked in the find-a-pearl oyster stand in the International Marketplace, then I sold gold electroplated cockroaches when they were in, then I sold paraphernalia and sex toys in back where Oriental Imports used to be, behind The Stop Light and the bikini store on King Street, then after that place folded I got a job in Crack Seed World, then I landed a job in luggage at Shirokya, worked at Longs Drugs checkout, and did inventory at The Good Earth. I was thinking about going back to Boston. Thinking a lot, Dr. Friedell—it was happening at an underground level. I realize you aren't interested in what kind of thinking a student who walks out of Augustine is experiencing, because you can't think about anything that hasn't been totally hashed out already by geniuses—that's the impression you give me anyway, all that stuff about us living on the last mushroom of the dunghill of Romanticism and standing on the shoulders of giants, and all you can do when you go back to school is learn how to use the library and document everything. Why do they make such a big deal about plagiarism if it's all been said already? Not that I think you're actually reading this, since it's written on onionskin in ball-point when you only accept typed stuff.

While I was working those different jobs I

taught folk dancing at Kaimuki Y (once) and the temple (five x). I went to a Hebrew class at the temple because I was teaching all these dances to Israeli music and I didn't know Hebrew, but every time we would get past the alphabet some new guy or some kid would come into the class and we had to learn the alphabet again, so I never got beyond the letters. A total joke. Rabbi Siegel up at the temple used to go on these digressions, so obviously we never got anywhere, and finally after class I went up and said, "Rabbi, aren't we all just wasting time in here?"

He looks at me under the fluorescent lights in the Learning Center, which is all white linoleum and woodgrain tables and green plastic chairs, and nailed up on the walls all the Old World stuff, those ticky-tacky pictures of the bearded men. Rabbi Siegel faces me in his suit with his silver tie pin. "Sharon," he says, "I'm sorry you feel that way."

"I want to learn Hebrew," I said. "Isn't that what we're here for?"

"Sharon, I think you realize that in the end the words are the least important aspect of what I'm trying to teach. Come here," he says, pushing me into the sanctuary. He was one of those big-time formal rabbis who wore black robes at services and had like a whole set of hand signals for the organist—I think he was a frustrated conductor or actor. We go into the sanctuary and he flicks on the lights, floodlighting the temple ceiling, stained glass, et cetera. "Sharon," he says, "Judaism is more than a few simple phrases. It's a culture, one of music & art, poetry & light, it is the intimate & the sublime, exalted &"—I forget the exact words. "Think of the lyric music of the Psalms," he tells me. "While the Egyptians were building tombs we were singing of life and love, while the monuments of the ancients were crumbling to dust we were treading over the ruins in a tradition that arced back over the millennia and forward to the future. Our friends in class may never remember a word of Hebrew, but if they can sense something of the grandeur of our tradition the historic sweep of the epic blah blah blah chosen people."

I guess I sort of gave him a look, because this chosen-people crap was always one of my big problems with organized religion.

He heaves a big sigh, folds his arms over his belly. "I think you know how strongly I feel about that one," he says. "Each people is dear to God in its own way, and I often make the analogy to the different states of the Union." He was a great guy, Siegel, but when you asked him a question it was like throwing a bottle in the ocean and just watching it drift away over all his metaphors and comparisons plus the incidents it reminded him of. And as far as where I was coming from in the folk movement, he hadn't a clue because he was into "High" art, which goes back to what I was saying about the past. Siegel used to say "When I say the Bor'chu—'Bless ye the Lord'—I think how fitting a trumpet fanfare would be right there."

Meanwhile I was getting really alienated, not so much by him but by life in general, and by the kind of things I was doing, and I sort of disappeared for a while on Molokai with a guy I was having a relation-

ship with at the time and grew pot out there on
government land, and I really got into the Hawaiian
way of life and just nature out there, the greenness
and the livingness of the rain forest. It's just so pure
out there where the hotel moguls don't have their
greasy colonialist paws on it yet, with the chrome
and glass and penned-in dolphins and chlorinated-
swimming-pool bars and the hills paved over with
Day-Glo golf courses and the electric patrol carts to
ward off trespassers and the guys who have to comb
the sand out with rakes every morning. We lived in
an abandoned toolshed/bungalow thing that this
botanist had originally built as a field station. The
roaches bit, although you understand out there because they're hungry too. You kind of got to understand the Jainists with their temples with the plank
floors over the insects and just that basically every
creature has just as much right to do whatever as you
do. So anyway we lived out there maybe a couple of
years and slowed way down, no telephone, newspaper, or any of that shit—shut out all the noise. The
problem was, the government was trying to wipe us
off the map—not that we were on the map, but the
Feds were always looking—and we had to move a
lot of times, plus there were naturally poachers and
we had to set traps, and so of course we had to worry
all the time some hiker would get killed walking the
wrong way. We had to keep a gun out there too,
which was a pain in the ass morally, because I've
always been a complete pacifist. Looking back, we
definitely would've gotten killed if we were any better at farming than we were, but we didn't grow
much surplus—the marketing scene was something

we were just not that into. I would compare what we did more to the eighteenth-century utopia "Make your garden grow."

As it turned out Kekui's (the guy I was living with's) father died, we heard through his sister Roslind. So we fly into Honolulu for the funeral, a shock, let me tell you, coming into Disneyland, with the high-school kids in aloha-print bathing suits with those plumeria leis on their arms or decapitated carnations strung together—"lei greeters" for the package tours and the Japanese honeymooners in their white white tennis whites. And in front of all of them is Mrs. Eldridge standing with her car keys in her red muumuu and her hair piled up on her head with a red hibiscus at her ear—a big woman, not fat, big like an opera singer, big like photos of Princess Ruth when she sat at the Summer Palace on her throne.

We got to the funeral up in Makiki at the church there, I forget the name, and after the ceremony in the car she, meaning Mrs. Eldridge, turns to Kekui and me, who she hasn't said a word to all day, and she says, "KK, you're coming home."

"What?" he says.

"Roslind and her kids have the back room, Minnie and her kids are in front, Earl and Matthew have Minnie's room, Leilan and Mitchell are upstairs," she says.

"What?" he says.

"We cleaned out your room," she tells him.

"Excuse me?" I say.

"Keep quiet, girl," she says. We drive up to their house in Aina Hina with two plumeria trees in front, not a flower left—they picked them all off for the grandkids' May Day pageant. She had six of the eight kids living in the house and about five grand-children. There were all these add-ons in back and a second story above the garage—Mr. Eldridge was a contractor. And there were something like seven cars in the driveway plus a boat and a tour van, just to give you an idea. We sit down inside, everyone depressed from the funeral, some of the babies cry-ing. Mrs. Eldridge takes them on her knee, she looks around like she was ready to take everyone on her knee. For what? To rock us? To hit us? "KK," she says, "you've come back home to stay."

"Excuse me?" I say.

"Quiet, girl," she says.

"I have an application for you," she says. She brings out a bunch of forms. "West Oahu College," she says. "I brought up all my children to go to college. Okay?"

KK looks down totally crushed with this heavy guilt—he never went to visit his parents or his father before he died, and this was probably some oedipal thing with his father dying and him coming home to Mother—the minister at the funeral gave a whole speech about obedience and duty to the parents in times of sorrow.

"Everyone in this family is a worker," she says. "You filling this out?" She gives him the application forms.

"Yeah," he says.

"Goddammit!" I get up off the floor. "You dickless idiot! Don't you care about me at all? You're going to leave me in Molokai so you can live with your mother?"

"Get your mouth out of my house," Mrs. Eldridge declares, standing up in her full dimensions. "Hippie girl, just 'cause you washed up here on Oahu you don't need to come invading my family. Go back to where you started—California, England, Holland, or whatever nationality you are. And don't you dare walk around taking the Lord's name in vain blaspheming my husband's funeral. Get your pakalolo face away or Earl'll get his badge out and arrest you!"

~~~

So the upshot was Kekui and I broke up and I ended up getting a job at Paradise Jeweller and actually picked up some Cantonese there and got kind of close with the family—went to a lot of the family functions and stuff like that. They were working on evangelizing me and we had some really interesting conversations—they were Pentecostalists—and I went to church with them a couple of times out of my interest in religion. This is what I think you don't realize about me, Dr. Friedell, that this has been my lifelong interest—don't tell me I haven't thought about the concepts. So that's when I started at the university and took religion courses. And they were great experiences, let me make that clear—I never had a problem until you. I got an A in Hindu Myth, I got an A in Jesus and Liberation, and only your course threw me for a loop—I mean, can I be honest? Religious Thinkers has been totally frustrating in that you keep sidestepping the issues and you are totally obsessed with detail—I mean, were you raised a Pharisee?

So the point is I sat there in Moore Hall, I listened, I read these books you were assigning, but what you couldn't see was how much more religion means to a person like myself who comes into a class like yours not with a lot of classical shit under my belt but with a whole life of experience and with these questions, the big ones I previously mentioned, and I knew when I walked out on you I had to find this stuff at the source, that I'd tried asking my questions to professors and rabbis and missionaries and lovers and to myself—sober, high, clean, dirty, unemployed, working, et cetera. In other words all states of consciousness, in other words I go for the empirical method, which is maybe the one thing I get from my father—he was an economist at BU which is besides the point, because obviously I am antiwealth, anticapital—I wasn't on speaking terms with him even when he was dying—and anyway I knew I had to go to the source of some of this religious debate, as in a quest. Like the great poet Yeats when he picked up and traveled to Byzantium—I picked up and took all my money, bought a ticket, came here to Jerusalem.

So you're probably saying "What the Hell is she going to do in Jerusalem and what does she think she's going to live on just out of the blue ending up in the Middle East without a dime." Actually I have close friends here who are putting me up—the guy I referred to earlier who I was in a relationship with twelve years ago when I went out to Hawaii and he decided to go to Fiji is currently in Jerusalem, now involved with the Torah Or—which means Torah Light—institute. He had written me a lot and extended an open invitation ever since he got here, and has basically become like what I have always defined as a holy spirit. He was always this quiet kind of guy, but the quietness just deepened in the last few years—I barely recognized him when I saw him, he used to be such a beer-swilling heavyset kind of guy and he's real pale now and thin as wire. At the airport I walked right past him, naturally being out of it after twenty hours flying. So I sort of wander off the plane into the Hebrew and all those guards. "Sharon," I hear. It's him, Gene, with this thin pale face, wearing a navy suit jacket. We just stood there, looked at each other. We both started to cry. It was mystical. "You've changed," he said, which was the real shocker. I'd changed? I've had the same hairstyle since '74, straight to the hips like Crystal Gayle, and I was wearing my old folk-dancing skirt plus an original Boston Folk Festival T-shirt.

We drove off in the Torah Or hatchback Hyundai, started ascending the hills. I was just staring the whole way as we were driving up. It was such a spiritual odyssey—I said, "I feel like this is the culmination of my whole life." I said, "This is the ancient city of Jerusalem; I'm going to get some answers." So the city rose up before us, made out of Jerusalem stone, naturally, and with the olive trees and even flocks on the hillsides—I felt like my whole spiritual experience was coming together like an epiphany. It was The Land.

Torah Or has its central office in the Old City right near The Wall, and the school is in Mea Shearim, where I've been the last two weeks. In the mornings I wake up—there's like a dormitory for students where we sleep—and I go to pray in the synagogue/cafeteria—it's kind of a small-scale school so they have to double up. There are about twenty-five women students, something like twenty young ones on their junior year abroad from college, like Queens College, Brandeis, and a couple from Barnard, then there are a few of us older ones. The college girls just speed through the prayers and sit down for breakfast while we older ones are still standing there with our books. Then eventually these women start finishing up, but I'm still standing there, praying till the cows come home, just because my Hebrew is so bad I'm spelling out the words—it takes me around four hours to finish praying every morning. The Yemenite women come in, clear away breakfast, I'm still praying. They fold up the folding chairs, I'm still praying. They start hosing down the floor around my feet, they start squeegeeing the water, I'm still standing there like the rocks and the planets. There's one other woman who also takes a long time. I've noticed she keeps looking over at me to see what page I'm on. Then she turns back to her book, bobbing up and down like a maniac. After about a week I figured out this woman is into praying with feeling, which means for each word you have to move your lips, knit your eyebrows, and shuffle around as much as you can, and so obviously the slower you go the more feeling you have, right? So she's like envious of me because I'm going slower than everyone else, so I must be the holiest one there, but she can't for the life of her figure out how to go as slow as I do—every morning I drive her up a wall, since I never told her I know hardly any Hebrew. She has to give up after about three hours. Stalks around glaring at me. There are some real lunatics in Jerusalem, these religious groupie types walking the streets. It kind of taints the atmosphere.

I mean I got here and I saw the city and had this sort of epiphany at the beginning, yet I still have all these major questions exploding in my head, but with the praying and seminars I have hardly any time to think, and also classes here are kind of low-level, focused on these questions like What is a Jew? and What is Torah? I guess it's kind of overcentered on the ethnic stuff for me. I've done ethnic stuff all my life. I mean, when you've been in the folk movement you've kind of already paid your dues as far as ethnic. I want to go beyond that. I'm ready to go beyond. So today I went in to see my friend Gene, who mans the Old City office. "I'm ready for more," I said, standing there right in the light of his slide projector—he was organizing slides on the carousel. "I want to talk about God," I said with this big projection of some Dead Sea Scroll across my arm.

"Sharon, by the way, you haven't paid the office," he mentioned, which totally pissed me off.

"You aren't hearing me," I said.

"I'm hearing you," he said, "but we're having a

financial crisis. Without tuition payments the school is falling apart. Then what are we going to discuss?"

This was so materialistic I would have walked out, but the truth is Torah Or gave me hope I was getting somewhere, so I asked him, "How much do you need from me?"

"Three hundred dollars."

"What?" This just stunned me. I mean, three hundred dollars is all the money I have in the world right now. I mean, holy shit.

Then, after I took the bus back to the school I got a real blow—an actual telegram. It's my cat.

I have this cat I picked up when I got back from Molokai. It kept moaning and screaming outside the building and I took him in and named him Ugly, which he is—so he's kind of lived with me through all my moves and now I've got him staying with a friend from the university and he sends me this telegram. "Tests back; diagnosis positive." I look at this telegram. It's like I've been trying to run away from this thing and it caught up to me. My cat has feline AIDS. It's just a big blow to me—I mean Ugly and I were never demonstrative, he's kind of mean, he's from the street, he likes to go off alone for a few days—he gets kicked around and comes back—but we've been together a long time, maybe seven years.

I just took the piece of paper outside and I walked and walked with my bag slung over my shoulder. I walked through the narrow streets and the vegetable markets with the Me'ah She'arim kids with the black hats like black Panama hats on one block and then round-brimmed hats on the next block—these are like their school uniforms—and I walked past the shops with the silver candlesticks and olivewood stuff and little stinky alleyways between them with clothes hung out to dry. Shirts, shirts, shirts, little shirts, little fringes, and then this satin wedding gown hanging on the line, I swear to God. And I looked in the wig shops and I saw the kids buying beige twisted candles and feathers on the street corners. I walked all the way up the road, up the hill, and I got to this park in front of the Jerusalem Nature Conservation Office, and I am sitting here with this paper and pen, I am sitting on this huge stone from an olive press, which looks like stone money from Yap or Yip, I forget, lying on its side, and it's getting cold out because April is not that warm, and I am full of all these questions and just mainly, What is God? Where is S/He? and What should I do? and What is the earth here for?

I know you don't take this, coming from me, seriously, but I am serious—I feel like I could explode. I read but I don't understand. It's like with Hebrew—I can sound it out but I don't know the meanings. That's the metaphor of how I feel. I came to Jerusalem but I don't feel gathered up and I mean I came from far; Honolulu has to be one of the four corners of the earth. But where is the canopy spread over me—forget of peace—when I look up at the sky at night I'm afraid, it's so dark you can drown in it, it's so black and they say the stars up there aren't even the stars, they're just the ones that used to be there and it takes so long for the light to get down here the real ones have died already. So is it just dead bodies up there? Are they messages from the past that we don't understand? Just words floating down but no one can read them? I've seen those people writing messages and sticking them in the Western Wall in between the stones like it's some kind of goddamn wishing well. They're writing these crazy things—who's going to read them? They're writing to the wall, Dr. Friedell. I'm writing to you.

The light is white lavender gray blue and there are two stars and the moon, I'm watching them, they aren't dead, they're definitely alive. I believe they are alive. Ha. I believe. What the Hell does that mean? Do you want to know the truth? I believe in God without any reasons. That's the part that drives me crazy—I know He exists but I'm not sure how I figured it out. Maybe you're born with it, who knows—maybe it's just basically because I've had a good life. I mean maybe more like Coyote than Road Runner and with those crackly bloodshot eyeballs once in a while and flattened like a cat under a truck once in a while and mad as Hell most of the time about these completely meaningless things like, no offense, your lecture that time, but inside me somewhere there's this person naive and ready to do something totally different—then boom, you get a telegram like this and you just wonder all over again if it makes any sense. I guess I'm basically an optimist with nagging metaphysical questions. Why else would I clean out checking and savings and come to Jerusalem?

And the thing that hurts most is that after getting here and driving up and seeing the flocks and the ancient walls you see that Jerusalem is just a

place. It's just such a place. I thought it was going to
be so much more—I mean, not like I thought I was
actually going to see the valley of the shadow of
death, but I keep seeing plain hills and valleys and
that's it. Which has got to be me, right? I know it's
what you bring, I realize that. It makes me cry because I don't have it in me. I just don't understand
and I want to. I didn't understand Augustine, which
is one of the reasons I hated him, because I read it
and read it and it doesn't make sense to me. Satisfied? And I can tell you I thought seeing this place
would make more sense but it doesn't, it doesn't at
all. I feel ashamed of myself sometimes, like I'm
constantly sidetracking from the bigger questions.
There is this whole spiritual existence out there and
I can't get there. What do you need to do? How
many books? How many journeys? What are the
words and what kind of food? macro? micro? do roots
feed the soul? carrots, turnips, potatoes? or the ancient songs? I lift up my voice in the wilderness,
eyes to the hills, my timbrel and lyre to the mouth
of the sea whence cometh my aid and dance on the
sand a song of praise with words I don't understand.
What can you do with just an alphabet when you
don't know the constellations, just that ayin is an
eye and a well, but what's down the well? You live
in this thin layer on the crust and you can never
delve down to the underground rivers or get onto
the other planets and get any perspective. And they
say you should climb to the top of the hill and cry
God is in this place! and lift up your voice along
with your eyes whence cometh your help, but what
if you do that and afterward it wears off and you're

just sitting there on the hill back where you started? Where do you go from there? Because I've had some real out-of-body experiences and you always come down afterward. I want to go further. My spirit has dancing feet. That's the one thing I guess that keeps me moving, being a dancer. I can dance without shoes, without music, without words, without partners. I look down at these two feet, they keep each other company. I guess you have to keep moving and dwell on the stars instead of the negative.

So I'll be back in Honolulu on May 1 to be there for Ugly, and I was wondering if you could possibly take this as my final paper for the course, since it basically summarizes some of my current views and independent research into religion. I realize it only mentions Augustine briefly, but since he was sort of the starting point of the research it was justified. I could type it up if you want—but the main thing is if you would give me full credit for it, because, obviously, your course is required. Thanks,

Sharon

Variant Text

Dear Aunt Ida,

Attalia is screaming under the piano. She has taken it into her head that she needs a pair of boots. Having explained that her mother and I are perfectly willing to provide our children with necessary items, but unable to supply their ceaseless demand for toys, clothes, and every extravagance, the vital necessity of which is impressed on them by seven-year-old peers, I have resolved to let her scream herself to sleep. I'd say she's good for at least half an hour.

Beatrix has been exhausting herself. She is in London for the topology conference. As soon as she comes back Sunday she will have to prepare her paper for Majorca. These conferences are always a strain and raise numerous logistical problems. Beatrix's parents, living upstairs, would seem the logical choice for baby-sitting, but they are really no longer

able to control the kids—especially now that Adam
can walk. Aunt Clare is out of the question.

Cecil looks fondly at the smooth black surface of his
Olivetti electronic and with a grim smile flicks off the
switch. If only Beatrix were home to manage the kids.
She goes to a three-day conference and they become un-
reasonable. Parents over forty-five should use the buddy
system. He and Beatrix had made a pact to that effect
when Adam was born. If either of them ran away he or
she would take the other along.

They had both thought the baby-sitting situation
would be better in Oxford than it had been in Brooklyn.
When Beatrix taught math at Hunter and Cecil had a
class at Brooklyn College their schedule had been much
more hectic, but there was always Aunt Ida to take care of
the kids. Then Beatrix got her chair at St. Ann's and Cecil
had to give up the part-time position in English at Brooklyn. He had enjoyed that—the resignation letter, the
packing. He feels he has made a small but significant
political statement by leaving America, voting with his
feet. American culture is dying. Apart from the museums
and the ballet, there isn't much left of the city. It was also
a relief to leave the Brooklyn shul, which had rejected the
books of biblical criticism he had donated in his father's
memory. But above all, Cecil was making a feminist statement by following his wife to Oxford. And besides, he
hadn't got along with his department.

The great domestic advantage of moving was that Beatrix's parents, the Cahens, owned this enormous Norham
Gardens house right here in Oxford, and glad of the company and the cooking, they had given over the first floor
to Beatrix and Cecil. It had seemed ideal: two live-in

baby-sitters upstairs. But naturally there were complications. The Cahens are in their late seventies; last winter
Mrs. Cahen slipped on the ice and broke her arm; the
cavernous house is unheatable; and as Beatrix is exhausting herself teaching her seminar and writing papers, it is
Cecil who is stuck with the kids. He doesn't really mind
baby-sitting up to certain limits, and he enjoys replaster-
ing the ceilings and shopping for pipe fittings, but keeping up with his research is difficult. Last year Cecil was
invited to apply for a position at Leeds, but nothing came
of it. Meanwhile, the house and the kids are time-
consuming but usually tolerable, except when Beatrix is
away and Attalia decides to scream herself sick. And except for Beatrix's older sister Clare, who has lived in the
Norham Gardens house all her life. Suddenly inspired,
Cecil flicks on the Olivetti and continues:

> Attalia is becoming more and more like her aunt
> Clare—ruining her voice with screaming, and aban-
> doning herself to increasingly frequent rages. Unfor-
> tunately, she follows Clare in her slovenliness. Even
> more unfortunate, Attalia shares her aunt's lack of
> artistic talent.
>
> In the three years since we moved from New
> York, Clare has insisted on making life in this house
> intolerable. She is sullen and angry, a bad influence
> on both children. But perhaps we will be spared the
> pleasure of living *en famille* in this battleship with
> Victorian plumbing if the sale on the Brooklyn
> house goes through. Or at least we'll have the cash
> to fix up this place. It will take at least two years to
> rewire the house. I don't see why Mr. Cahen won't

subdivide it. Most of the other Norham Gardens castles are now quite nice twentieth century. . . .

Cecil gives up on the letter to his aunt in New York. He leafs through the new June issue of *Shavian Studies*. Finally he walks to the piano and the screams and whimpers stop. He bends down heavily under the keyboard. "Come to bed now."

Attalia glares at her father through the strands of her slippery brown hair. She screams rather loudly for her size. Fine pair of lungs. Pity she doesn't have an ear for music. Cecil had tested both of his children early on for any signs of musical aptitude. When Attalia was two he set her on the piano bench. She struck at the Steinway with her fists, banging the ivory keys. Cecil had waited a few minutes and then given up.

"I'll read to you in bed," Cecil concedes. The tired children scramble up and pad to their room. Cecil glances about for something readable. A stack of *Times Literary Supplements* balances on the sofa; the dining-room table is weighted with Beatrix's mathematics, Adam's crayons, Attalia's homework (probably not done), a bunch of bananas (probably soft).

"This puts me to sleep within minutes," Cecil tells the kids. He opens *Shavian Studies* onto Adam's bed. "Well, well—Lewis has found a variant text of *Major Barbara*." Now both children begin to cry.

⌒⌒⌒

The next morning Cecil puts up a pot of coffee for his in-laws, the Cahens, and rushes to put on his tefillin before the children wake up and the Cahens and Clare come down to be served breakfast. For a moment the house is quiet. The sun glistens on Cecil's black-framed glasses and glows red through his ears. Then the kitchen stairs begin to creak as the old couple make their way down in the dark, and little shrieks escape from the children's room, where Adam is trying to comb Attalia's hair.

"Molly," Morris Cahen calls out hoarsely. "Molly, it's dark, turn on the lights."

"I can't see the switch."

"Above your head."

"Do you want me to break my neck jumping for a light bulb?"

At the bottom step a wooden door blocks the way to the kitchen. Morris grasps the doorknob, pulling and twisting until it is jammed.

"Cecil, you've locked us out!"

Cecil shuts his eyes tightly.

"He's locked us out, what do you think of that?"

Cecil opens the door and the Cahens stumble in. Morris has a gray suit and a quivering, jowly face. Molly wears a shapeless dress—conservative, she calls it. Cecil unwraps his tefillin and pours the Cahens their coffee. Attalia runs in.

"Daddy, I can't go to school."

"Oh, yes you can." Cecil lifts her up and seats her at the table.

Adam toddles in with nothing on. "Pot," he says plaintively, "pot."

After cleaning the living-room rug, Cecil makes an enormous quantity of porridge. Attalia watches morosely as her father dishes out the mush. She is dressed in dark green corduroy overalls and a brown-and-blue striped jersey. Cecil and Beatrix Birnbaum are nonsexist, so they dress their children in unisex clothing. Attalia's hair has never been cut. All ballerinas have long hair. Cecil takes Attalia to ballet class every week. Even though she is the smallest girl there, Attalia is the most meticulous about the steps. She always watches her feet to make sure they are in the right place. Cecil pours each of the kids a glass of milk and a glass of orange juice. Adam drills a hole in his oatmeal with the back of his spoon and pours the juice and the milk into it together. Quite a chemist for a three-year-old, Cecil thinks. Delightful fellow.

"Cecil, I want to know why you are sending Adam to that Jewish kindergarten ahead of his age with the four-year-olds." Molly's voice gathers strength at the end of the sentence.

"Daddy, I can't go to school." Attalia whimpers.

The phone rings.

Upstairs on the third floor, Clare shuffles out of bed. She is wearing a dark pink velour skirt, three sweaters, and a shawl because she knows that if the radiator is left on she will catch fire, and if the windows are closed she won't be able to escape. Clare's hair hangs like water weeds; she pushes the stuff out of her face, puts on a pair of boots, and kneels down to examine the bottom of her bedroom door. The match she wedged in the door jamb is still in place. Then quickly Clare bolts the windows shut. Her room is the most dangerous in the house. The walls slant inward with the sloping roof, and at night Clare lies in bed knowing that if she sleeps the walls will crush her. Clare never bathes. She is wanted by the police for writing poetry. Why should she wait for them like Marat, alone and naked in the bathtub? Clare's life is doubly dangerous because she knows Hebrew. She pauses on the kitchen stairs, sensing she has forgotten something. Windows locked, door bolted, what could it be?

The kitchen always makes Clare nauseous. Adam is throwing oatmeal at his grandparents.

"Bad boy." Cecil frowns; then back into the receiver: "No, I was talking to my son. Sixty thousand—that's below appraisal. I know the house is in Brooklyn. The neighborhood was fine when I was there last. Just some perfectly respectable Puerto Rican fellows. Never any problem at all—Let them drink their beer on the front steps—they'll keep away the crazies. I'm throwing in the appliances. No, not the fridge. I'm shipping it to England. What do you mean irrational? They don't make that model anymore. It would cost as much to buy a new fridge as it would for me to ship the fridge from Brooklyn! Ben, are you there? . . ."

Clare walks slowly to the sink and drops her bowl and spoon in. "Burnt," she states flatly.

"Well, we do our best," Cecil answers. But Clare is already deep in the hall closet pulling on a black trench coat.

"Clare, it's seventy degrees outside," Molly protests. "There are going to be patches of sun—you don't need the umbrella."

But Clare slides the thin steel point of the furled spear through her belt loop, and she is gone.

✌

The kindergarten is housed in an annex to the Oxford shul. All the money for it was given anonymously by Marv Pollack, the father of Children's Vitamins. The playground reminds Cecil of a hamster habitat he once saw displayed in a pet-store window. The sandbox is filled with cedar chips. Sand becomes dirty and stale and transmits common childhood diseases. There is no jungle gym or slide or swing set. Instead an enormous complex of smooth wood has been built in the shape of an amino-acid chain. All the classroom furniture is made out of natural woods and fibers. There are seven computer terminals. The art center is decorated with laminated Chagall posters. It is here that Adam fingerpaints creatively, listens to Bible stories about *HaShem* (a/k/a God), plants pumpkin seeds, and during naptime learns deep relaxation. In the third-grade classroom Attalia will soon be sitting in a circle of tiny chairs for Good/Bad Talk. On the blackboard Ms. Nemirov has printed today's question:

HaShem or Darwin?
YOU
decide.

"I can't go to school, Daddy." Attalia wails. She clings to the foam seat of the Hillman Minx. Cecil pries her loose, grasping her arms and hair. "Daddy."—Attalia howls—"I don't have any teeth!"

"Well, of course you don't; it's part of the human life cycle," Cecil reassures her. "If you could compose yourself, no one would notice. Right now, you're crying and looking ugly as the very devil," he tells her, quoting Henry Higgins, "but when you're all right and quite yourself, you're what I should call attractive." Not having read *Pygmalion*, Attalia sniffles off to class.

Another father passes by with his little girl and fat wife. Cecil looks at the heavy woman and whispers softly, "There but for the grace of God . . ." thinking of all the

similar types his mother and her anxious friends had introduced to him. They all had the three Ds: They were
dumpy, dowdy, and devout. Beatrix is none of these
things. She is lean and brilliant—and as for being devout,
she agreed to keep a kosher kitchen and let the kids
attend the *gan*. Cecil does not expect more. He himself
had been brought up in a house of strict observance,
exquisite baking, and strenuously fond academic expecta-
tions. And although he does not believe in God he
remains observant. His friends find it contradictory and
even hypocritical, but Cecil has always enjoyed the con-
tradiction, and still nurtures it. He finds spiritual suste-
nance in his academic discipline and intellectual structure
in the rituals of his childhood.

He was thirty-five when he married. His parents
hadn't lived to see it. His friends, of course, were flabber-
gasted. They remembered Cecil from his Columbia days
when he refused to go to dances or talk to women. He
swore he hated children, traveled to the Middle East, and
enjoyed Swedish pornographic films.

He had met Beatrix on a bus in Israel. And in fact had
written to his father in the hospital about the "ugly
woman." "She's nothing to write home about," he had
written. He showed Beatrix the letter soon after their
marriage and she loved it. Cecil's father had died just
before the wedding and left him the Brooklyn house. And
so they spent the first years of their marriage there, with
the old letters, the dusty furniture, the faded Schumacher
drapes, and the framed pictures of Cecil that had been
propped up on all the tables by his mother. They
changed nothing.

In the evenings Beatrix would tell Cecil about the
mathematical problems she was working on. He had been

a math major before he switched to English, and so he knew just enough to see how beautiful the schemes were. He loves the way physicists come to Beatrix's seminars to see if they can apply her ideas to their work. But it makes him strangely happy when it seems there aren't any real-world application for her ideas. The formal structure of Beatrix's mathematics has to be appreciated for its own sake. He's often said the same was true of *halakhah*, Jewish religious law.

∽∾∾

In the schoolyard Adam is already rolling in the cedar chips and rubbing dirt in his face and hair. The only clean thing about Adam is his eyes. Yes, he is a charming fellow, Cecil tells himself as he maneuvers out of the parking lot. There seems to be a bottleneck at the exit, where Margo Bettleheim is standing. Cecil reaches for the flyer stuck on the windshield and peers at the bleeding purple mimeograph.

To Whom It May Concern
As a specialist in Jewish early-childhood education with a masters in the subject from the Hebrew University, and as a parent, I am compelled to speak out against a situation which I feel threatens the learning environment of the entire *gan*.
I will state flatly and unequivocally that I am appalled at the deception and irresponsibility of certain parents who have falsified official *gan* records and have registered their child under false pretenses. In short, by misrepresenting the age and

stage of development attained by this child. Thus endangering the learning process of all involved.

It has been shown by Piaget that perceptual development and physical hand-eye-mouth coordination as well as other behavioral processes require a definite time period to develop. I am not convinced that this child has developed these skills, or that this child is ready to interact at the level of food-and-toy sharing interpersonal interplay required at a more mature level.

We know the preschool years to be the most significant formative experience in the educational process (Golding and Simon, 1978). Join me in protecting the future of the next generation: fill out the form below.

Margo Bettleheim

_____ Yes, I want to focus on the issue of an ordered educational process—and allow each child to develop as an organically centered person.

_____ No, I am unconcerned with the process of development, which is uniquely important to the success of the prescholastic learning environment. I am unconcerned about the interplay of persons of the same age.

Signature. . . . .

Inching toward the exit in the line of cars, Cecil reads the letter and checks the space marked Yes. He signs on the dotted line:

Cecil Eugene Birnbaum

and hands the form to Margo, who stands firm at her post with a mass of blond curls and two hard lines of lipstick.

ᗫ

On High Street, Clare takes one last breath of fresh air and dives into Laura Ashley Fine Clothes and Fabrics. The place is lousy with sweet summer perfume, bolts of dizzy little prints, mulberry sailor suits, and American tourists with loud voices pulling all the flowered dresses off the walls. Clutching her black umbrella, Clare squeezes her way to the dressing-room corridor. Rose-ruffled chintz is drawn between the women struggling into harebell-blue puffed sleeves and twenty-three-button dirndl skirts.

"May I help you, miss?"

Clare stares at the new salesgirl wearing a starched pinafore.

"I'm afraid all our dressing rooms are occupied at the moment. Was there something special you had in mind? I have some lovely linens. But perhaps you want something more of a gamine look."

Clare walks to the great beveled mirror at the end of the corridor. She taps the mirror lightly. "Henry," she whispers hoarsely. The mirror swings open.

"Clare, dearest, how *are* you?" Henry puts a motherly arm around Clare and ushers her into his office. The walls are bare except for a bookcase that contains Henry's Rupert Brooke collection and the bound copy of Henry's life work, a bibliography of the Lost Generation. There is no sign of chintz, flowers, or perfume at all. On the desk is a very good reproduction of a pre-Columbian statue of a fire god.

"Oh, I'm simply marvelous, Clare, simply marvelous. Pardon the mess." Henry points to the computer printout on the desk. "I've been checking the sales figures." Henry has dark shadows under his eyes because he works nights. After he finishes the day as manager of Laura Ashley, Henry turns to his real work, Equinox Press—known as Bleak House to its competitors. Equinox publishes a small dark circle of poets. Clare is now bringing out her second book with Equinox.

"I think you will be so pleased. I know I am," Henry tells Clare. He lifts a cardboard carton onto his desk and slits the strapping tape. "Two thousand copies, and this is the first one." He gives Clare a small rust-covered booklet. The cover is printed:

22 poems
by CLARE CAHEN
Equinox Press

"I got the paper from Holland," he continues. "I knew when I saw it that the texture was perfect. Absolutely exquisite. Just between us girls, the good Holland paper is worth the extra money."

∾∾∾

Just a few blocks away, Cecil is appalled by the prices in the Covered Market. He buys eggs, Greek olives, currants, but rejects the outrageously expensive sole just as it is about to be rung up. "I'm not made of money," he tells the old woman behind him in line. She looks at him strangely and moves away. New carts of vegetables are being unloaded. The market is full of exotic produce, and the prices are being driven up. They are even selling kiwifruits and orange-brown mangoes. Next thing you know, they'll put in a cappuccino bar and gentrify the whole neighborhood. Grasping his carrier bag and his *Times*, Cecil makes his way to the car. A violinist is playing on the sidewalk, and Cecil drops his change in the musician's open violin case.

∽∾

At home Clare has barricaded the kitchen with her carton of books. She is reading a poem to her enthralled mother and her dozing father:

Roman Ruins

Sun bones
Stand white—
Unlying in the grass
You swore was unafraid.
Strange song of my death
You left me lone—
Remembering the hollow
Of marrowed bone
And seeping sand.
Forgotten blood,
Numb, unpitying—
The sorrow of it is
You are
All—
And I—
I saw a black rock—

Alive in knowing death
Skitter away.

"Correct me if I'm wrong, Clare," Cecil says from the hallway, "but the ruins are gray, are they not? I don't remember a black rock either—the area is hilly and green—that is, if you are talking about where you were sent as a kid during the Blitz." Cecil trips sprawling over the carton in the doorway. "Get this wretched trash out of my way!"

"Cecil, you are screaming at my daughter!" Molly screams. Cecil limps into the kitchen doubled over. He dumps the groceries on the table and eases himself into a chair, eyes smarting with pain. "I think I've thrown my back out." He states it with an icy coolness lost on his three in-laws.

Clare picks up the carton of books and moves slowly up the kitchen stairs. "Clare," Morris calls after her, "I don't want you to carry that load yourself. Cecil, go help her with those books."

Cecil doesn't move.

"In our family we were brought up to help and sacrifice for each other," Molly says. "Cecil, what are you doing for your family? I'll tell you what you're doing. You are working Beatrix to death. You are taking the grandchildren away from us."

Cecil turns around gingerly to face Molly. "I've been meaning to speak to you about this. Beatrix and I will be going to Majorca next month. . . ."

"Why do you send them to that *frumnik* school?" Morris breaks in suddenly. "You want them to grow up Israelis?"

"The *gan* isn't an Orthodox school, or *frumnik* as you

so quaintly call it. Besides, it's not any of my business what the children grow up to be," Cecil says matter-of-factly. "I am forty-five now, and so I'll be too old for it to matter when they do grow up."

"Morris, did you hear that?" Molly shouts. "Pawns is what they are. Innocent children destroyed."

"Hello. Yes, this is he." Cecil speaks loudly into the telephone receiver. "Oh hello, Miss Greenberg. No, I was not aware there could be any difficulty with Adam at the *gan*. Yes, he is at a mature stage of development. No, I would not say *completely* trained, but very nearly, yes. I'm afraid I can't collect the children yet, I'm off to the Bodleian in just a minute. Yes, I consider myself a concerned parent. What you are saying, then, in layman's terms, is that my son has peed in the prereading center. No, I do understand the seriousness of the problem, but I'm afraid I really cannot collect him at this time. Well, smack him one. Psychological scars? You don't encourage this kind of behavior, do you?"

In the cool dim rooms of the Bodleian Library, Cecil muses on the hysteria of adults involved with small children. Taken in the proper perspective, one's children are really rather amusing, actually. Spread before him are his notes on Shaw's music reviews. He may have found a connection between the theory of sound that can be extrapolated from Shaw's music criticism and the form of Shaw's language theory suggested in Higgins's phonetic experiments. A subdued sense of righteousness fills Cecil as he checks the originality of his idea by searching the bibliographic citations of *Shavian Studies:* Sound Theory. Nothing under that heading. Music Criticism. Nothing there. Confidence rising, Cecil checks under Phonetics. He winces. The idea must be discarded stillborn. There, in the column of papers on Shaw's phonetics, is the listing: "Musical Intonation in Higgins's Phonetic Theory," *Shav. Qt.* Apr. '59. Bitter, Cecil pushes away the book and goes to collect the kids.

∾

Miss Greenberg wears a bright green dress printed with daisies. She has white plastic daisy earrings to match. "Dr. Birnbaum, as grade-level chairperson, I have been delegated to ask you to withdraw your child from the *gan*. I think it is clear from our discussion on the phone that Adam's presence at this time could disturb, or even traumatize, the classroom environment."

"My good woman," Cecil begins, and then bursts into laughter.

"It may seem a trivial matter, but an important principle is involved. The *gan* is an extremely selective school, and there are many children on the preschool waiting list. Margo Bettleheim, for example, is particularly anxious about her son, Moshe."

"Well, I hardly know what to say," Cecil replies dryly. "Perhaps I should let Adam speak for himself."

Miss Greenberg is relieved. "Yes, do discuss it with your son. This discussion could play a beautiful part in the bonding of your relationship. You know, whenever I have to speak as a teacher to a child, I try to think of the experience less as an evaluative encounter and more as an opportunity to nurture growth and understanding."

∾

The Cahens always sit at the kitchen table and watch while Cecil prepares Friday-night dinner. Cecil can't decide which is worse, Attalia and Adam underfoot or their grandparents, who ask plaintively: "Could I trouble you for a little something in a tiny glass—very sweet?"

Cecil lifts Adam onto the kitchen counter and says briskly, "I hear you made a fool of yourself in school today." Adam giggles and crawls into the sink, then he stands unevenly with one foot in the drain.

"My God, he's going to maim himself." Molly gasps.

Cecil pulls Adam out of the sink and places him on the floor, where he begins to scream.

Attalia runs in from the living room. "Daddy, I have a new tooth." She shrieks. She opens her mouth and points to it.

"Congratulations," says Cecil. "I can't see anything, but I'll take your word for it."

"Clare, where are you going?" Morris calls out to his daughter, who is almost out the door.

"To dinner," she mumbles.

"To dinner where?"

"At the house of my publisher, Henry Markowitz."

"I told you, I don't like the looks of him," Molly says suspiciously.

"Clare is forty-eight years old," Cecil reasons. "I should think she can go where she pleases."

The Cahens are taken aback by this flat statement that their daughter is forty-eight. But Molly asks just the same, "You are going alone?"

"Sid Berglund is coming!" Clare screams suddenly, and escapes into a waiting cab.

"That dinner sounds like a silent auction," Cecil remarks as he sets the table. "Clare speaks very little, and Berglund . . ."

"What does this Berglund speak?" Morris queries.

"Well, he's one of Beatrix's ex–graduate students. Some kind of shell-shocked physicist. He speaks math, I suppose."

Cecil sets out the dinner on the dining-room side-board: challah, choucroute garni (with corned beef, of course), couscous with baked eggs and onions, kosher wine and currant cake with a double measure of currants sunk to the bottom. Molly looks at the dinner with a practiced eye. The egg in the couscous is overbaked, the kosher wine is like vinegar, the currant cake is burned on the bottom. She looks at Cecil and says sweetly, "Could I trouble you for a piece of bread?"

<p style="text-align:center">~~~</p>

Clare has never been to Henry's house. It lies in a new development near Summertown. Henry has lived here for three months, and he could not have visitors until his things were in place. Henry has many things.

"Clare, welcome!" Henry draws her into the parlor. Each parlor armchair is covered with swatches of fabric because Henry is in the process of choosing colors and textures for reupholstering. "Dear girl, I'm so glad you could come—forgive me—I'm making a hollandaise." Henry clatters into the kitchen with his white enamel pan and calls back to Clare, "Won't you look at the azaleas? They're just—just—I took photos of them this morning at dawn with one thousand ASA, because you never know if the light will hold, and I do hope they came out. I would be so disappointed if those lovely colors got caught in the sprockets. There by the window in the blue. I've left some books by the lamps that might amuse you. Quarto leather—did you know I got a personal letter from Blackwells at Christmas? Don't ask how much I spent." Clare does not ask. She is looking at Henry's decanters. The cut crystal is clouded with the mossy stain of old, still liquor.

"Ouchy! Ouchy!" Henry is taking little biscuits out of the oven and burning his fingers as he pops each one into the basket lined with starched linen. The door opens softly and Sid Berglund enters with a bottle of Scotch. Sid wears a tattersall shirt tucked into his gray wool trousers; he has a flat nose and a receding chin.

Clare greets him, and Sid nods. He walks into the adjoining dining room where he puts the Scotch on the sideboard. Above the sideboard hangs a framed drawing. Sid leans toward it, squinting at the clear face behind the glass.

"I've willed it to the National Portrait Gallery," Henry tells them at dinner. "I wanted them to have my Dürer. Partly because they already have the oil from this study. And partly—oh, one really can't explain these things—the attachment to an institution." Henry spoons hollandaise onto Clare's salmon and asparagus and then dishes out the potatoes au gratin. "But I must tell you," Henry continues, "the exhibit at the British Museum is simply unbelievable. It is an Egyptian linen exhibit. We are all used to the preservation of stone, but that this delicate material can survive through the ages—Sid, I bought the catalogue. I want you to see it. I am really much more expert in silver, a maven really, but I have a few nice linen pieces. But silver is just so much more, somehow—you know. I felt that somehow I experienced a tremendous coming of age when I bought my service for twenty-four. I always associate it with that tremendously exciting yet frightening experience of renting one's own apartment and buying one's own books for the first time."

Clare and Sid look away, respecting Henry's emotion. Henry sets each piece of china on a tray and goes to fetch dessert. Suddenly Sid and Clare are alone.

"There will be an animal-rights demonstration at Wantage," Sid tells Clare urgently.

"When?"

"Ten o'clock. Bring lunch. Be there?"

For the second time that day Clare thinks she has forgotten something. She looks behind her quickly, feels for the purse between her feet. At her side the sharp spike of the umbrella is sheathed.

"I will come," she whispers furtively.

Henry sets down three Venetian glass bowls of pear sorbet. Each sorbet has on it five thin slices of kiwifruit arranged to form a flower. "I am sorry I didn't bake; it's just that I take such childish delight in using this set of sorbet spoons. They were made by a very important woman silversmith. But, Sid, Clare, you have hardly said a word all evening. Sid, how is your dissertation progressing?"

"Much the same."

"Clare? This dinner must be quite different from Cecil's concoctions. I will never in my life forget the last meal I had in that house. Those children! On the floor, on the table. Good God!" Henry laughs. "Adam simply reached across the table—took a chicken leg and began to eat. No plate, no knife, just began to eat. I can't tell you! But Clare, this is your day. In honor of your book. I do wish you would be a good girl and let me give you some of our lovely dresses. Come to the store and pick out anything you like. Anything."

Henry looks at his two solemn-faced guests. "Well," he chirps brightly. "Perhaps now would be the time to break out some champagne!"

ᴄ✑ᴄ✑

At home even the children are asleep. Clare steps on the edges of the kitchen stairs so they won't creak. She holds the umbrella close to her so that the tip won't scrape the wall. Softly Clare eases open the door to her room. Then she shoots her arm around the door jamb, flicks on the light, and bursts into the room. A slight shadow flickers on the wall. With all her energy Clare lunges. She pushes the button of the automatic umbrella and the black shield unfurls, shooting the steel tip at the wall. Nothing. Clare closes the umbrella and wearily crouches down on her bed. Slowly the ceiling lamp fades and Clare begins to dream:

> She stands on the dark pavement of Regent Street. She senses that Cecil is behind her. And there he is in the lamplight with his Olivetti electronic taking down her thoughts. Henry confronts Cecil. "My dear man, why are you troubling this poor girl?"
>
> "I am merely recording her accent," Cecil replies. "I can locate anyone by his pronunciation. You, for example, are from Vienna, Brooklyn, NYU, Cambridge, Princeton, and Los Angeles."
>
> "Good God. You *are* good. Have you met Cecil Birnbaum, the phonetics expert?"
>
> "I am Cecil Birnbaum."

"*Really?* I am Henry Markowitz. I came from Los Angeles to meet *you!*"

Cecil disappears, but Henry puts on a white apron and ushers Clare into Laura Ashley. He helps Clare into a wedding dress while he chants an incantation:

"The white taffeta is pure silk. Marvelous design. / Off the shoulders. / Notice the details at the waist. / Fan-shaped train. / Just between us."

Clare looks into the beveled glass. The bodice hangs loosely on her. The satin train is tangled at her ankles. The sleeves fall off her bony shoulders and show the shaggy hair under her arms. She is untransformed.

∽∾

The next morning Cecil and the kids walk to shul. Attalia loves shul. She is allowed to wear the pink dress that her American aunt gave her. Beatrix is against pink. But out of courtesy to the relatives, Attalia should wear it once in a while. Adam wears an Oxford United sweatsuit. Cecil sports an "Abortion Rights" button. When they reach the shul, there are two strollers on the steps of the building. One of them is labeled in black ink along the awning M. BETTLEHEIM.

Attalia stays in the cloakroom to play with the Goldman girls. Adam follows his father into the men's section. The shul was originally designed for an egalitarian congregation that never made a go of it. Now the sanctuary is rearranged for separate seating, and there are red velvet curtains in front of the ark. But the walls are still covered with cork bulletin boards. One of the notices pinned up is Margo Bettleheim's open letter to the *gan* parents. Next to it is an advertisement for a cantor:

> Young, vibrant Jewish group in Honolulu seeks like-minded lay leader to energize holiday services.
> Will provide plane fare.
> Write to The Bet Knesset Connection, Unitarian Church, Old Pali Rd., Honolulu, Hawaii, USA.
> Ref. required.
> MUST KNOW HEBREW!

"Good God," mutters the man standing next to Cecil.

"Oh, I quite agree, announcements like that in the sanctuary," Cecil says in sympathy. He recognizes the speaker as George Lewis, the very man who found the variant text of *Major Barbara* and was written up in *Shavian Studies*.

"I was not referring to the notice on the wall," Lewis replies coldly. "I was speaking of the obscene statement you are making by wearing that button on your lapel. I find it extremely offensive."

"Do you, now? Well, if we are to be perfectly candid, I found your little book rather offensive. I can imagine that twenty years ago a book like yours could accrue some kind reviews. But at this time, when the whole question of the variant text has ceased to be an issue, when the very concept of a normative, authoritative text has been discarded . . ."

"I do not talk about these things on Shabbat," Lewis replies scornfully. "You know, I'm always amazed at your lack of sensitivity. This congregation is not a place for statements, political or otherwise. If you want to critique me, write to *Shavian Studies* and see if they'll go so far as

to publish the letter. I can promise you this, I am pre-
pared to write a response such as the pages of that review
have never seen."

Today is Ezra Ben-Zion's bar mitzvah. Cecil walks to
the back of the shul to congratulate Jonathan Collins, the
wiry-bearded anthropology lecturer who instructed Ezra.
"He did a fine job with the morning service. It's nice to
hear the proper consonantal values for a change, and not
those twisted Hungarian and Rumanian vowels from the
old-timers. I compliment you on your teaching."

"Oh, it was nothing, really," Jonathan demurs. "He's
Israeli."

"Jonathan, before the Torah reading starts, I'd like to
have a word with you." They duck out of the sanctuary
and stand in the quiet atrium.

"We have discussed this many times," Cecil continues, "but nothing has been done about it. You still allow
Jack Bettleheim to come up to the Torah. Now, you know
as well as I that he isn't a Sabbath observer. And as if that
isn't enough, he flaunts it by pushing a stroller to shul."

"Well, if we must be technical, Cecil, Margo Bettleheim pushed the stroller."

Cecil is not amused. "I am not talking about techni-
calities."

"Why, Cecil!" Jonathan whispers, fascinated. "Do
you mean to say you are talking about the principles of
Jewish law as they are connected to *God*?"

"God has nothing to do with the problem at hand."

Jonathan looks closely at Cecil's stern face. "Oh, I
see," he says slowly. "You've heard about Margo Bettleheim's open letter."

"Don't try to trivialize this," Cecil says seriously.
"What I am saying is that I cannot participate in a service

in which men who are not *shomer Shabbat*—who don't observe the Sabbath—are called to the Torah. I thought I made my position perfectly clear when I resigned from the religious practices committee."

"But Cecil, Jack was the Ben-Zions' choice."

"Where is it written," Cecil says sarcastically, "that the parents of the bar-mitzvah boy are allowed to choose a man who is not *shomer Shabbat? Halakhah* is *halakhah.*"

"And God has nothing to do with this?" Jonathan chuckles. "You know, Cecil, you're what Mary Douglas used to call a primitive ritualist—the term 'primitive' meaning nothing derogatory, of course. It's quite the best thing to be in anthropological circles."

Cecil presses on with quiet restraint. "I cannot and will not suffer a violation of Shabbat. I come here to pray and find Bettleheim's stroller at the door; I go into the sanctuary and George Lewis threatens me and impugns my freedom of expression on reproductive rights."

"Oh, Cecil, they've found your soft spots."

Cecil turns away.

"Though I always have felt Lewis was a complete loss," Jonathan adds sympathetically. "I mean, there he is, filling up an academic post, with an office, a telephone, and half a secretary."

"I don't complain," Cecil says stiffly. "This is a matter of principle."

Jonathan coughs politely into his beard. He jumps nimbly into the service and Cecil follows more slowly. As Jonathan calls Jack Bettleheim to the Torah, Cecil folds his prayer shawl deliberately and kneels down on his hands and knees to search under and between the seats for Adam.

Attalia puts on a full-scale show as they leave the social hall.

∼⌣∼

At home, Morris and Molly Cahen are waiting for lunch in the kitchen. Cecil puts out a plate of herring, a basket of challah, and for Adam a bowl of mashed salmon. "PINK!" Adam screams. Carefully he flattens the salmon with his fork.

The doorbell rings five times in rapid succession and Cecil hears a deep female baritone cry out "Hello! Are you home? Hello!"

"There is an Israeli accent at the door," Cecil tells Morris.

"So answer it," Morris replies.

The door swings open in Cecil's face, revealing a fierce woman in a fuzzy brown skirt, gray sweater, and hairy stockings. She grasps Cecil by the arm, "My name is Yaffa Yehuda-Yardeni. I am here for Clare Cahen."

"In what capacity are you here for Clare, Miss Yardeni?"

"My name is Yaffa Yehuda-Yardeni. I am here for Clare Cahen," she repeats. "Take me to her."

Yaffa Yehuda-Yardeni enters the kitchen darkly. She sits down and crosses her legs—one hairy gray knee sock over the other. She glares with disgust at Adam on the table. "I dislike children," she tells him. "I should explain my presence here," she continues.

"What is this woman's name?" Molly begins to ask, but Cecil cuts her off.

"As you know," Yaffa Yehuda-Yardeni announces, "I am not unknown as a novelist in Israel. For one of my most important works, by the name *Induction Currents*, I have been urged to seek greater audience in the West. I am staying at the Wantage Center for Study of Jewish-Arab Relations until my rebound in August. The novelist and the novel is a parent-child relation of love and hate. I have entrusted this child of love and hate to Clare Cahen." She pauses dramatically. Then, in a dark, urgent voice: "Clare Cahen was to translate that child."

"Watch it, Adam, or I'll translate you!" Cecil moves the orange juice out of his son's reach.

"I have come for Clare Cahen. I have come for the money that I gave her."

Cecil begins to understand. "You mean that you paid Clare to translate your book and now you want your money back? You aren't going to get any money back from her. You have paid her, and she has spent the money. The exchange is completed."

"I have given to Clare Cahen eight hundred pounds from the one thousand that the British Council gave me to translate my novel into English for the English and American audience. I will get it back."

"I'm afraid you underestimate my sister-in-law. She has a tremendous capacity to spend money. She believes she is wanted by the police, and when she doesn't take her pills she calls a cab and tries to get a flight out of Heathrow. Just last winter she managed to get as far as Spain."

"I want my money back and my manuscript. Take me to Clare Cahen. I will sue."

"Cecil," Molly calls out. "Who let this woman in the house?"

"I think that before you sue," Cecil says with growing

interest, "we need to establish whether Clare has translated your book."

Yaffa Yehuda-Yardeni pulls a thick sheaf of pages in English from her bulging black bag.

"Is this Clare's translation?"

"This is not translation, this is fraud." She thumbs the pages of the manuscript. She reads:

> Yellow soap. Yellow hands. The egg bled into the
> sink from the surgical disks. The inner moan of the
> grinding garbage disposal gnawing at my flesh.

"Where is the passion? Where is the shock and the pain? I will sue. Take me to Clare Cahen."

Morris rises and walks over to the novelist. Bending down, he speaks loudly into her ear. "My daughter is a very sick girl."

"Your daughter is a psychotic! My ex-husband has experience with lawsuits. I have the name of his firm's solicitor in London. I came all the way from Wantage! I will sue!"

"Well, I am sure if you had an appointment Clare would be here." Cecil speaks with a strange mixture of defensiveness and formality. "As it stands, it seems she had an unavoidable conflict."

Yaffa stands up. She straightens her lumpy gray sweater and pulls up her hairy socks. "This is an overheated kitchen," she hisses.

"Only when people are in it," Molly snaps.

At the front door Cecil gives one last piece of advice. "Look here, Miss Yardeni, Clare is schizophrenic. You won't be able to get a penny out of her in court. To put it simply: She's got you."

Yaffa grips Cecil's arm. "Clare Cahen has not seen my last."

⌒⌒⌒

Clare walks slowly on the dirt road outside of Wantage. The fields hide a network of mines in the long grass. She sees a man walking a leashed terrier. "Morning," he calls out. Clare panics. She turns out of the road and her boots sink into the deep mud. Fighting the tall grass, Clare sinks deeper. She lifts herself dripping from a small weed-strangled pond.

"Clare." Sid crouches on a rock near her. "Clare, I miscalculated. My directions to the caucus ground were insufficient. Apparently the site was too obscure." He points to the damp stack of animal-rights leaflets at his feet. Clare says nothing. They sit among the reeds in silence. A brown-feathered wild goose gathers her goslings into the weeds. At last Sid stands up. Clare follows him.

They climb the overgrown bank to the railway bridge. "Is this bridge high enough to die from?" Clare asks Sid.

Sid wipes his glasses with the bottom of his tattersall shirt. He peers over the edge of the bridge. "The distance can be calculated using a falling object and a stopwatch. Simple equation."

"And what if you had no watch in the wilderness?" Clare asks.

"In the wilderness there are no bridges," Sid replies.

The sun slips behind a cloud. Clare intones the opening lines of her work-in-progress. "Darkness": "Black, black, / Spiral down the sun."

"Spiral down the sun," Sid repeats. "That's lovely."

Clare is silent. Then slowly she unsheathes her umbrella, unfurling it over the railing. She lets it float down open—spinning to the ground. It catches on some brambles and snaps inside out in the wind.

"Abandoned umbrella; false trail," Clare says, smiling. They bend into the wind and walk back toward the village. A dirty Fiat swerves off the road, narrowly missing them.

"You want to get killed?" screams the deep-voiced driver. The Fiat races on, leaving the couple unrecognized and alone.

∿

That night Cecil sits down at his Olivetti. The letter to Aunt Ida is still in the typewriter. "Most of the other Norham Gardens castles are now quite nice twentieth century. . . ." Suddenly Cecil is stricken by a terrible thought: Where will he put the refrigerator when it arrives from Brooklyn? The only clear kitchen space is in front of the door. Never mind. When Beatrix returns she will work out the math. He will have to shop in London for that transformer on Monday. So much to do. Tickets for the Royal Ballet. The linen exhibit at the British Museum—who was it told him about that? The paper for Helsinki still to write. Run down for milk. The Bodleian closed. That ass Lewis.

Cecil unrolls the letter to Aunt Ida and inserts a new piece of paper. "As an active member of the Society for Shavian Studies, I was surprised and not a little disappointed to see . . ."

"Daddy." Attalia stands sleepily in the lighted hallway. "Can I say *shehechiyanu* for a new tooth?"

"And while Lewis claims . . ." Cecil types.

"Daddy?"

Cecil looks up. "I am not really qualified to rule on whether that benediction is appropriate. You'll have to ask a rabbi."

Attalia shuffles back to bed. Cecil feels a twinge of regret. He flicks off the typewriter and turns out the lights. Never mind, he tells himself, Beatrix will be home tomorrow, and Clare returned in a cab, not an ambulance. He walks down the dark hall and looks in on the sleeping children. The little beasts are lovely when they're sleeping. "Attalia," he whispers, "I think it might be all right to say *shehechiyanu*."

Attalia rolls over in her sleep, and he adds, "Or some sort of blessing. I'll look it up first thing in the morning."

Young People

*T*he Checker Cab cuts in front of a tour bus and screeches to a stop at the St. Moritz. "Brooklyn Jewish Hospital, please," Henry Markowitz tells the tiny Yemenite cabdriver.

"You got it," she says without turning around. The cab lurches forward, narrowly missing a doorman loaded with suitcases. "Watch it!" the cabbie screams out the window.

"Dear God." Henry breathes. He swabs his fleshy face with a white handkerchief. "I had forgotten what the traffic was like."

"You used to live here?"

"I was a student at NYU."

"Ah." She leans forward and shoots her cab into the next lane. The cab license identifies her as Tiki Sofer. Her little face is shadowed by a poof of grizzled gray hair. Tiki's quickness makes Henry nervous. He feels huge and swollen in the heat. Suit coat crushed over his bent legs, he holds the tulips for his mother cradled in one arm and leans his other on the ledge of the open car window, drumming his fingers on the door.

"I was an NYU student as well," Tiki continues, "and now I am a poet. I write poetry in Hebrew and English. And I run this cab with my husband. I was an anthropology major. But the professors were such shits I'm driving a cab. If you don't sleep with them, or do their work for them, or both, you're going to get some kind of shitty recommendation, guaranteed to keep you out of the department."

"You don't have to tell me; I know," Henry sympathizes. "Let me tell you, I've been denied tenure at some very fancy institutions. They did everything they could to keep me out. Finally I said the hell with them. I got my degree at Wharton Business School, and since then I've been living like a human being."

"Yeah," Tiki breaks in, "but the point is they couldn't keep me out of the field. I'm publishing oral histories of Yemeni women, and I've branched out into linguistics and poetry. Then there's the cab, and I've got three children. So I'm pretty threatening on a lot of different levels. There was a time when I was interviewing for every academic job. But now they've got to read me in the journals. I've had some real findings too. Did you know that nearly all traditional Yemeni women were raped on their wedding night?"

Henry shakes his head. He can't help staring. He's lived in Oxford so long, spent such a lot of time among soft-spoken people. Mathematicians who dominate conversations with their silences, old historians who have grown so eminent that modest qualifying phrases encumber every statement like clinging ivy. Even the shop

Henry manages has a rarefied air. The deliverymen themselves speak in muted tones.

"Only one woman I interviewed wasn't raped," Tiki
tells him. "But she'd run away. You really have to understand the Yemeni tradition to understand that. I was for-
tunate to live in three cultures as a child: my parents'
traditional home, the Orthodox shul, and Israel. But my
kids are really lucky. They're growing up in at least five
cultures: the traditional Yemeni at their grandmother's,
the Orthodox *shtieble* on the corner, Israel every summer,
my friends from the Institute of Social Analysis and
Greenwich Village, and our black neighborhood. That
combination is just about unbeatable. Their father, by the
way, is a real person—none of that academic crap. He
runs the cab twelve hours, and I run the cab twelve hours.
But don't think we deprive ourselves. There are some
things in life that are important, and we make time for
them. Since I've started with the cab, I've written a play
and almost been assaulted twice. But I handled it. You
learn about networking: One friend did the costumes
with a telephone tree, and a painter friend did the sets—
avant-garde with the lights. We got grants from the park,
the rec center, and the Borough Council on Culture and
the Arts, and put it together with traditional mideastern
dancing and instruments. The whole thing was a huge
life-cycle pageant of traditional village life. Another
friend did the food. Another one reviewed it. Once you
have the network going, you expand. We're going to do
something big in Central Park next summer. So that's the
way it is. I'm an artist. And I live in the real world."

Henry stops drumming the car door. What an extraordinary woman! he exclaims within. An entrepreneurial
artist living in the very thick of urban crime and decay.

An artist adapted to the city, somehow managing a symbiosis. The little red fish living in the poisonous sea anemone, thriving among those poisonous tentacles. It astounds him. He had never thought it possible, and he feels he's made a discovery.

Henry searches for talent in his own small way. He's begun Equinox Press for that purpose, and slowly he's finding poets to enter in his lists. It's because even after he left academic study of the English moderns, he still savors the oblique and new, poetic voices with their own odd rhythms, their particular timbres—too delicate for a world of shopping malls and corporations. He searches usually in the country, and has found poets in Vermont and Brittany, and a writer of verse plays outside Binghamton, New York. There are several, of course, from Oxford—not from Oxford the city, but from the more essential place, the university, the *idea* of the city. But now to hear a poet speak from the thick of this slum, from the black heart of this monster—it seems miraculous to him. Underneath this coarse language lies, perhaps, a brilliant voice, a source of new sounds! "I hope you won't be offended if I compliment you on your courage," he says. His right eye twitches earnestly. "You see, I have great admiration for artists and art in general, and I feel there is such a tremendous need in the world to support beauty. There is so much cruelty, such inarticulate violence in the world." He gestures toward the litter-lined street. "I would like to do everything in my power to help you— the artists, the creators. In fact, if I can find my card . . ." He reaches into his pocket and pulls out his pastel Laura Ashley business card. "No, that's not it." He rummages some more. "Here we are." The card is printed: *Henry Markowitz, Publisher. Equinox Press, 217A*

High St., Oxford, England. "You must be a little startled at this," he apologizes.

"Not at all." Tiki smiles. She pockets the card and gives Henry one of her own.

❧

"Look, taxi lady," mutters the driver of the tour bus. He tries it several ways—once with a chilling calm, once with a sliding sneer on the word "lady."

The bus inches forward in the morning traffic.

"Can we get there on time?" asks Ms. Froelich, the head foundation rep.

"No," the driver answers precisely. He glances at his passengers in the rearview mirror. The kids don't look worried. Just sprawling across the chairs into the aisles. Stretching their legs longer—all bone and muscle. The girls, just bones.

"The rehearsals are going to run late," worries Ms. Froelich, behind him.

"If you can figure out a way to get crosstown faster . . ." the driver starts. How old could this "advisor" be? Twenty-one? Just old enough to hold a clipboard, and they put her in charge of thirty huge teenagers. Dancers, yet. *Encouraged* not to sit still.

"Wait, stop the bus!" Froelich clatters her clipboard and points to a kid out on the street, running toward the bus.

The air brakes shriek, setting off all the car horns. The driver opens the pleated door to the bus, swinging the arm handle for the kid dodging traffic.

Sean's duffel bag slips off his shoulder as he dives for the door. His tap and clogging shoes have sunk to the bottom. He can feel his steel-braced Irish dancing shoes through the thin material.

"You're Sean McCole," Ms. Froelich tells him, and sticks a name tag on his sweater. The bus jolts forward, and Sean sinks into the seat next to Brian Wattley / Chicago IL / ballet. Brian is slim and black and wears a white muffler.

"What happened to you?" he asks Sean.

"We drove down from Binghamton, and my mom forgot her camera, so we were going to go back for it, but then we thought: When we get to Grandma's, why don't we take hers? But she was out of film. . . ."

"You can't take pictures at Lincoln Center," Brian announces.

"Yes you can," the girl across the aisle breaks in. "You get that film you don't need flashes for."

"That's the kind she was out of. I mean my grandmother . . ." Sean's story trails off. Cara d'Avanzo / Concord NH / ballet. Her hair is long and smooth over her thin shoulders. Sean wonders whether the fuzzy stuff on Cara's sweater will come off with the name tag. He wants to peel it off and see. He says instead, "I love your shoes. They're so . . . blue."

Cara looks down at her turquoise sneakers. She points her toes out into the aisle. "Yeah, aren't they cool? I got them at Woolworth's."

"Are all your shoes like this?" asks Sean.

"Why do you ask?"

"I don't know."

"Do you have a thing about feet?" she asks mildly.

"No. I just like looking at them."

Brian leans back in his seat and lights a cigarette. He

smiles at Sean's freckled astonishment. "What?" he chal-
lenges.

"Nothing," Sean says, "but doesn't it do terrible
things to your breathing and all that?"

Cara fans away the smoke with her rehearsal schedule. Then she kneels on her seat and tries to open the
window.

"I'll help you." Sean lurches across the aisle as the
bus turns sharply.

"I got it." The window snaps open, and Cara leans
out.

"Head and limbs inside the bus," the driver booms.

"I can't believe I'm here," Cara tells Sean. "I mean,
Dad tried to make the audition tape on this thing that
wasn't even a video machine. This old movie camera. I
looked like Charlie Chaplin."

"What do you mean, old movie camera?" Brian
laughs. "Better than nothing. My teacher couldn't even
find anything till two days before it was due. She went to
all those clubs—I mean, like every animal: Elks, Lions,
Mooses. Finally she got the camera from the Kiwanis.
And my sister works for Video Hut, so she got the film.
Fuckin' pain in the ass for three point five minutes. I
totally can't believe I'm here. Hey, let's have some
fuckin' music! Isn't that a radio up there?" Brian vaults
up the aisle, pushing off from the chair backs.

"Look, young man," the driver hollers. "This is my
bus, and it's my radio. I'm going to play my music if and
when I want to. And I don't care who you are, or where
you dance—there's going to be no profanity on this bus.
You stand in back of that red line."

⌇⌇⌇

Clutching Tiki Sofer's card and the orange-red tulips, Henry takes the groaning elevator up to the hospital room. In the bed by the door, a young black woman with hennaed hair lies stiffly in a body cast. She whispers and giggles into the telephone receiver. Henry's mother, Rose, dozes in the next bed. Gray hair is swept back from her sharp forehead. She has kept her Tuesday hair appointment, even in the hospital. Henry bends down and kisses her cheek quietly.

"Hello, Henry," she says without moving.

"I brought you flowers. Would you like them by the window? How are you feeling now?" Henry puts the flowers down and draws a chair to the bed.

"I had a terrible night. Racking pains."

"Come, Mother, it couldn't have been that bad. Does it hurt in your eye?"

"I can't see."

"You have to give it time."

"Oh, it's not a question of time." Rose laughs sarcastically. "He did the wrong eye."

"He did not do the wrong eye, Mother; we've been through this before."

"Henry, let me be the judge of my own eyes. I know which eye had the cataract."

Henry sighs and tries another tack. "Well, you're going home tomorrow; you must be looking forward to that."

"Four walls. Four walls and some furniture," Rose amends.

"What's this you've been reading?"

"There on the night table? The new Howatch book. It's my only diversion. I can't see the television."

"Then how do you read this?" Henry picks up the

thick paperback gingerly. The cover is blue, embossed with silver lettering: "She is Young and Desperate— Ready to Gamble Everything for Love in—*RUSSIAN ROULETTE.*" "You can't really be reading this. This is filth, literary masturbation, pornography at best!"

"It's not as good as *Penmarric*. But it's all I have. I can only read a few pages a day." Rose begins to cry. "Put it down. And stop destroying everything dear to me. You don't understand the kind of pain I'm in."

"What kind of pain could you have? It was a tiny operation. Dr. Feldman told me it went beautifully."

"That man doesn't know or care. He looks at me and sees the new car he's going to buy. He doesn't see my pain, and he won't prescribe me more pills."

"Mother, you've got enough pills. You don't need pills. Look at the girl in the next bed. She had a real operation. Is she complaining about pain?"

"Some people don't have pain."

They stare at each other, baffled. "Guess where I'm having dinner tonight!" Henry tries to restart the conversation. "Do you remember Jemmy? He's vice-president of Eastern Trust now. He's taking me to some fund-raising thing for young dancers."

"How kind of you to fit me in."

Henry stands up and walks around the bed impatiently. "You know I came all the way from England to see you. But if you insist on making this visit painful and turn it into an empty gesture, I refuse to argue with you. I can only say that it hurts me deeply that you are never satisfied with, or for that matter the least bit interested in, my life. And I must ask what I could possibly do to earn your approval."

Mrs. Markowitz looks deliberately at her balding,

overweight, thick-featured son. "Get married," she says
clearly.

ᴄᴜᴇᴏ

Sean slouches down in his seat and leans his head back.
In the empty concert hall the tiered lights of the balcony
railings stand distant as constellations.

"My mother has this thing," says Cara. "She has this
thing about summer jobs. But not dancing. I mean, other
people did *Nutcracker* at Saratoga, and I worked on this
blueberry farm. I had to dance in the *barn.* And then I
worked at a dessert place in Maine. It was supposed to
make me eat. I cut up peaches and I made this thing:
gingerbread, then vanilla ice cream, then gingerbread,
then ice cream, then peaches. And last summer I worked
in a candy store. That really turned me off food."

A modern dancer runs through her dance on the bare
stage. She takes a little hop, representing the leap she
will make in tonight's performance. Then she hurries
through the rest of her dance in tiny steps, as if she were
humming to herself a remembered tune.

"You know what I used to like?" says Sean in the
audience. "That rubber candy."

"Gummi Bears. They've got gummy rats now.
They're like a foot long, with these huge tails, and they
come in black, white, and pink."

They applaud loudly for the dancer when she finishes
her run-through.

"Look at her tights!" Cara points to the dancer's
bronze metallic legs.

"She looks like a Halliburton Zero suitcase," Sean
says.

Ms. Froelich hears them laughing and walks toward them.

"There's Brian," Cara whispers. Her arm brushes Sean's on the armrest between them. He wonders whether he should move his arm away. "Look," she whispers.

The stage darkens, and Brian centers himself, kneeling. He balances on his knees, arching his back. He holds one arm above his head and one arm behind him, fingers braced against the floor. The technicians are having trouble with Brian's tape. Brian holds still, clenching his teeth. The cords of his neck stand out. Suddenly the stage lights up with the sprightly music of *Coppélia*. Brian walks to the edge of the stage and shades his eyes, peering out into the cavernous hall. "That's not my music," he tells the stage manager, who follows the script from a lighted music stand.

"We understand that, Brian."

"And I don't want the lights to come up that fast. I want it gradual."

The sweating manager walks down the aisle to the stage. "Cool it, kid."

Brian stands in a side drape, with one hand on his hip. All the house lights blink into darkness.

"All right. Pumpkin time," announces an advisor. "Everybody into the musicians' lounge."

Sean gets up reluctantly. "What happened?"

"It's the union," Cara says wisely. "The stagehands have been working four hours without a break. So that's it; they stop."

They follow the other dancers backstage. In the lounge, tables are laid out with tuna salad sandwiches, potato chips, fudge brownies, and sticky tarts. "Just relax," Ms. Froelich tells the sullen group.

"Oh, right," Brian says. "When all the dancers after intermission haven't rehearsed. What are we supposed to do? Slow down so they can follow us with the spotlight?"

"I hope I don't get Brian's music." Cara bites into a sandwich and continues with her mouth full. "My whole town'd freak out. They all drove down from Concord in the school bus—I mean, my sister's coming with her whole softball team."

∽

Henry rings the bell of the restored Brooklyn brownstone. There is no answer. Six-thirty, Jemmy had said, because they had to go to the young dancers. He backs away from the door and checks the address nervously. All the houses on the street look the same, and they have little signs on the grass informing intruders and visitors of protection by Castle Services.

The door cracks open so fast that Henry and his Glenfiddich nearly topple off the brick steps into the hybrid holly bushes. A stern, dark-browed kid stares wordlessly at Henry.

"Philip? Good lord, you are getting so big. I always used to hate it when people said that to me, but you make me feel ancient. Do you remember me?"

"I'll get my father, Mr. Markowitz." Philip takes the Scotch and leads Henry into the house. They walk past the nearly vertical flight of stairs facing the door and enter the white living room with its parquet floor, Boston ferns, antique chairs, and new Steinway piano. The room is immaculate, except that the carpet is littered with empty cassette wrappers, extension cords, microphone heads, and pages of home video camera instructions. Jemmy kneels on the floor, filming, with his back toward Henry. The rest of the family crowds around, helping.

"All right, you should see a green light." Jemmy's wife, Angela, is a broad-hipped woman with a pageboy haircut. She wears a dress of black silk that looks like Qiana. "Do you or don't you see a green light?"

"I don't know!" Jemmy bursts out.

"What do you mean, you don't know? Honestly, Jeremy, you're mechanically inept."

"Let me see, D-D-Daddy." Fourteen-year-old Nicole kneels down next to Jemmy and wrests the camera from her father. She doesn't stutter as much as she used to. "No, he's right, Mommy. You're not sup-pup-pup-posed to see the light. You just push it here."

"Nicole, give him back the camera," Angela orders. "Your job is to keep Josh out of the reflectors." Josh, the fat baby of the family, is rolling his walker steadily toward the shiny silver umbrella reflectors near the piano.

At the center of all this stands three-year-old Sara. With her white smocked dress, curly brown hair, and blue eyes, she waits patiently for the camera to roll.

"The test light is off," Jemmy tells Angela.

"Finally. Nicole, check the microphone. Just tap it. That's enough. All right, we're ready."

"Jeremy!" Henry calls from the door. But Philip puts his finger to his lips as Sara smiles into the camera and begins to sing "The Eentsy Weentsy Spider."

Every person in the room watches intently. Sara's mother mouths the words to herself; her father focuses the camera on her little fingers as they enact the motions. Her older sister pushes baby Josh in a gentle orbit away from the microphone. Her older brother stands guard at the door.

> *Up came the sun and*
> *Dried up all the rain—and*
> *The eentsy weentsy spider*
> *Went up the spout again.*

Sara smiles for the camera and holds out the hem of her skirt.

"Print it," Jemmy announces, and stands up stiffly to greet Henry with: "Well, what did you think?"

∽

At the table, the housekeeper brings out chicken soup. The bowls for Sara and Josh contain bright pieces of carrot, green pepper, and sweet red pepper. "We'll go to any lengths," Angela tells Henry. "Sara is a terrible eater."

"She wasn't until Josh was born," Jeremy corrects cautiously. "When Josh was born, she got a little j-e-a-l-o-u-s."

"It must feel very strange to be so much older than your brother and sister," Henry says to Philip and Nicole.

"It's a l-lot of fun," Nicole stammers amiably.

"They've been awfully good with the kids." Jeremy adjusts his round glasses. "Sara and Josh really have six parents, with Philip, Nicole, the baby-sitter, the housekeeper, Angela, and myself. You're a happy girl, aren't you, Sara? Are you a happy Sara? No. Not now. Sara, *no*."

"Traveling has gotten really ridiculous," says Angela. "When I was nursing Sara, I had to take my breast pump through security at every airport, and it kept setting off the alarm. They insisted on taking the whole thing apart every time, because the guards didn't understand what it was. And I'd have to repeat over and over: 'This is a breast pump. It is used for pumping milk from breasts.' And then in Greece, when I was pregnant with Josh, my placenta started to unravel, and I had to be rushed home, and Jemmy had his leg in a cast from the skiing in Gstaad, so he couldn't help much. The doctor ordered me to stay home in bed—you can imagine what that was like. I was stranded here, up on the third floor. I couldn't go up and down stairs. That was when we installed the intercom system and the furo—you know, Jemmy, we've got to show him the top floors after dinner—so I was stuck up there, workaholic that I am. I planned my day around the flavor of ice cream I'd get Philip and Nicole to buy me when they got home from school. We've got the flagship Häagen-Dazs on our street, you know. I blew up like a blimp. Must have gained forty pounds. Four, zero."

Henry looks up wanly after this graphic description. Angela has such a way of talking about bodily functions! He admits it to himself: The whole dinner is a bit much for him. Watching the babies mash their food together. Watching the older girl pick at her beans. He can smell diapers and talcum powder, and it makes him feel quite faint. He wonders how Jemmy can live in such an atmosphere. It seems impossible they are the same age—that they were both students. What happens to people? he wonders. What makes them want a life of bottles and diapers? My God, Jemmy volunteered to do it twice, with a second set of kids. Same wife, four kids! When did Jemmy undergo this transformation and become fixated on little children? He never seemed interested in them before, in college. When was it he changed? It must be

Angela. Her influence. Jemmy hardly seems to speak for himself. He's dominated by his family, but he doesn't notice. Does he read books anymore? Or is it just parent manuals? Get married, Mother told him. Her orders from the hospital. But how can married people bear it? Feeling he should say something to Angela, Henry asks, "Did the firm give you trouble about taking maternity leave?"

"Well, I'm a senior partner now, so we've solved some of those problems." Angela passes the fruit salad to Jeremy. The fruit is served in a hollowed pineapple cut lengthwise, so that half its prickly stem hangs over the edge of the platter. As Jeremy maneuvers nearsightedly, the stem topples a glass of red wine.

"Jemmy." Angela moans. And Henry thinks: Marriage—an insulting intimacy.

"I'm sorry," Jeremy tells the housekeeper as she swabs the table.

Sara squirms out of her booster chair and dashes around the room, holding her doll by the hair.

"When is her bedtime?" Henry asks hopefully.

"Whenever she decides to go to sleep." Jeremy sighs.

"We're sending her to the Newman Preschool," Angela says proudly. "That's where she learned the song. You know, they make such a fetish out of preschools now. It's incredible. They say that you have to send your kids to the Newman School because it's a feeder for Buckley Country Day, which is a feeder for Andover, which is a feeder for Harvard. But we just send Sara there because we think it's a good school."

"How's business in Oxford, Henry?" Jemmy asks.

"Marvelous. Simply marvelous. The store is doing brilliantly, and my little publishing company is losing less each year. Oxford is such a beautiful place. You really

must visit." He looks at the children and adds, "Unfortunately, I live in a microscopic flat. You know, I grew up in
the city, but I'd forgotten how beastly it was. To venture
onto the street for a taxi is to take one's life in one's
hands. And the exploitation of it! I am almost afraid to
talk to the drivers, because they invariably have a Ph.D.
in art history or anthropology. Today I took a cab to visit
my mother at the hospital, and my driver was a petite
Yemenite woman who was forced out of academia: simply
driven out and forced to run a cab. I was very nearly
moved to tears."

"How is your mother?" asks Angela.

"Impossible. Absolutely impossible. She'll outlive us
all."

"I never have trouble g-getting a cab," Nicole puts
in. "When they don't want to take me, I just say, 'I sup-
puppose you don't know who my father is. He's
p-p-president of the Checker C-Cab C-C-Company of
Manhattan.' And it usually works. Some of the girls at my
school haven't ever been outside Manhattan at all. They
d-don't even know where Brooklyn is."

"They don't know what planet they're on," says
Philip. And then, in a completely different voice, to the
baby: "But we like those mashed potatums, don't we,
Josh? Yes we do!"

Nicole struggles on. "That's why this week was
c-c-career week, and c-c-career women c-came to speak. I
went to the banking seminar, and the woman banker
t-talked to us about getting jobs. She said the most important thing to do at our age is to make sure to c-c-call
ourselves for an interview, be-c-cause if our parents
c-called the employer would get the wrong impression.
She also t-t-taught us how to sit." Nicole demonstrates by

straightening up, leaning forward slightly, and lifting her chin. She wears a string of pearls with her pin-striped blouse and parts her frizzy hair on the side. "Actually, I don't want to marry a b-businessman; I'd rather marry someone with b-b-billions of dollars."

"When I was your age," Henry tells Philip, "I used to escape to the library and just read and read. Jane Austen, E. M. Forster, Dickens—each of these writers was, to me, like discovering a new world. The language was so exquisite. I never had any ambition to write myself, only to read and study every intricate detail of these delicate plots, these characters and places, which seemed to me then, and still seem to me now, so much more subtle than those in the so-called real world of the twentieth century."

"Yeah. Well, I play squash," says Philip.

"He's ranked third nationally in his age group," Angela adds.

After dinner, Philip carries Josh off to bed, and Jeremy and Angela give Henry the tour of the house. The furo is a black bathtub, with a three-line phone built in. The second-best part of the house is the third floor—devoted entirely to the children. Sara opens the door to her room, announcing "*Please* enter."

"I'm afraid she's terribly spoiled. She's got every toy on the market," Jeremy says proudly. "And duplicates in Amagansett." Sara's bed is covered with dolls and stuffed animals. Fisher-Price maps the floor with urban sprawl. Sara has every model: the House, the Barn, the Garage, the Castle, the Store, the Shopping Center. She has taken all the little plastic cars from the garage and stacked them in the castle. The farm animals ride the elevator in the garage.

The tour continues past Nicole's room, with its larger-than-life posters and equally overscaled stereo, and they walk past Philip's tiny rectangular room, with its built-in drawers under the bed and shelf of squash trophies over the bed. The largest room on the third floor is the playroom. Philip sinks into a huge beanbag chair and flicks a soccer match onto the VCR.

"What a beautiful computer!" exclaims Henry. The IBM is hooked up in its own wall system. "You must use your PC a great deal."

"No, not really." Philip yawns. "Just for games and term papers."

"I have to write a term p-p-paper on street life in ancient Rome," Nicole tells her mother.

"*Street* life?"

"Well, all the buildings were t-t-taken, and the upper c-c-classes were already picked."

"And so you have to write a paper on street life? I don't like that. I don't like that at all. Jemmy"—Angela turns to her husband—"Jemmy, I want you to phone that woman."

"Mrs. D-D-D . . ."

"Yes, Mrs. Dalton. I want you to phone her tonight. I find her assignments offensive. In fact, I don't like her whole attitude. You might as well start by phoning the principal."

"I'll phone first thing in the morning, dear," Jeremy says. "We're taking Henry to the Young Dancers of America benefit."

Angela snorts. "I'll stay home and phone."

"It's one of the bank's causes," Jemmy says mildly. "We're doing gifted children."

"You *should* be doing addicts and runaways," Angela

tells him. "We've got some life-and-death issues here in this city."

"But surely," Henry protests, "the survival of the arts is a life-and-death issue as well."

"We're also giving to A Better Chance and the Fresh Air Fund," Jemmy points out firmly. "Really, Angela, you should come."

"There is no way," Angela declares, "that I am going to go and watch a bunch of teenage fairies prance around the stage."

"It is shocking," Henry puts in to make up for provoking her earlier. "Some of them have become so blatantly obvious."

∽∾∽

Sean stands in the open doorway of Cara's dressing room, watching her make up. "Sean, you look so cool!" she says, catching sight of him in the mirror. He wears a blue wool kilt, with a royal-blue velvet blazer and a narrow tie. "This guy wore a kilt to our prom," Cara tells him, "and this other guy called him a faggot, so the guy with the kilt pulled a switchblade on him."

"Why are you putting red circles on your cheeks?" Sean asks her.

"Because I'm Coppélia, and she's a doll. I've got to dance her in character."

"I took an acting course once," Sean says. "We all had to get down on the floor and pretend we were horses. Then we had to pretend one horse died, and we had to think how we as survivors would react. It was really crazy. We were all on our hands and knees, trying to make sad horse noises."

"Floral arrangement for Miss Cara d'Avanzo," the room attendant calls through the door.

"Oh, wow! It's so huge!" Cara shouts as she takes the box. "It looks like a coffin!" She lifts out a dozen long-stemmed coral roses and reads the card aloud: " 'For Cara, from her fans.' "

"Who do you think sent it?" asks Sean.

"My parents, who else?"

They run to take the elevator up to the stage.

∽∾∽

Advisors stand in each of the wings. They wear head-phones and check their lists of entrances nervously. Sean and Cara try to see out onto the stage, but the advisors block their view.

They slip back to the narrow passage behind the stage. The sounds of a brass ensemble drift back behind the curtain.

"I can't see your eyes," Sean tells Cara. Her lashes are thick with mascara.

"It's gross," she says matter-of-factly, "but you have to plaster your face so they can see you."

"That much?" asks Sean.

"You're not supposed to stand so close," she says im-patiently. "It's for the cheapies in the back rows."

Sean puts his hands on her waist. "I'll teach you a German dance," he says. "Chassé right, two, three, left, two, three, hop right, hop left, turn." She follows the steps twice through, then spins out on a turn and starts jitterbugging to the band music. They dance smoothly, careful of Cara's tutu and Sean's heavy shoes.

Someone calls Sean's name over the intercom. They

look up, and suddenly both see the dark shaft of the theater vault opening infinitely above them. They hold still, trembling with excitement.

"Sean!" Ms. Froelich calls desperately. She pushes him into the wings. "You've got five minutes; do you want to sit down?" She offers him a stool.

"I'm fine!" Sean reassures her, in what seems the next moment, when he jumps out onto the stage.

He stands poised center stage, in the pool of light. Suddenly bright piano music fills the darkness, and he hops up, clicking his feet. He jumps forward and back, arms held straight down—and all the while his feet are dancing together without any help. Sean kicks up his legs, and they fling themselves easily into the air. His tapping quickens with the music, and he whirls around in the circle of light. As the music fades, Sean clicks and turns off the stage and comes back to bow, one leg pointed in front of his straight body.

"You were so good!" Cara whispers in the wings, and he realizes the dance is over. An advisor gives Cara a push, and now she is balanced in the light, her head turned slenderly.

"She has a pretty good figure for a ballerina," Jeremy tells Henry in the audience. "At least she has some kind of bust."

"But that Irish dancer was absolutely brilliant," Henry murmurs. It wasn't just the dancing. He was so young. It really saves him to see a young person like that, after such a day. You're surrounded in the city by such machines, such—what did he tell the cabbie?—ugliness, insensitivity. You can feel it on the streets, the buildings shadowing the sidewalk, the pollution from the buses filling the air. There isn't any courtesy left for strangers.

There isn't any grace. The books, the music, the dances are only left in libraries and theaters; the beautiful things are preserved behind glass, the graceful lives retreat behind the proscenium. Because there aren't any books left in the home. Look at Jemmy, who used to read—he has boxy cars and athletic children, an ambitious wife, nothing beautiful—there isn't any music left in his home. A piano, and his little child with the video equipment. Precious to him, to be sure. But nothing excellent. Jemmy's little girl, so photographed, how could she compare to these few chosen on the stage? It does Henry good to see this. A young man who comes from outside the city and excels with an innocent art. Without the vulgarity of the street—which clung even to the cabbie like a shell. Without the complacency of the home—another kind of vulgarity, to be sure. "I do hope we see him at the reception," Henry says of Sean now.

"Actually," Jemmy confesses during the applause, "I can't stay after the show. I've got to give Philip a driving lesson tomorrow before squash practice."

❧

After the last curtain, the caterers roll white tables onto the stage. Still in costume, Brian sprays a champagne bottle over the dancers heading backstage for the showers. "Hey, to us," he toasts. "There better be towels down there!"

In the tangle of guests and champagne flutes, Henry sees Sean, out of costume now, his face still glowing.

"My name is Henry, and I must say I thought your dancing was just lovely. This Aran sweater is marvelous;

it is so appropriate." He fingers the wool. "You simply cannot get wool like this in America. Was it imported?"

"Well, I don't know, but my mother knitted it, and she's American."

"What I simply cannot get over is the intricacy of a dance form that yet remains a kind of folk art."

"That's what I like about it too," Sean agrees uncertainly.

"How did you learn?"

"Watching my father. And when we had parties, someone would yell, 'Give us some dancing, Sean!' So that's how I started. I still dance for them on tables and stuff, but I keep it low and easy, unless I really warm up." Cara rushes by, with her second glass of champagne. She has changed into an emerald-green backless dress. "This summer I'm going to the Morris Dance Festival in Oxford, England," Sean continues.

"*Are* you? Bless your heart, that's lovely!" Henry puts his arm around Sean. "You see, I *live* in Oxford. It's absolutely the most beautiful place on the face of God's earth. Look, I'll give you my card, and if you need any help finding a place to stay, just ring me up. . . ."

"Sean!" Brian calls out from the other end of the room. "Get the hell over here if you want to be in the picture."

Sean hesitates, confused. "Oh, don't mind me," says Henry. "Here, just take the card and run along. I'll expect to hear from you soon."

Sean kneels next to Brian in the front row of the picture. The photographer is reloading his camera. "Who was that fag you were talking to?" Brian asks. "He was fuckin' weird."

❧

After the reception, Henry takes a cab back to the St. Moritz. His mind is alive with the young images of the evening. He imagines his own heavy body jumping and leaping, heels clicking high in the air. They're still serving dessert at Rumpelmayer's, bless their hearts. With a little hop, Henry pushes open the glass door. He sits at a pink table, half dazed by the pink-and-white light of the bakery. A waitress passes, carrying a glossy peach melba. It's just too much: this rich pastry wet with sweetness, this sweet ice cream, Sean's sweet open face. It redeems him, it makes him feel alive again, that he has had a glimpse of youth. How odd that what Jemmy does is called life-begetting. Driving lessons and ground baby food and tired looks from Angela. Where is the life in that? Commuting to the bank and competing for the proper preschools. Where are the ideas? It is a mystery, Jemmy's transformation, but it's clear the change has killed him. Only the husk of Henry's old friend is left. Jemmy is dominated by the pattern of his own ties, he is fully described by his furniture and his vacations. No essence left. But that is what Sean is completely—without other accoutrements. An idea of youth and grace and joy. An artist without the least protective shell. Sighing with happiness, Henry orders a piece of chocolate cake and a glass of milk.

❧

In the chartered bus, the dancers are delirious with their success. Brian runs down the aisle of the bus and chins the luggage rack.

"Do that one more time, son, and I'll stop the bus," warns the driver.

Cara has smuggled a carafe of wine from the reception. She puts her roses in the red wine and tells the advisors the carafe is a vase.

"Cara, you're drunk," Ms. Froelich scolds.

She just laughs. Everyone is so funny. When she tilts her head back, the bus veers strangely. The wine spills over the pink roses as she sips from the bottle through the stems. Her hair comes loose and falls over her shoulders.

"Have some." She offers Sean the carafe.

"Oh, I don't drink," he says, fascinated.

"Just one sip." She giggles, holding the carafe to his lips.

He sips slowly. "Oh, goodness, that went right to my head!" Cara tosses her hair back, laughing. "I think I feel a little tipsy," he tells her.

"That's good." She puts down the wine and settles onto Sean's lap. "Let's go swimming," she whispers.

"Where?" he asks stupidly.

"I don't have my bathing suit; what could I wear?" Cara wonders. She pauses to consider the question. "I'll have to wear my pajamas," she concludes seriously.

Sean pulls off his sweater. A white card falls from his pocket. *Tiki Sofer, poet*, it says. *Hebrew and English. 370 Richmond Rd., Brooklyn, N.Y.*

"Brian was right," Sean whispers to Cara. "That fat man was weird."

She nods sleepily and closes her eyes. Sean wraps his sweater around her shoulders.

Brian chins the luggage rack and sings out, "When you're a Jet you're the swingin'est thing . . ." He chins the rack again, and the bus stops. Brian drops to the floor quickly. "I just thought of something," he says in a hushed voice. "When you get old, does your pubic hair turn gray?"

The bus is silent. Brian crosses the aisle unsteadily. "Shit," he says solemnly. "I never thought of that."

Wish List

A sheik rushes through Heathrow, followed by his wives and children and his children's servants, each pushing a Smarte Carte. A young American couple cuts through with a screaming baby. "Where's the plug?" the mother asks desperately. Her husband fishes out a pacifier from his load of baby gear and plugs the baby's mouth. "We really shouldn't do it." He sighs guiltily.

Rolling their tiny suitcases, a group of stewardesses scud across the terrazzo floor. "And so," says the youngest, "I just told him, 'I would hardly worry, sir. Our security is excellent. But if you are disturbed by your neighbor, we have one vacant seat in the smoking section.'" A young Hasid runs to catch a 10 A.M. flight, closely followed by a group of middle-aged women wearing double-knit polyester pant suits, then a Japanese school tour, the students dressed like French schoolgirls.

Swaying a little in the crowd, Professor Edward Markowitz stops for a head count: four kids—Miriam, Ben,

Avi, Yehudit—two friends, Grandma, six suitcases, three duffels, and the goddamn violin. Ed and his wife, Sarah, look warily at the group they have brought to England for the summer, the whole summer. A bunch of teenagers and other nongrown-ups waiting to be transported to Oxford, fed, and amused. Two of the kids are fighting already. The others want to get some real breakfast. Then there are the friends the boys have brought along: Noam, the gum chewer, and Ben's friend Scott, who leans against the wall reading *Zen and the Art of Motorcycle Maintenance*. Ben lifts the left side of Scott's Walkman. "Living in the sixties?" he asks.

Ed clears his throat. "Sarah, could I talk to you for a minute?"

His wife gives up fishing for a brush in her huge leather-thong bag. As they walk out of earshot, Sarah calls back, "Ben, get a chair for your grandmother." Ben flashes Grandma a pearly smile and offers her a suitcase to sit on.

"What we should do," Sarah tells Ed dryly, "we should get two cabs and a limo. One cab for the luggage, one cab for the kids, the limo for your mother. We'll send your lectures along with them. Then just the two of us can cash in our tickets right here and bicycle through Brittany."

"Not bad," Ed mutters, "but I wouldn't trust my lectures to that group."

Noam has gone to sit next to Grandma. "Piece gum?" he offers.

"I wear dentures," Rose Markowitz says in a terrible voice.

"Okay, okay," Noam says. " 'scool, 'scool."

"This was not what I had in mind when I was invited

to Oxford," Ed tells Sarah. "The centre is very elegant. Badly endowed, but elegant. It's got a kind of genteel poverty and . . . *Christ*, what am I going to do with six stir-crazy teenagers out in Wantage? This is not going to work, Sarah. This is a lecture series, not a youth hostel. Israeli novelists and medieval Arabists—and these people take themselves very seriously. Not that anyone in Oxford comes," he adds. "What do Oxford philosophers and Russian historians care about Jewish-Arab relations? Half the speakers don't know anything about any relations after the thirteenth century." Ed looks again at the kids and begins to smile. "Well, people are going to come to *my* lectures. Looks like I've shlepped myself an audience."

They squeeze into two cabs: the older Markowitzes in one, the younger tribe packed into another with Cadbury chocolate bars. The gray airport lifts away from them, and they speed through bright June fields.

The Wantage Centre is housed in an Elizabethan manor or, as the kids dub it, "Jesus, the real thing." The cabs approach the manor on a long, curving drive shaded with yew trees. Green lawns surround the house, sunken gardens, and flower beds. Beyond the gardens, the cottages, barn, and greenhouse are also owned by the centre. In each cottage lives a scholar and his or her family. Some stay for the summer, some for a sabbatical. The manor itself is built of gray stone. It's a three-story, heavy-browed building with deep walls, massive windows, and chimneys.

Dick Frankel greets the Markowitzes at the door—a huge oak door with iron claw hinges and a mezuzah. Frankel has pale-blue eyes and a delicate beaklike nose.

"Edward, Sarah, welcome to Wantage!" He beams.

"Do come in. How was your flight? My goodness, there are so many of us. The cottages seem quite crammed, so we've roomed you in the manor. Would that be *too* awful? Oh, excellent, then we can push on. Yes, all the way at the top of the stairs," he tells the kids, who have already pushed on. "McBride would help with the bags, but I don't want to trouble him." Frankel laughs nervously. "He is very probably the most important person at the centre. Sees to the heaters and the grounds. I am certain we should all collapse without him. He has that practicality—well, I suppose we academics will always live in awe of it."

❧❧❧

As Frankel utters these words, McBride is stirring in the second-floor blue bedroom. He grimaces and sits up in bed. "Yoffa," he grumbles, "where's my clothes?" Yaffa is already dressed. She sits at her writing desk, watching him with dark, burning eyes.

"Why do you not say my name in all?" she demands in her heavy Israeli accent.

" 'stoo long." McBride groans, trying to find his pants without leaving the warm bed.

"I think sometimes you do not know me—my name or my art. I am Yaffa Yehuda-Yardeni. Do you read me, do you know my soul?"

McBride flops back in a tangle of sheets and shuts his eyes.

Her voice softens just at the sight of him. "But you do not need novels," she murmurs fervently. "You are a novel. D. H. Lawrence gave birth to you."

"She did?" McBride asks distantly.

"My God," Yaffa breathes, "your hair, your eyes. My God, your shoulders. That mustache."

"D'you think I should shave it off?" McBride asks with sudden interest.

"It would kill me."

"Oh."

"I thought yesterday of your arms," she tells him. "They remember to me *Anna Karenina*. The meadow mown with peasants. Their muscling arms around the scythes."

McBride takes a towel and stumbles toward the bathroom.

"When will I see you again?" she asks.

"When I come out," he says, with his mouth full of toothpaste.

"Tonight?" she persists urgently. "If you see the hall light burning, come to me tonight."

"Ease off, woman," he bellows, and slams the door.

⌒⌒

Ed stops on the landing to catch his breath. The great staircase is carved, with dusty banisters. Below him lies the tiled entrance hall, with its dark-paneled walls. The front door is bolted shut with a massive wooden bar. Above it gleams a red EXIT sign.

The kids bang up the stairs with the cleaning lady. The attics have been finished and partitioned into bedrooms. "There's been seen a ghost in these attics," the maid tells them breathlessly.

"Yeah? Was it a girl or a guy?"

"She is the ghost of the lady who lived here and hung

herself because she loved a Moor and her parents locked her up and wouldn't let her see him."

"Good deal," says Noam, looking around the rooms with new respect. He opens the diamond-paned window and looks out at the grounds in the back of the manor: a wide green lawn and then a low stone wall; beyond that, a sunken garden, a higher wall, then an apple orchard; and beyond that, stretching out to the horizon, wind-ruffled fields of wheat. The others join him at the window. "Football!" he yells. The kids charge downstairs to take on the field.

᭙᭙᭙

On the second floor, Frankel shows the older Markowitzes to the rose bedroom. Grandma has a green room next door. "It's small," she says, "but I'm glad of any place I can lay my head. Edward, would you draw the drapes and bring me my book? Thank you." She eases a chair to the desk and turns on the little desk lamp. "It doesn't burn very brightly," she observes.

Frankel touches the desk pensively. "A brilliant graduate student used to live here." He says it much as the maid told of the ghost. "He was short-listed for a position at Leeds but was edged out and forced to go to a ghastly university in America." Frankel shudders. "Texas, I believe."

"Austin?" Ed laughs. "He'll have the highest salary and the lowest cost of living in the country. Somehow I wouldn't pity him."

"Oh, not *pity*. No one wants pity. In fact, when he left we didn't speak of it. He was very proud."

"Come now," Ed says. "When you consider the money that school has."

"But you come from America yourself, Ed. So it wouldn't affect you the way it would him," Frankel says gently.

～

As Frankel drives home that evening, he waves to Mc-Bride, who stands at the gate, doing something clever with the hinges. Splendid. And when one thinks that five years ago the place was used as digs and cut up into little rooms! Mrs. Frankel was very unkind about that. Hotel for academics, she had called it. Cheap place for Israeli aesthetes, sanatorium for languishing Orientalists, half-way house for Persian miniature cryptographers after budget cuts.

It is absolutely untrue. Frankel's lips twitch in indignation. "We have a mission of peace," he says aloud, quoting the centre brochure. Even Mrs. Frankel admits it was quite a coup getting Ed Markowitz for the summer. A Georgetown expert in terrorism. It certainly modernizes the lecture series. "Professor Markowitz spent his undergraduate years at Cornell," Frankel murmurs, formulating a little off-the-cuff introduction for Thursday. No, perhaps something a bit more dramatic. "Understanding the motives, the practice, indeed the science, of terrorism has always been, though we hope will not always be, of much concern to students in the field of Jewish-Arab relations." Yes, that has a nice ring. Personal, but solid and well considered. Frankel turns on the little black radio perched on the dashboard. A modern string quartet prickles against his skin. He supposes it's very interesting but turns down the volume just the same. Have they ordered the cakes for the centre's anniversary? Little white chairs on the south lawn. He'll have to say a few words. "We have done much, but there is much to do." Yes. Frankel smiles at the modesty of the phrase. He hasn't spoken of it publicly, but he sees unlimited possibilities for the centre. It is even possible that in future years, Arab scholars will accept invitations to Wantage.

∾

As Frankel muses on Progress, Ed Markowitz wearily drives a rented Fiat to the Oriental Institute. He had not wanted to go on the day of his arrival, but this is the only time he can be sure to see Mujahid Rashaf, who is returning to Saudi Arabia within the week. Rashaf is an Oxford fellow and the son of a merchant prince. He will provide just the reasoned yet religious opinions that Markowitz seeks for his book, *Terrorism: A Civilized Creed*.

"A provocative title," the institute director says languidly at tea. They sit in dark-green leather chairs and sip Lapsang souchong. A dozen scholars chat at the inlaid tables, leaning forward from the shadows of their hooded chairs.

"But it's meant to be provocative," Markowitz replies. "Terrorism must be understood as part of an ethical code. To study terrorism with any dispassion, we have to begin from the understanding that it is a logical, rational, and ethnically valid form of action. The real issue in the Middle East is cultural absolutism—something we must recognize in ourselves as well as in Arab nations."

"Hmm." The institute director bites a chocolate-glazed biscuit delicately. "Not to press you to divulge

your conclusions, but I suppose there are no easy answers."

"Exchange, moderation, tolerance," Ed answers con-
fidently. "Not easy, but certainly answers."

Markowitz rises to refill his cup at the buffet table,
glad to leave the director, who always speaks with such a
flat, bored voice. He joins the livelier circle around
Mujahid Rashaf. The young man wears white slacks and
a simple linen shirt. He speaks with the natural, artless
manner of one used to an audience. His features are not
as delicate as his accent. He has a fleshy face and small
bright eyes. Ed sees at once that Rashaf is absolutely
brilliant. His dissertation is a study of the early industrial
influences that shaped Fitzgerald's distortion of Omar
Khayyám.

Ed is nearly faint with exhaustion when he leaves the
tea. He shakes hands with Rashaf and suggests corre-
sponding about the changing role of terrorism in Israel.

Rashaf smiles and presses Markowitz's hand. "There
is no change," he says gently, patiently. "We will drive
you into the sea."

∽∾∽

At Wantage, a few scholars gather in the library after dinner. The small oak-paneled room contains a strange collection of chairs—some overstuffed and Victorian, some
anorexic and modern. Books have overrun the shelves
and advanced to the tabletops: Saadya, Bellow, Imru 'l
Qais, Amos Oz, Rosenfeld, Abu Nuwas, Kissinger. A new
history of Lebanon, an old study of international law in
the West Bank, Hourani's classic, almost elegiac history of
Arabic thought. Bound in green-and-red leather, the rival

Arabic dictionaries compete for space. The French-Arabic version edges out the German-Arabic by a tome. The fellows of Wantage talk placidly in a room of books uncatalogued and wild, competing for space in precarious layers toppling toward the light.

Itzak Tapuz, the great Israeli playwright, confers in a corner with his illustrator, a young cousin he has commissioned to draw sketches for his forthcoming collected stories. A quick-eyed Yemenite anthropologist perches on the movable library stairs. "So. Are you the scholar or the spouse?" she asks Sarah Markowitz.

"I earn my living as a teacher, and I'm writing a novel, so I'm probably—"

"Got that. I'm Tiki Sofer. I'm the scholar. My husband drives a cab. We run it in the city. The centre invited me to speak, but the plane fare came from the cab. That's the way it is; the real work supports the fancy stuff. What is this leisure of the eighteenth century? Ha, Leisure!" She pronounces it with a succulent mock-English accent. "I write poems on Ocean Parkway. Driving on it. In the car. I even got myself a cheap publisher right in the cab. From Oxford, yet. Just sitting in the backseat. And none of this vanity press shit. I pay only expenses. That's the way I work."

"I have to use a desk," says Sarah, amused and discomfited. Tiki Sofer must picture her typing eccentrically after hours beside a skull-shaped candy dish, like Penny in *You Can't Take It with You*. Or as a languid housewife shuffling through chapters in bedroom slippers. These images are new to Sarah Markowitz, who likes to think of her desk in Washington as an emblem of the Great Tradition: Jane Austen, George Eliot, Tillie Olsen, Cynthia Ozick.

The door opens and the resident anthropologist Jonathan Collins steps in, his beard meaning to get trimmed. "Sarah!" he cries. "Come here, old thing. Knew where to dig you up. How are you? Where's Ed? What—tucked away in bed already? After all those hours on the plane? I always do a good run to reorient the spine. I've only just returned from the field myself. Now, now, oral history in Albania is every bit as much fieldwork as the Ituri forest. It's at least as much of a shlep and every bit as wild. I would tell you, but you would never believe me. That synagogue! All octogenarians, and still fighting and squabbling like men half their age. But really, we're all frightfully glad to see you. Especially Frankel. The thing is, it's been a horrible winter. Peace institutes are simply becoming a drug on the market, and in terms of funding—well, I suppose you know about the Moonies. It did get to be a nasty business with solicitors and such. Ed will explain. No, they sued *us*. But now the great American capitalist is coming to save us. Oh, didn't you? Our Ed is the whole show. Going to be relevant to the times and talk up the peace process and other American things."

Tiki looks at Jonathan shrewdly. "And what does this American get?"

"Oh—glory, of course. The one who gets is the little bourgeois fund-raiser who found him."

"A commission for bringing in money?" asks Sarah.

"What commission? Terence Glueck finds and brings this donor, and he gets the centre. One more donor like this, and he could have full feudal rights to the place. We'll all labor in the cottages and pay a tithe of our pages." Jonathan laughs at his medieval vision. He himself can't tell whether he speaks bitterly or from an instinct to amuse.

❧

That night the Markowitz kids sleep deeply, as only the jet-lagged can sleep: legs and arms extended without seat belts, cramped necks and shoulders slowly melting into relaxation. Only Ben's friend is awake. Scott is still reading *Zen and the Art of Motorcycle Maintenance*. On the second floor, Ed leafs through the centre brochure. The photo of a dark-eyed woman fills the back page, with the legend: "Wantage is so precious a place for the majority of us. Even if I write only one chapter here, I will know I wrote it at the Centre. —Yaffa Yehuda-Yardeni, novelist." Ed yawns and turns out the light.

Except for the hall light, the last light in the manor is Grandma's. Rose Markowitz never sleeps. If she did sleep she would be the first to notice, but sadly sleep is impossible, because of the pain. She feels it most when she is alone and when the rest are talking about things that mean nothing to her. It is an agonizing pain. It tears through her so fast that she could not tell you where it hurt. Rose closes her thick paperback romance. A loathsome thing and badly written. Not at all tasteful, like *The Thorn Birds*. She pads to the night table and bravely takes out her bottle of pills. There are now only sixty-one pills left. In the lighted hall, the door to that Israeli woman's room stands ajar. Rose walks past it to the high-ceilinged bathroom. A scalding bath is the only thing for the pain besides the pills. She floods the claw-footed tub with steaming water. The sound reassures her; reminds her of bubble baths and white lace dresses. She had been a picture in that dress. The water rushes on. Who had told her that? She turns off the tap and suddenly is afraid to step into the brimming tub. It is too deep for her, and she cannot climb out alone. She would sit down and sob, but no one would even hear her. She looks at the water and wonders briefly how to drain it, then turns off the hall light and shuffles back to her room. How she would like to sail again to Sweden or the Orient. The destination never matters. Ed could arrange it. Rose smiles—how could she be old? She has never lost her youthful wander-lust, the impatience for excitement and the vague sense of future possibilities. The only difficulty is that there are now only sixty-one pills left.

∽

The next morning Yaffa thunders into the kitchen. The manor's kitchens are remnants of the building's days as student digs. Now the scholars use them. On the third floor a mangy medievalist piles dishes in the sink; on the second floor a young Arabist grows bean sprouts. And here on the first floor Yaffa slams a frying pan on the stove and takes out a stick of butter. She wears a man-sized shaggy plush bathrobe and orange terry-cloth slippers. Keys clatter down the hall, and McBride enters, whistling. He stands in the doorway with his cocker span-iel, Lorna. The two of them look at Yaffa, bright-eyed. "Make me an egg, Yoff," McBride orders.

"What?" She snarls, with her back to him.

"Not too runny."

She tilts the pan to spread the melting butter. "My only weapon," she whispers dramatically. Then she calls out, "Let *her* do it."

"The wife hates eggs. Can't stand the sight of them. Calls 'em liquid chickens."

Yaffa slams the pan on the stove and whirls to face

him. "Look. These shadows. These lines," she cries, pointing to the dark circles under her eyes. "I never slept last night."

"Huh," McBride says thoughtfully. Lorna thumps her tail at his feet.

"Where were you?" Yaffa explodes.

"In bed," he answers. "Look, are you making my egg?"

Yaffa takes an egg from the icebox and hurls it at him. The egg smashes on the door frame and drips down to the floor, where Lorna licks it up.

"In bed. With *her*." Yaffa roars. "You lied."

"You said come if the hall light was on, but it was off," reasons McBride.

"Liar!" Yaffa screams.

"Bloody mess," mutters McBride. He whistles to Lorna and ambles down the hall.

The Markowitz kids run past him into the kitchen. "Food! Breakfast!" they scream. They freeze in the doorway as Yaffa slaps into the seething pan three strips of fat-marbled bacon.

❧

The manor orangerie has been converted into a three-bedroom house for the Albert and Joyce Siedenstein Fellow on sabbatical leave from the Hebrew University. This year's fellowship funds Gavriel Ben-Zion, his wife, and their two children, who eat Rolos behind the couch and watch the neighbors through the glass walls of the converted greenhouse. "People are coming," thirteen-year-old Ezra whispers to his younger sister, Naomi.

"Back to the table," orders Geulah Ben-Zion. Her

voice carries. Ezra and Naomi push their Rolos under the couch and join their parents for blueberry muffins. The orangerie is filled with modern furniture, in keeping with its glass structure. In the winter it's the warmest place in the centre, but in June the greenhouse effect overheats the place. Geulah Ben-Zion has put up green curtains to screen against the sun and passersby. She has covered the picture window in the lavatory and the glass walls in the kitchen. "You can hardly blame her," the cleaning women in the manor said to one another. "It's like living in a cucumber frame."

"Can't you see them?" little Naomi calls out. She draws the curtains by the kitchen table, revealing a long line of Markowitzes winding toward the door. Gavriel Ben-Zion puts down the *Times* and goes to greet the visitors. He stands in the doorway imposingly, a tall Yemenite man with a military haircut.

"Hi!" Sarah Markowitz says hopefully.

Ed puts out his hand. "I don't suppose you've ever seen us before, but I'm Ed Markowitz; we just got in last night. Uh, this is my family." He gestures hurriedly.

"Edward," Grandma whispers disapprovingly at his elbow.

"This is my mother, Rose Markowitz," Ed adds.

Rose looks at Gavriel appraisingly. "I am pleased to meet you, Mr. . . ."

"Ben-Zion," Gavriel finishes.

"As I said, we just woke up this morning; I mean, we just got here last night," Ed continues.

"Food, Dad," one of the kids prompts from behind.

∽

"We had no idea the kitchens weren't kosher," Sarah tells Geulah at the table.

"They are kosher on the second and third floors." Geulah reaches for the plate of blueberry muffins. Only crumbs are left. The kids have finished off the muffins and run outside. At the window, Geulah sees Ezra and Naomi leading the teenagers to the sunken garden. Mc-Bride passes, naked to the waist and carrying a rake. "*That* is a beautiful man." Geulah opens the green curtains a little wider for Sarah to see.

"Yes, he certainly is," agrees Rose.

"You have beautiful children," Sarah says, embarrassed. "The little girl looks just like you."

"Oh, no." Geulah comes back to the table. "They're both adopted. And they're Yemenite, like Gavri, not like me."

∽∾∽

"I am so glad to find you here, Gavriel," Ed says in the study. "I've heard a great deal about you."

"Really," Gavriel replies dryly. "What have you heard?"

Ed searches quickly for something repeatable. Ben-Zion is one of two Yemenite professors in Israel. He is a Communist. He married money. She is six years older. He has a whole house in Jerusalem. "Well, about your eminence in the field." Ed beams with vague joviality. "I was riveted by your book *Jihad as Proletarian Uprising*. I'm hoping to get a lot of work done this summer. I'm just finishing my new book about terrorism."

"A difficult subject." Gavriel shifts his weight back in his swivel chair.

"Oh, yes, of course. Very difficult," Ed agrees. "But not necessarily tragic. In fact, I do something I haven't seen done in any of the literature. I've been talking about terrorism as a dynamic process involving elements of anarchic creativity. In fact, we see in the four terroristic elements the mirror image of so-called constructive action. In simple terms, both the terrorist and the rescuer use the four elements secrecy, surprise, team or theistic loyalty, and escape. You're smiling. You think this is shocking."

"No," Gavriel says bluntly. "I think you're a jackass."

Back in the kitchen, Sarah and Geulah are planning for both families to go to the Eights Week boat races.

"None too soon," says Sarah. "The kids are going to do and see everything in the village by tomorrow."

"It's important to plan activities," Guelah says earnestly. "I work with the children every day on their projects, but they must have outings."

"You sound very scientific." Sarah laughs. "I just let the kids scrounge."

The women hear rising voices from the study.

"Listen!" Gavriel shouts. "You know nothing about rescue missions."

"What do you mean, nothing? I was on-call consultant for *Entebbe*—the movie."

"Right!" Gavriel shoots back bitterly. "The movie. Creative dynamics. You don't know."

"So you were there?" Ed asks sarcastically.

"I was in Yemen. Operation Magic Carpet. I was sixteen, and I knew the language. I was ordered to go to villages and gather up the people. So I did, and they followed me to the landing strips. Sold everything to get there. And here they are. We got them here. Is there organization? Dynamic? Not enough planes, and the flights came late. Families died on the landing strips without food or money. No shelter. Waiting for the planes I promised them. Don't tell me about creativity. There's a fifth element, you see: the success factor. And terrorists have more success than rescuers. It's a lot easier to blow up people than to keep them in one piece."

"Hey," says Ed, abashed. "I should have been more sensitive. This is heavy stuff. We run into this a lot."

"Go to Ethiopia," Gavriel says. "More of you experts should go out into the field."

"Oh, no. The field is very crowded at the moment," Ed demurs. "You don't know the number of grad students."

❧

Outside on the lawn, the kids tramp past the little garden study built for Tapuz. They peek in the window and see the Israeli playwright scribbling furiously in his undershirt. Ezra and Naomi take the Markowitz kids through the Elizabethan grass tennis courts, where Ian Scott and his wife, Gwendolyn, live in the converted tennis pavilion. "This is not a Jewish centre," Frankel likes to tell prospective donors. "This is a centre studying Arab-Jewish affairs." He always mentions the Scotts' excellent work in ancient siege archaeology at this point. The Scotts are charmed by this, and try to come every winter to Wantage. "It's lovely at Christmastime," Gwendolyn says. "I get out all my traditions and we have a great big Advent party for all the Wantage fellows. Not everyone eats, of course, but everyone can come, because there

aren't any other Advent parties competing. The whole
thing seemed a bit Jewish at first. But we hardly notice
anymore."

The kids walk past the barn, now the library, and the
other cottages. They climb over the low stone wall and
jump into the orchard. "A rabbit!" Naomi gasps. She
points to a tiny gray rabbit with quivering ears, startled
from under an apple tree's gnarled roots. Naomi moves
toward it slowly and takes it up in her hands. The rabbit
sits in her cupped hands, paralyzed with fear. "It's a girl
rabbit," Naomi announces without looking. "And her
name is Shlomit."

～

After the Markowitzes have gone, Geulah gathers up the
wash in her wicker basket and walks to the gray stone
horse stalls at the side of the manor, which now house the
washing machines. Red roses cover the stalls outside, and
inside, iron rings still lie embedded in the stone. Tiki
Sofer is folding towels from a pile on the dryer.

"Hi," she says briskly.

"I didn't know you did laundry, Tiki." Geulah has
heard Tiki expound on domestic philosophy.

"I take my turn. You should put your husband on the
rotation system. Why slave? I learned that from watching
Yemeni women. Even in America they want to kill themselves. I say: Look—they want peeled vegetables, I'll buy
them peeled. Diced? I'll get prediced from Birds Eye.
They want child care? I'll send the kids to day care."

"I'm not like you," Geulah says defensively. "My
children are a full-time occupation. I have to fulfill their
needs."

"Ima!" calls Naomi, running into the laundry stall. Naomi holds out the baby rabbit. "Ima, we have to take her in."

"Please, Ima," says Ezra. "We'll keep her in our room. Her name is Shlomit the Rabbit."

∾∾∾

Jonathan Collins's worst fears gain new substance that afternoon. Frankel drives up with the American fund-raiser and the multimillionaire the American has found for the centre.

As Jonathan watches at the library window, the fund-raiser emerges from the car. He is a tall, bony man wearing white pleated pants and a sapphire-blue silk shirt unbuttoned at the chest. He carries a small leather purse under his arm. "Oh, my God, my God." Jonathan gasps, in real horror. "Is he a pansy, or is he just American?" A woman follows the fund-raiser. She wears a red silk dress and also carries a purse. She wraps her arm around the American's waist and whispers something into his ear. The couple help an elderly man out of the car. He walks, bent and wispy-haired, toward the stone manor steps. Frankel pops out, looks around for McBride, and then opens the boot to carry the suitcases himself.

Jonathan turns away from the window miserably. He picks up a copy of the *Economist* and tries to read. He puts it down again. What will become of the centre? Can Frankel really be that desperate? He'll give it to the Americans, and they'll send over students. Girls taking their junior year abroad. The old man will die, and the Americans will take on the trust, carve up the lands. Start high-tech concessions.

"This is the library," says Frankel, opening the door grandly. "Oh, Jonathan! What a pleasure! Jonathan, this is Terence and Pat Glueck from Miami. And this is Mr. Armistead Buchsbaum, also a Miamian. Mr. Buchsbaum, Jonathan is one of our treasures here at Wantage—an anthropologist doing marvelous things with the study of fundamentalism in the Middle East. I think he's taught us all how much common ground there is for extremists *qua* extremists."

"What do you do?" Jonathan asks Terence.

"I'm an art historian," Terence answers with unaffected boredom. "I focus on the Mannerists."

"You all make me feel terribly unacademic," Pat asserts comfortably.

"Oh, heavens." Jonathan moans after they have left. "An orthodontist. The wife is an orthodontist." The American Dream: stainless-steel teeth. They'll hollow out the centre and fill it with silver.

〜

That evening two desk lights shine in the library. At one desk, Ed Markowitz is revising his lecture for Thursday— "Melanin and Miasma: The Racial Factor in the Bekaa Air Strikes." At the other desk Sarah is revising part three of her novel. It's the story of a woman named Rachel Meyers who grew up in the 1950s in New York and studied English at Barnard. After she moves to California with her husband, Bob, Rachel finishes her master's at UCLA. The job market is tight, and Rachel takes a job on a research grant with a group of draft-dodging linguists. By the end of the seventies, the soft money is gone, and Rachel takes time off to paint. She joins a painting group and starts to discuss her work with others. Friends urge her to develop her talent, but she decides to go back to school and finish her Ph.D. in English. With Bob's support, she does this. After she has earned her Ph.D., she leaves the field to paint full time.

"Sarah." Ed looks up from his desk. "We're going to have to do something about my mother."

"You make it sound like euthanasia."

"No, no. I mean, you're going to have to take her to see Henry."

"Why me?" Sarah unscrews the parts of her ballpoint. "He's not my brother."

"But she's been kvetching about this all day: 'I only came to England to see Henry. I must see my son.'"

"Then you should take her, Ed. How is Henry going to feel if his sister-in-law brings her? He knows we're all here."

"I can't go to that house."

"You mean you won't."

"No; I can't. And don't do that to your pen. You're getting ink all over."

"Don't tell me what to do with my pen. I want to know why you can't take your own mother to visit your own brother. You don't have to stay very long."

"Can't do it. I'm allergic to that house."

"You are not."

"Yes I am. Look—don't use that tone of voice with me."

"You don't have any allergies," Sarah reminds him.

"Yes I do. It's just that I'm allergic to very rare things that we don't have in Georgetown."

"Like what?"

"Cracked leather bindings, moldy shmatas from the seventeenth century, old wine with cork fragments."

"You mean you're allergic to his whole lifestyle." Sarah huffs. "I think that's extremely insensitive."

Ed gives her a look. "Since when have you become my brother's great defender?"

"He's part of the family. To be specific, *your* part. I don't see why it's such a sacrifice to take your mother to spend a few hours with him. You'll all survive."

"I don't have time for this." Ed growls. "What none of you seem to understand is that I am not on vacation. I have lectures to write."

"And you have allergies," Sarah snaps. "I have allergies too. I'm allergic to bull."

"Don't start." Ed points at Sarah emphatically. "If you think this is because I disapprove of Henry, you're wrong."

"Oh, ho." Sarah laughs. "Tie that little bull outside."

ᗑᘉᗑ

In the end, they decide to take Henry on neutral ground. Henry will meet them at the boat races, with all the kids and the Ben-Zions. Grandma will be happy, and Ed can escape his allergies in the open air.

The Markowitzes rent another Fiat for the overflow of kids. After long and violent disputes, the oldest daughter, Miriam, gets to drive it. Miriam secures this right by convincing Naomi Ben-Zion that Shlomit the Rabbit doesn't want to go to Eights Week.

The day is hot, the lines long. Students drink beer in Edwardian clothes. The men don't dress up much, but the women wear long skirts and white starched blouses with high collars and muttonchop sleeves. They sport straw boaters with wide ribbon bands. One woman, her hair piled up, wears a blue dress with a bustle and carries a parasol. The Markowitzes meet Henry in front of the boathouse of St. Edmund Hall—Teddy Hall.

"Darlings!" Henry cries, and runs toward them with wet kisses. He wears a Greek fisherman's cap incongruously small and flat on his large, domed head. "Mother!" Henry beams. "You're looking well!"

"As well as can be expected." Rose sighs.

"Children!" Henry moves on. "Tell me everything!"

"I'm at Georgetown," Miriam begins.

"She's doing very well," Sarah continues. "And Ben will be applying to Georgetown in the fall."

"Are you still playing that tuba?" Henry asks Yehudit.

"Sax," she corrects.

"She just made the Northwest Washington select band. And Avi got the Most Improved award in all of high-school gym."

"Mom." Avi groans.

"And who are these young people?" Henry points to Scott and Noam, who watch the oarsmen carry the boats down the cleated boathouse ramp to the river.

"The boys brought their friends, Scott and Noam."

"Hey," says Scott.

"'t's happenin'," says Noam.

Ed appears, having dashed off for several minutes to tend the parking meters. "Good to see you," he hails Henry.

Henry takes Ed's hand and presses it between his own. He looks into Ed's eyes and says, "You mean a lot to me."

"Uh, yeah." Ed laughs to himself like a bad stand-up comedian. "You look well," Ed says.

"I feel good." Henry clings to Ed's hand. "I've decided to be happy. I've decided. It's really a conscious decision, like deciding to go to the theater or switch analysts."

"Is that what you've done?" asks Ed.

"What have I done?" Henry echoes. "Is that what you're asking? Well, I went to Stratford and saw *Romeo and Juliet.* You really must go. They did it as an episode from *Miami Vice.* With the commercials. But I tell you, there was something there that was absolutely compelling. First of all, the use of the rock video as Mercutio's vehicle for the Queen Mab speech was just technically astounding. You know, Tammany was the director, and he has a very eclectic vision. As a whole it seems incoherent, but as fragments there is a sort of anarchic realization of pattern in his productions. Especially during the commercials, one had the sense that the tragedy was transposed from the slight and, you know, rather flawed structure of early Shakespeare to a searing indictment of American society."

"It sounds terrible," Ed says.

"Oh, it was terrible, but after all, that was the point. The ass in the *Times* headlined his review: 'More Pity than Terror.' But I personally thought that was just his bit of egoistic fun. Yes, obviously a theater critic has read the *Poetics.* The fact that he has to prove it so vulgarly really speaks to us about the educational system. But I tell you this, Ed, because I think you should go—as a student of violence."

"A student of terrorism," Ed corrects as they follow the Ben-Zions to the bridge.

"Well, it's the same thing," Henry says.

"No, it is *not*, Henry." Ed's face reddens. "Terrorism is a technical sociological term."

Henry takes a deep breath and closes his eyes. His brother's opinions always make him ill.

The starting gun fires, and the boats pulse forward, oar blades skinning the water.

On the other side of the bridge stand Terence Glueck and his wife, Pat. The two had been at Oxford as students and find the American tourists extremely funny. Just yesterday Terence saved a young man whose punt got stuck in the mud, while his girlfriend glared from the boat.

"Darling," Pat says now, "do you really think old Armistead is going to give a million to the centre? It's not very hope-of-the-next-generation-looking. I haven't seen any students."

"They're working," says Terence.

"In their little garrets," Pat muses. "Manual typewriters. If I were Frankel, I'd get the whole place Wanged. Wang gives matching funds, and they would have some word processing."

"It doesn't matter," Terence asserts. "Armistead Buchsbaum doesn't know from high tech. Frankel has charm and English teas, that Oxford stumble in his voice."

"Well, I think that before Buchsbaum pops off, he's going to give it all to the cancer society or the lung association."

"He doesn't have any major diseases."

"Then he'll give it to the osteoporosis fund."

"Oh, Pat, don't be morbid. He's going to live a long time and give the money here. And we'll have a nice little chair at Wantage for the summers. Without the children."

"I wonder how they're doing with Mrs. Dimauro."
Pat gets out her binoculars to watch the faraway boats.

"I wonder how she's doing with them."

～

The weeks pass, and the Markowitz kids take over the television room to watch the Wimbledon matches. "It's live," says Ben.

"It's there," says Noam.

Ed Markowitz delivers his weekly lectures on terrorism in the paneled ballroom. He has the largest audience of any summer fellow: a core number of seven and a half people (Rose comes about half the time), plus an occasional student. Sarah has finished revising her novel. Despite the fact that the heroine's mother-in-law, Iris, comes to live with the family, Rachel's future as a painter is assured. In the orangerie, Shlomit has grown from a tiny ball of fluff into an enormous gray hare. She shreds her newspaper, knocks over her water dish, and thumps across the carpet, leaving behind a trail of brown pellets.

～

On the day of her lecture, "The Novelist as Peacemaker of Nations," Yaffa walks with McBride in the orchard.

"Why will you not come to hear me?" she asks, gripping his arm.

"I don't want to come."

"It's *her*," Yaffa thunders.

"No."

"Someone else." Yaffa holds him by the shoulders and stares into his eyes.

"No, but I have to go into town and rent chairs for the anniversary lunch."

"They exploit you," Yaffa whispers. "Let's run away. I would sleep on the moors."

McBride looks at her, puzzled. "You're a funny girl, Yoff."

"It's crazy," she hisses. "They walk on you."

"They pay me," McBride states practically.

"You no longer want to leave." Yaffa's black nylon skirt catches on the rough bark of an apple tree.

McBride says dreamily, "What I really fancy is a ladies' hairdressing shop."

"A hair shop! A head shop! You want to finger ladies' hair after I leave! You have no money!"

McBride smiles. "I'm going to hock the silver tray Frankel gives me for ten years of service."

∽∾∽

"The Novelist as Peacemaker of Nations." Yaffa pronounces the title of her lecture slowly. Then she throws up her hands and cries, "What can the novelist do?"

She clasps her hands behind her and paces the floor, as some members of the audience scribble: "novelist peacemaker nations," and others note down: "what can novelist do?"

Yaffa stands against the dark wood paneling and continues. "What can she do but work and learn, developing her own work in the singular experience that is her own? I can only tell you the method of my own. The life of my own days. The novel is work and blood. A love child of mysterious parent. The birth is long. A longing for the soul to speak to a companion. A desire great like the lust of the crops in the earth."

Frankel creeps into the back row to take full-length pictures.

"And," Yaffa continues, "the novel is a tension, an inner fight of split identities. Rain and Piss. Stream and Consciousness. Dream and Illusion. Pregnancy and Barrenness. Woman and Male."

The Markowitz kids slump drowsily by the end. Ben Markowitz's friend Scott lies with his head thrown back, Adam's apple exposed on his long neck.

"Ms. Yehuda-Yardeni," Sarah Markowitz says during the quiet question period, "how valuable do you find the writing workshop experience."

"*In*-valuable," Yaffa spits disdainfully.

Sarah writes in her notebook: "workshops invaluable."

∽ᗺᗂ∾

That night McBride directs the caterers as they set up white tables in the great hall for the Wantage Dinner honoring Armistead Buchsbaum's visit and his lifelong commitment to peace. McBride sets out place cards according to Frankel's seating chart. Ian and Gwendolyn Scott sit with the Israelis Tiki Sofer and Itzak Tapuz. Dr. Ben-Zion sits next to Dr. Markowitz, and the Gluecks sit with Buchsbaum and Frankel at the head of the table.

At dinner Terence Glueck talks to Frankel with earnest rapidity. "You see, what we'll do next year is have the same dinner, same food, but for two hundred pounds a head."

"Dear me," says Frankel. "I certainly wouldn't pay

two hundred pounds for a bit of trout. Though it *is* superb." He smiles up at McBride, who serves the fish with heavy silver tongs.

"No, no. That's not it at all," says Terence. "The two hundred is a donation to the centre; it's not really for the food. Maybe ten pounds for the food. That's the way it's done in America. You'd need more tables, of course. Then if you want to make it a *real* gala, charge three hundred pounds. Open up the ballroom for dancing. Wine tasting on the tennis courts. No-host bar in the Blue Room. Strolling violinists. If you got out a mailing, you'd be in good shape. You'll have to cull your list and put together a group of donors good for five hundred or more."

Frankel stares at Terence. "It sounds rather frightening."

"Just a matter of organization," Terence replies. "I hope you have someone working on bequests."

Armistead Buchsbaum looks up vaguely and mutters, "Good fish."

At the other end of the table, McBride takes a trout in his tongs and says, "Well, Yoff, do you want it with the head?"

After McBride clears the dishes away, Frankel stands up and taps his spoon against his glass. "All of us at Wantage would like to welcome and honor Armistead Buchsbaum, one of the greatest friends of Wantage in America. And surely one of the greatest friends of peace in the world. He is a man who has visited India and Russia and served as an ambassador of peace in his position as one of the most prominent leaders of the world's scrap metal trade, both ferrous and nonferrous. Accompanying Mr. Buchsbaum are his two young friends and fellow Miamians, Terence and Patricia Glueck, new and, we hope, frequent visitors to Wantage. . . ."

McBride appears in the doorway with a tray of Key lime pie slices.

Frankel continues. "In honor of these three distinguished guests, I would like to propose a toast: for peace in the Middle East, an end to war among nations, and better understanding through culture—and, as Ms. Yardeni showed us so eloquently—"

The sight of McBride serving pie is too much for Yaffa. That magnificent body stooping to serve Geulah Ben-Zion! Yaffa's eyes brim with tears. She pushes back her chair and rushes from the room.

"Oh dear, oh dear!" Frankel gasps. "The poor girl. Is she ill? Should someone go after her?"

"Contact lens trouble," Gwendolyn Scott murmurs.

"No, no," Tiki tells Gwendolyn. "She is lusting for him."

"Who?" Gwendolyn whispers, laughing.

"The old lech McBride," Tiki answers, more loudly than she intended.

"Oh, God. Tiki!" Gwendolyn gasps. "You're such a card."

"But he *is* a magnificent specimen," Geulah sighs as she watches McBride pick up a fallen fork. Geulah glares at her bullet-headed husband, who eats placidly, allowing Ed Markowitz's insights about Libya to float by him.

"I wish Yaffa's books were in English," Sarah Markowitz tells Geulah.

"Oh, it's all rubbish." Geulah sniffs. "She has written no good books since the first one. Now, that book was a work of genius. *Induction Currents.* That was *takeh* a bestseller. Not a cheap best-seller. A real seller of excellence.

That book had a power—men just could not understand it. It had new ways of writing Hebrew never done before. *That* was a *book*. But now? She has nothing. Nothing."

Jonathan picks at his pie miserably. He watches Terence Glueck draw out a plan for the Wantage Campaign on a cocktail napkin. "Well," Jonathan says to Frankel's wife. "Exciting new developments for the centre, eh?"

Mrs. Frankel spoons in more pie. "Hmm," she replies. "About time, I'd say. Dick has done enough. I've told him time and again he should leave the administration to an administrator. Dick has his own books to write."

Jonathan groans. "You don't *really* think this Glueck is going to take over the centre?"

"We can only hope and pray he does," Mrs. Frankel tells him briskly. "You know, Dick originally wanted to live here in the manor. Like living above the shop!"

McBride finishes serving the pie but takes Yaffa's piece back to the kitchen and eats it himself.

ᚥᚥᚥ

The next Thursday Ed delivers his last lecture on terrorism. The lecture is a special layman's summary for Armistead Buchsbaum and a tour group of seniors from Temple Beth Shalom in Cleveland, Ohio. Ed begins his lecture: "One man's terrorist is another man's freedom fighter." He looks up mildly at his audience. Suddenly Tiki Sofer stands up.

"I object!" she says.

Ed sighs. "I assumed," he says, "that I wouldn't have to delve into relativist methodology. All right, let's backtrack. Let's take a look at what cultural relativism means. When a man—"

"I object," Tiki repeats, still standing. "I object to you using the male noun."

"Oh, I see," says Ed, relieved. "Thank you. I was afraid we were going to have to deal with some epistemological stuff here. Well, there you go. All right, once more, with feeling. One person's terrorist is another person's freedom fighter."

∽✑∽

After the applause, the Markowitzes pile into the two rented cars and drive off to the Cotswolds. "A picnic in the fields." Rose sighs. "This is what I came for."

"I thought you came to see Henry," Sarah teases.

"Henry? Never. I just saw him a few months ago, and he knows I don't like to travel."

They spend the day spreading out food and picnic blankets and then packing up to move as cows graze closer. Rose sits on a folding chair and falls asleep under a tree. The kids drive off in one of the cars, in search of ice cream. As the sun sets, the Markowitzes walk along the river and watch the swans.

It is late when the family returns. Ed gets into bed, pulls up the covers, and falls asleep.

In the distance, a telephone rings. Thudding sounds on the door and a woman's husky voice. Sarah shakes Ed awake. Yaffa stands, backlighted, in the hallway. "It's long distance. The public radio in America. They want Edward Markowitz."

Ed stumbles out of bed to the bathroom. Splashes

water on his face. He pulls up his pajama bottoms and runs to the telephone in the common room.

"Hello. Hello," he says.

"Hello, Professor Markowitz? This is Peter Henkey from NPR in Washington. We've been discussing to-night's hijacking with several specialists, and we would like to ask you for your insights. I understand you are at work on a book about terrorism."

"Yes, I am," Ed replies in a clear voice as he gropes frantically for a copy of the *Times*.

"Well, Professor, as you know, the hijackers have allegedly killed three and wounded eleven. The terrorists claim to be members of the radical Shiite group Black December. How would you describe the mind of a terrorist Shiite to our American listening audience?"

Ed shakes himself. "Perhaps the most important motive for a Shiite terrorist is his belief in the rise of Islam through jihad. This term is commonly mistranslated as 'holy war,' but the actual meaning of the Arabic word is 'moral struggle.' As for the mind of the guerrilla fighter, I would like to stress that terrorist tactics are justified for him by his extreme dedication to certain communal mores. However, it is a dangerous oversimplification to say—"

"Yes. Now, we understand that the two young men on Flight Fifty-two have no other supporters in the plane. The captain reports three passengers have been shot in three hours by one young man, while the other guards the plane. Very briefly, what further developments do you envision?"

Ed feels suddenly nauseous. It must be the mayonnaise from that chicken salad.

"Professor Markowitz?"

His stomach tightens. He has to get to the bathroom, but he clutches the phone and continues. "We must take a closer look at what terrorism means on a deeper level than the ideological—the human level, if you will. . . ."

"Three killed in the last hour," the announcer recaps for the radio audience.

"It's unspeakable," Ed whispers.

But the announcer has already finished the interview. "Thank you, Professor Markowitz. That was Professor Edward Markowitz, expert on terrorism from Georgetown University."

Ed hangs up and takes two Pepto-Bismol tablets. He climbs back into bed, a pillow under his stomach. He feels fat and soft and angry with himself. Always overeating, oversleeping, overachieving.

～

The day of the garden party is clear and cool. The maids lay out the tables with petits fours and chocolate-covered strawberries. Tiki follows the girls, questioning and taping them with her little black machine. "English oral histories," she writes home to her husband. "I've found publishable material. This Jonathan Collins has to go to Hawaii, Albania, and I find data under his own nose!"

"Who told you about the ghost in the manor?" she asks a maid.

"My mum."

"Who told her?"

～

The garden fills with people. The Markowitz kids mob the tables. The Ben-Zion kids clutch their sprawling rabbit. Yaffa arrives, all in white. She wears a white lace dress, white stockings, white shoes, and long white gloves. McBride pinches her behind the punch table. "Yoff," he tells her, "this is my last day. They're going to give me a silver tray, and I'm going to hock it."

"We'll hock together," Yaffa whispers.

Women in silk dresses gather in little groups, spike heels sinking into the turf. The American and English men wear three-piece suits. Gavriel Ben-Zion feels awkward with all this formality. He wears a long-sleeved white shirt, open at the collar. He makes his way to Tapuz, who wears a clean khaki jacket. Gavriel looks the playwright up and down. Jacket, suit pants, new shoes, champagne flute in his hand.

"Bialik," he says, invoking the classic Hebrew poet.

Eyes glittering, Tapuz clicks his heels and bows in return. "Tchernichowsky."

Rose Markowitz pulls Sarah by the elbow during Frankel's anniversary address. "I feel ill," she says. "I can't bear crowds."

Sarah guides her to a chair as Frankel concludes: "Peace is an elusive quality. One which seems, at this point in our culture, almost ineffable, impossible to grasp. Only through scholarship, I submit, can peace become graspable, effable, if you will."

The audience applauds, and Frankel continues. "Like peace, the subject of funding has always been problematic. I know I am among friends today, and so I can confess I have a little list." He puts on his reading glasses and unfolds a piece of paper. "As the centre director, I am a bit of a librarian, a bit of a housekeeper, and so I've compiled a wish list I thought you could help me with. First on the list—and you must excuse me mentioning this just after eating—new toilets for the first-floor lavatories."

"Oh, my God," Terence Glueck says with a shudder to the man next to him. "The centre needs a *program*, a major gift committee, a fund drive, *leadership*! He just never learns."

"No," Jonathan Collins agrees happily.

Naomi Ben-Zion begins to cry. Shlomit has jumped out of her arms and run away.

"Naomi, you are nine years old," Geulah scolds. "And high time the rabbit goes. She's too big, and she ransacks the house."

"Oh, Shlomit." Naomi wails. "She was such a sweet rabbit."

Ed sees Shlomit dash behind the punch table. He jumps up and tears after her.

"Oh, Ed!" Geulah tries to call him back.

"Don't worry." Sarah laughs. "He won't catch her."

Frankel presents McBride with his silver tray, engraved in huge script letters:

For Lt. C. P. McBride
On the Tenth Anniversary
of the
Wantage Centre
for
Arab-Jewish Relations
in recognition and gratitude
for his ten years
of
Outstanding Service

"Mm." Tiki smiles. "He can't sell it with that whole citation." And just at that moment, Ed appears red-faced and panting from his run around the garden and entanglement with a tablecloth. Even he cannot quite believe he holds Shlomit in his arms.

"My rabbit!" Naomi screams.

Even many years later, Ed would still remember the look of disappointment on Geulah's face.

The Succession

*R*abbi Everett Siegel walks stealthily through the mall, carrying a Woolworth's shopping bag. Tall and stout, he cannot hope to hide in the crowd of young mothers and strollers. If he is to avoid recognition, he must rely on speed, and so he trots along, puffing with little quick steps. He is nearly out the door when George Kugel runs up, calling "Rabbi! What are you doing in Hawaii Kai?"

Siegel stops and holds his shopping bag uncomfortably. "Well, George," he counters, "what are you doing with your Friday nights? You should come back to the temple."

"Ha!" George says bitterly. Even here in the mall he can see the temple as if he were standing in front of it.

Martin Buber Temple stands in one of Honolulu's oldest neighborhoods. Old Pali Road is no longer residential. Its 1930s colonial mansions now fly the consular flags of Japan and Indonesia and the king of Tonga. Outnumbering even the consulates are churches and shrines:

Methodist, Greek Orthodox, Episcopalian, and Shinto. Next door to Martin Buber, the Cochran estate houses the Kwan Yin Temple and seminary. A two-story gilt statue of Kwan Yin Bodhisattva beckons serenely in several directions, caressing the Cochran garden with the sinuous shadows of her many arms. John and Susan Cochran lie in the Congregationalist churchyard with their son-in-law Prince Pauahi. It was their great-grandchildren who converted the old mission house into the Cochran estate. Now the white pavilions ring with temple bells. As John and Susan had always hoped, the house of their descendants remains a house of prayer.

It was the bells that caused architect George Kugel to resign from Martin Buber Temple. Kugel says he left MBT because he underwent a personal crisis. He needed to become Unitarian in order to come to terms with his Jewish roots. But this is not the real reason Kugel left. The main reason is that the board grossly mismanages the development of MBT property. Kugel hears the bells of the Kwan Yin Temple and is overcome with aggravation that the MBT board didn't listen to him back in '71 and buy the Cochran estate when it came on the market for fifty thousand dollars.

Even without the estate, MBT is a large temple. "We're not talking size," Kugel still argues, "we're talking market potential." In any case, MBT presents a noble modern profile on Old Pali Road. Kugel designed the sanctuary. But contractors slapped together the religious-school buildings. This was the last straw. Kugel submitted a three-page letter of resignation to the president. It began with cool formality but warmed at the end. The architect wrote: "I am an artist. I pour out my soul in my work. When you massacre such work, you spit on my soul." He left while the Samoan construction team built a lava rock wall without fitting the rocks together. They spray-painted between the rocks to disguise their white mortar in black shadows. Kugel did not return in 1979 to see the new rust carpet in the sanctuary or the bean bags that replaced the conference table in the library. Years later the earth-tone chairs still stand, as do the coarse lithographs of the old country and the abstract sculpture that is said by some to look like a cross. Kugel refuses all conciliatory offers. "I sweated blood for this building," he tells Rabbi Siegel. "You don't know what it does to me when I see those add-ons. This design was an original. This was my plan."

"What can I tell you?" the rabbi answers in his deep, mournful voice. "I also had a plan."

Everett Siegel, rabbi emeritus, has served MBT for a quarter century. He is known for infusing Friday-night services with pathos and dignity. He still presides in black robes, and his deep tones fill the sanctuary even when he turns his back to the congregation to lift the holy scrolls. He has a special microphone built into the ark. Siegel's sermons are long, and many find them deeply moving. When Dr. Sugarman came to say Yizkor for his first wife, the new Mrs. Sugarman was moved to tears by the rabbi's words. Siegel does, in truth, have a gift for speaking to the bereaved. His secret is that he does not try to comfort or give hope. Instead, he gives eloquent voice to the pain and anger of the mourner. He speaks of the injustice of the world, the enormity of personal sorrow, and the everlasting, unhealing scars of grief. He understands that this is what the mourners want: the reassurance that they are inconsolable.

With the passing years, the rabbi has become more

eloquent. His sermons are longer and more profound. Siegel is a community figure in Honolulu with his work in interfaith relations. He joins priests of Buddhist and Christian sects in ecumenical services. On these occasions with the other religious leaders, he officiates in Hawaiian-print vestments. He listens to the hymns and mantras sung in turn at Thanksgiving; and, like all the other ministers, the rabbi believes he is Gauguin among strange blessed people, holy in their exotic rituals.

Two years ago the MBT board decided that Rabbi Siegel was old, and before Siegel could resign, President Steve Gottlieb appointed him emeritus. Siegel will never forgive Steve for that. Next the board conducted a national search for a rabbi who would be good with young people. They made an offer to the third-choice applicant because they were convinced that the first and second choices would never come to Hawaii, and if they did, they would never stay. "Look," Gottlieb reasoned, "we're not going to get Stephen S. Wise out here, so don't push it."

And so on Saturday, Rabbi Barry Liebowitz presides at Elijah Oshin's bar mitzvah. Rabbi Siegel watched from his place of honor on the bimah with Gottlieb and Betsy Sugarman, the Sisterhood president. The altar rises in flaming tropical flowers: anthuriums, proteas, orchids, and birds of paradise. The choir soloist sings to soft organ accompaniment while the congregation stands in silent meditation. Gottlieb glances at his gold pavé diamond watch. The new rabbi nods to signal the end of meditation, but he can't get the organist's attention, and so the music rolls on for several more minutes, while the friends and family of the Oshins shift from one foot to the other. Finally the organist notices Rabbi Liebowitz and resolves his last chord. Liebowitz is thirty-one years old. He has light-brown hair and a limp mustache. He seems short, with his slight build and tight, bent shoulders.

Rabbi Siegel leans forward, adjusting his legs uncomfortably. He is keenly interested in the performance of the young rabbi. Over the years Siegel has become known for his words on bar mitzvahs. He speaks for at least half an hour, developing plays on the child's name, elaborate metaphors about the future, the planet, love, and life. His homilies are collected and published in the book *On This Your Bar Mitzvah Day*. Siegel knows that Liebowitz could never provide sermons of this caliber. But Liebowitz doesn't even try! He lays his hands on the head of the Oshin boy and whispers something to him away from the microphone so no one else can hear.

While Mrs. Sugarman is presenting the Sisterhood kiddush cup, Siegel leans over in his chair and glares at Liebowitz. "No sermon?" Siegel asks.

Liebowitz smiles quickly. "I always talk to the bar mitzvah boy, because it's really his day. I mean, this is his experience; it's not for the parents."

The older rabbi knits his brow and declares, "Young man, you are mistaken."

Siegel feels like a black cloud among the celebrants at the reception. How many of these people even know he is the rabbi? The social hall is bright with expensive tropical clothes: muumuus from Carol and Mary, Reyn's subtly patterned reverse-print aloha shirts. The elegant set stand apart, in darker clothes. This may be Hawaii, but Mrs. Steven Gottlieb will never wear white shoes in February. Siegel moves his lips in silent argument as he spreads cream cheese on a whole-wheat bagel. These people don't remember what it was like before Hawaiian

Bagel opened. Transients is what they are. The overflow from California. They come in and push out the people who worked and built for twenty years. Siegel walks outside through the packed parking lot. The rabbi's reserved space now belongs to Liebowitz and his Mazda. Siegel has to walk all the way down to the Kwan Yin Temple for his gray Lincoln, parked under a dark banyan tree that drops sticky berries and the mess of mynah birds.

Siegel lives with his wife, Grete, in an olive-drab apartment building with a view of the Ala Wai Canal: canoe teams paddling on the dark water, tourist couples in their matching aloha wear, local kids fishing for tilapia, deep sunsets, a symphony cellist practicing outside. Above all this, the Siegels don't often look out the window.

Grete gives Siegel an appraising look as he walks in. She has a face much given to appraising, piercing gray eyes and a sharp nose. "So they ignored you at the service," she says. Grete sets out a plate of Sara Lee cheese Danish. She stopped baking years ago, when she stopped wearing makeup. "What did I tell you?" she prods. Siegel retreats into his study, but he lives in a non-Austenian world. Grete follows him through the open-plan apartment and sits in his desk chair, elbows on his desk. "Why did you go?"

Siegel turns his back and scans the bookshelves. At one time he worked here on a monograph on Martin Buber. He stopped writing around the time Grete stopped baking. Grete stands up suddenly. "What did they serve? Did they serve you lunch?" She shoos him into the kitchen and gives him two pita halves filled with tuna salad mixed with celery. Siegel is on a diet and always ravenous. He has to eat lunch before he gets home in order to survive. He sneaks to the Woolworth take-out counter and buys yakitori chicken and vegetable tempura. He hides muffins in the first-aid kit of the car. Now, remembering the Danish on the coffee table, Siegel decides to go into the living room to await Grete's company.

Evelyn is Grete's oldest friend in Hawaii. When the two women sit down to talk, they speak in their own learned tongue. All common words become technical terms; all names are replaced with pronouns.

"I told her," Grete says, "I said, what do you mean, a bridal shower? Have you seen this boy? Have you met the parents? So she's twenty-nine years old, and she's not getting any younger. Who is? But if you ask me, the mistakes in the long term are the ones to worry about. And that kind of boy is long-term trouble."

"Israeli," Evelyn murmurs.

"Exactly what I thought," Grete sparks. And Evelyn nods in mystic understanding.

"Ach!" Grete points to Siegel, stealing his second Danish. "They retire him, and still he's working like a dog. Finally they bring in a new slave, and the phone rings even more. I have to fight to get him an hour's rest. They'll kill him yet. He's not going to any meetings this week. I called and canceled." Siegel smiles indulgently at Grete, because he knows this infuriates her. "They want to work him into the ground," she fumes. "Even after he retires. What do they give him? The same job at half price. They keep this genius here at half price, and they give the little nebbish double the money. Do you know how much this Barry Liebowitz gets? You don't want to know. I hear it's the wife. She demanded sixty thousand dollars. Salary plus child care. For one *shtickl* kid!"

Evelyn pats her napkin to her lips and says earnestly, "They say he's very good with the young people."

Siegel smiles at Evelyn, because she is so beautiful. She has soft white hair and amber-brown eyes. Her hands are delicately wrinkled. After her husband's death she remained a widow for three years. Then Max Engel snapped her up.

ᴘᴄᴇᴐ

Grete and Evelyn clear the dishes and leave together for the Honolulu Symphony. When Grete starts the car, Evelyn automatically takes out her compact and touches up her lipstick. After Evelyn's first husband died, Grete tried to teach her to drive. But Evelyn only cried and took cabs and then remarried. After forty years of marriage, she could not learn to see the world from the driver's seat.

They walk from the car to the concert hall. A musician bikes past, violin strapped to his back. "It must be sixty degrees!" Evelyn shivers. She drapes a white cardigan over her shoulders. The evening is so cool, some of the women in the concert hall pavilion have an excuse to wear their little fur capes. Grete sniffs at them, the women in their imported silk dresses and their scraps of fur. All claws and tail.

In the concert hall, the *nebbisheh* rabbi and his wife stand talking to the Gottliebs. "Just look at that," Grete whispers to Evelyn. "Look at Liebowitz already playing up to them. He thinks the rich ones are big *yichus*." She shakes her head at the developer, who flashes a glassy diamond ring as he talks rapidly.

"What we do," Gottlieb explains to Liebowitz, "we sell all the units before they're built."

"Yes, I see," says Barry. "Good thinking. This sounds very good."

"You know," Grete whispers again to Evelyn, "there was a time when a temple rabbi was a spiritual man and he cared about learning, not real estate." And then, in nearly the same breath, she greets Linda Liebowitz maternally. "Well, the young *rebbetzin*," she says.

Linda looks pained. "I am not a *rebbetzin*. I don't derive my personhood from my partner's social role."

"How is little Benny?" Evelyn asks soothingly.

"He's great."

"Doing well in school, I'm sure," Grete presses.

"Oh, yeah. He's got an amazing vocabulary. We play dictionary games. He just eats them up."

"Oh, you're working with him," Grete utters significantly. "Is he reading okay?"

"He reads fine," Linda retorts.

Grete draws closer and whispers, "You have to work with them early, or any little problems could grow out of proportion. They reverse the letters or have some little eye problem, and suddenly dyslexia. You've got to check the eyes all the time. I have a niece legally blind because they didn't start the eye-muscle exercises early enough."

"So this is how she uses all that child care," Grete tells Evelyn as they sit down. "What kind of mother . . . I tell you, she never sweated from a day's work."

∽ର୍ଉ∽

At her aerobics class, Linda glows with sweat. "It's the one thing I do for me," she says. Linda hates aerobics. She takes class three nights a week and leaves the kid with the sitter. She could come in the mornings, when

Benny is at school, but the evening class is much faster-paced. The women are younger, tighter, more driven.

"Higher! Higher! Knees! Get them higher!" the instructor says, gasping. Linda had a lot of trouble finding a high-powered aerobics class when she got to Hawaii. Out in Mililani Town, where Linda lives, the women are cows. At the YMCAs, the women work, and they begin the class exhausted. The Honolulu clubs are twice as expensive as New York, but what can you do? So Linda pounds down on the polished floor of the spa. "Breathe! Breathe!" screams the instructor. The other women gasp like fish, eyes drooping open, dulled with exertion. Linda clenches her teeth and holds her mouth shut as she jumps. In the mirror, her determined face is tight-lipped, unbreathing except for a slight flaring of the nostrils.

Linda's aerobic glow wears off quickly as she drives back to Mililani, buys milk for the morning, and takes the sitter home. By the time Barry comes home from his board meeting, Linda feels hot and fat again. Looking for a V-8, she has her head in the fridge when Barry comes in. "Hi, sweetie," he calls. Linda faces the milk cartons, Wonder bread, ketchup bottle, and the bruised eggplant that won't fit in the crisper. Barry sits at the kitchen table as Linda announces there is no more V-8. She slams the fridge door and starts unloading the dishwasher. Outside, the moths bat against the screen. "I'm bored." She sighs.

Barry looks up, surprised. "But, honey, we went to the symphony just last week."

Linda grimaces. "Thanks. I don't need to spend my free time with Grete Siegel and her sicko, hypochondriac advice on child rearing. I'm so *tired* of talking to these women twice my age. Barry, there aren't any fun people here. There's nothing fun to do here. I could die. I run around all day, and there's nowhere to go." Tears start in Linda's eyes. "Barry, I'm so *bored*."

Barry reaches over and pats Linda's hand. "That's why Steve Gottlieb's idea sounds so good. He's putting together an investment group for a new development out on Kauai. We could put up money for a condo and make quite a bit renting it out. We'd have a retreat for vacation and even a place for retirement."

"What!" Linda shrieks. "I'm not moving to Kauai. My God, you remember that weekend we spent. I'm trying to tell you I'm bored. *Bored*. I don't play golf. I don't play tennis. I don't sit on patio chairs. We're not spending our retirement money on Kauai."

"But, Linda," Barry says, "I thought you'd love it. I mean, I sort of said yes."

"Did you ask *me*?" Linda hisses. "I'm saying no. We're not doing it!"

Barry's eyes widen. "Baby, I just want you to be happy. I'll call up in the morning and pull out."

"Damn well better! Oh, God, I am so . . . Seriously, I just want to *scream*!"

Barry gives her a soothing look. "I'm hearing you," he says. "I'm hearing you."

"This is not a seminar," Linda screams. "This is not a workshop! This is my life. I'm telling you I'm *bored*. You're not getting the message. I am not sixty-five. I am a young person. I need to go out. I need to go dancing. For Christ's sake, we don't even live in Honolulu. We don't go to any clubs."

"I understand," Barry says. "I really do. I think we need to spend more time together. Just the two of us."

Barry phones Gottlieb Investment at nine the next

morning. Steve is in conference, but his administrative assistant takes the message.

❧

Sunday morning Linda drives Benny to Sunday school. She walks him up to the first-grade classroom and his teacher, Becky, runs out covered with flour from the challah unit. "Linda!" Becky calls. "Linda, I couldn't reach you yesterday. Rachel Katz's wedding is off. She called me from Israel. Apparently this guy never cared about her as a person."

"Uh-huh," says Linda. "So I take it Rachel isn't coming home."

Becky dusts off her hands, "Oh, yeah, she's coming. That's the thing. We've decided to carry on with the shower as a celebration of Rachel."

"Oh, come on." Linda groans. "That's going to be such a downer. Listen, I don't go to wakes."

Becky stares. Screams rise from the classroom. "Linda, the shower was for Rachel anyway. You should follow through. Her self-esteem is probably really low right now. You probably already bought her present. You've got to come. Rachel needs your support."

Linda turns away. "She doesn't need *The Liberation Ketubah*."

❧

At Rachel Katz's surprise welcome-home party, Ruth Katz sends her daughter's friends out by the pool for chips and dip. Mrs. Katz has always sent Rachel's friends outside to the pool. It makes no difference that the girls are now in their late twenties. Ruth remembers when they were born. Some of them were named at the temple, and Ruth took pictures. She is the self-appointed photographer of temple events and has filled albums. The temple pictures are jumbled with the Katz family pictures: Rachel naked at three, the Kantor wedding, Tu Bishevat picnics at the beach, the kids playing volleyball, numerous bar mitzvahs, the dedication of the Sunday school. She's forgotten the occasion for some of the photos. One mysterious black-and-white print shows what look like the Sugarmans dressed as each other in a mock wedding ceremony. Dr. Sugarman wears a white veil, and Betsy holds eighteen carrots, which symbolize an eighteen-karat wedding ring.

Ruth Katz ushers her own friends, Betsy and Evelyn, into the living room for drinks. The room is cool and hung with textured wall tapestries Ruth made in her weaving class years ago. Betsy Sugarman sits in a straight chair near the couch. "Ruth!" she exclaims. "I cannot believe that Linda Liebowitz refused to come."

"Believe it," Ruth says. She sits down heavily, and her queen-size muumuu billows around her. "She didn't want to spend on a present now that . . . No, no, I'm fine. It's my sinuses, you know. I'm trying to cut down on the allergy medicine. I think it's carcinogenic. So no rats have died *yet*. That doesn't mean a thing. Meanwhile I've been taking the stuff for years."

"Linda." Betsy clucks. "She should have come for Rachel. That's selfishness. It makes you wonder about the Liebowitzes."

Ruth shrugs. "They seemed like nice people. It's just at times like this I have to say I miss Rabbi Siegel."

"Siegel could write," Betsy announces. "Siegel could

speak. When I heard Siegel at Yizkor, it was really one of the most moving experiences of my life. And when I came back this year—such a change. I was in shock. Liebowitz stands in front of people who are literally grief-stricken and he gives a sermon about how his *Zeide* died in his sleep and what peace it brought him to see *Zeide* go at ninety-three with no pain. This is not what a mourning person needs to hear! No person tearing his hair with grief should have to listen to this. The rabbi should be there to comfort, and I felt this year my husband was not comforted when he said Kaddish for his first wife, may she rest in peace. And I'm going to bring this up at the renewal meeting." Betsy folds her arms across her chest.

"Well," Evelyn says in her gentle voice, "they do say he's very good with the young people."

∼∼∼

Rabbi Liebowitz holds weekly meetings with Yoel Brodsky. Yoel came to Hawaii as a *sheliach* and never left. Now he is director of the MBT religious school. It seems that every week there's a crisis. Yoel pounds his fist on the rabbi's desk. "Barry, tell me you'll make a stand. The parents are screaming for three days. They want your decision. Should we continue the contraception and safe-sex unit for the confirmation class? Steve Gottlieb is withdrawing his child if you say yes. Irving Glazer is withdrawing the twins if you say no."

"What do you think?" Barry asks.

"My feeling is clear: better to lose one tuition than two. But they want rabbinic opinion. And they want it yesterday! I'm up to here with this."

Liebowitz massages his temples. Finally he looks up

at Brodsky and says, "Yoel, I know you're under a lot of pressure. But don't put this on me now. Not now, when the whole community is so divided. Don't put this all on me. Please, please don't raise your voice like that. Look, I'll go during juice break and talk to the kids themselves."

The confirmation class lolls under the litchi tree in the courtyard. Their teacher is packing up a clear-plastic model of a uterus. Barry squats down among the tenth graders on the grass. "Hello, people," he says.

"Hi, Barry," the teacher calls out cheerfully.

"People," Barry says, "I hear you've been studying contraception. That's pretty heavy stuff. There's a lot of issues in contraception. What do you think about that?" He pauses. One of the kids is blowing a condom into a balloon.

"I want to know your views," says the rabbi. "Because I think you should make decisions and discuss things on your own. How about some ideas. Emily Gottlieb?" he asks, looking around.

"Gong," intones one boy. The kids roll on the ground with laughter.

"Oh, Rabbi," the teacher whispers quickly. "I guess you didn't see the paper. All the Gottliebs have disappeared. The paper says Steve was involved in some kind of investment scheme."

Barry stands white-faced in front of the class. He feels suddenly that they knew all along and watched him sign the check and could have warned him but chose to laugh among themselves as if his fly were open. Why didn't Steve return that call? Steve had his number at home. He must have been gone before Barry even tried to reach him. The rabbi feels hollow, as if Gottlieb had eaten out his stomach along with his savings.

Alone in his study, he puts his head down on the cool, smooth desk. He wants to close his eyes and sleep. Curl up alone with his books and never go out again. He looks at his shelves. *The Book of Job*. He could read that. Or maybe *When Bad Things Happen to Good People*. Good books about men who face disaster. But nowhere do they answer the darkest question: How do you tell your wife?

❧

"Aw, shi-i-it," says Linda, and she slams the bedroom door. Barry waits a few minutes and then follows her. She looks like a monster, lying on the bed with a white mud mask on her face. Barry stands by the door uncertainly.

"Don't you have anything else to say?" he asks.

"No," Linda says.

"Nothing?"

Linda thinks for a moment. Then she adds, "It's your fault."

Barry starts to cry. He looks like a man rocking with silent laughter. "We aren't communicating," Barry says.

Linda sits up suddenly. The white mask is cracked and dry. "I don't know what the hell you thought you were doing with our wedding money," she says. "I don't even want to hear it."

Benny runs down the hall and jumps on the bed. "Ooh, gross," he says, touching Linda's mask.

❧

Grete examines the Olga brassieres at the Liberty House foundation sale. She tests the wire in solid black and then systematically empties the bin, looking for ecru.

"Grete!" Ruth Katz calls from Sleepwear, and she sails out with a pile of nightgowns cresting over her arm. Grete looks up, annoyed, and moves toward Ruth and the less personal zone of bathrobe racks.

"So tell me," Ruth whispers loudly. "Any more news on Gottlieb? I'm still in such shock I can't believe it's true."

"I know nothing at all." Grete idly shuffles hangers on the rack. "I never follow the Hawaiian business news."

Ruth smiles. "I take it that's Everett's part of the paper."

Grete's eyes narrow. "We did not invest in Steve Gottlieb, if that is what you're trying to say."

"So you know about Barry," Ruth says slyly.

"What about him?"

Ruth leans forward. "He gave Gottlieb twenty-five thousand."

Grete gasps.

Ruth smiles. Gossip well played is a dramatic art. In college she loved the Restoration comedies. "I always suspected he was mafioso," Ruth says. "He used to walk around with that huge diamond ring. I mean, honest people don't wear rocks like that. Obviously," Ruth adds, "this is all confidential."

"Obviously," Grete echoes.

That afternoon, just after Grete phones Evelyn, Everett comes home. "It's in the papers," he tells Grete. His voice is mournful. "Gottlieb sells three hundred units in a two-hundred-unit building not even built. Then he fun-

nels out all the money from Gottlieb Inc. into a new corporation, declares Gottlieb Inc. bankrupt, and leaves
town in the dead of night. Our president of MBT. It's a
shame to the last good souls in this community. This
Sodom. This Gomorrah. This pillar of salt. Even ten worthy men are impossible to find."

Grete closes her eyes and listens to Everett's dark
voice. Eloquent he always was. He dictates sermons like a
prophet. Even now in the kitchen when Everett speaks,
Grete's fingers lift, ready to fly over the typewriter keys.
Everett was not made for small talk. His mind is too large
and sweeping. His voice is an orator's, ranging for vast
audiences. Grete opens her eyes and reports the news on
Barry Liebowitz.

༺ཨོཾ༻

"Benny," Linda calls. "Come into the kitchen, punkin.
Daddy and I want to talk to you."

Benny plants his fully jointed Predator doll in the dirt
and runs inside, growling airplane noises. "I'm a
Blackbird." He screams. "Fastest plane in the world."

"Do you want some ice cream?" Linda offers.

Benny sits down. "Chocolate," he tells her.

"Please," Linda adds.

"Ben," Barry starts, but he can't go on.

Linda looks intensely at Benny. Ben looks up and
then continues spooning ice cream.

"Honey," says Linda, "when people get married,
they love each other very much, and they want to live
together all the time. But people change and grow, and
sometimes they start needing more space. So we decided
Mommy and Benny are going to go see Grandma and

Grandpa for a while. I need some space, and Daddy needs some space too. That's part of what a separation is all about. Daddy and Mommy don't want to see each other anymore, but that doesn't mean we're ever going to stop loving you. Honey, we know it hurts inside, but we're going to try so hard to make it feel better. You'll see Daddy every summer, and you'll see Mommy all year long. Don't you think any of this is your fault. There's just a change between Daddy and me. That's why Mommy is going to take you to California."

Benny puts down his spoon. "Okay," he says. "Can I go to Disneyland?"

Linda and Barry stare at each other. "Doesn't he care about us at all?" Linda sobs. "Little beast!"

"He's breaking my heart," Barry whispers.

Linda turns on Ben. "Did you hear that?" she cries. "You're breaking Daddy's heart. And me too. We're just tearing up inside. Can't you see that? We are in such *pain*!"

Linda's voice frightens Ben, and he starts to cry. Tears run into the chocolate ice cream on his face. "It's okay," Barry says. "Don't be afraid to cry. It's all right to—"

"Shut up." Linda cuts him off. "You've traumatized him enough." She wipes Benny's face and whispers, "Don't cry. Everything's going to be all right. You'll see Grandma and Grandpa and Aunt Laurel and Uncle Matt and . . ."

ᬒ

Before services on Friday night, Evelyn cooks dinner for the Siegels and the Sugarmans. This is Evelyn's first dinner party at her new apartment, and she feels claustrophobic in the tiny kitchen. While Evelyn fusses, in the kitchen, Max pours himself a generous rye and ginger in the living room. Max loves to watch the sun set over the lagoon. That sunset sold him on the apartment. The Realtor jabbered about closet space and footage and the fitness spa at the Hawaiian Village, but Max just looked out the window. The water was golden in the warm light, and a young couple walked along the sand. They seemed so happy leaning together, feeling the water with bare feet. Max chose the apartment for the view. Sunsets and young love. Even his first wife called him a sentimentalist. He longed for youth even when he was young.

Max owned a business that made nurses' uniforms: white dresses, starched white wimples, white arch-supporting shoes. The shoes proved unprofitable. He moved to Hawaii when he won a contract with Tripler Hospital. Then, after his wife died, he retired and became religious vice-president of MBT. That was where he met Evelyn.

When the Sugarmans arrive, Betsy walks into the kitchen and watches Evelyn cook.

"Evelyn, this is beautiful." Betsy purses her lips with pleasure as she nicks a carrot stick from the salad bowl.

"Mm-hm," Evelyn half answers. She dashes out with the butter dish and runs into Dr. Sugarman, who smiles beneficently.

At the table, Grete leaves her salad untouched. Raw vegetables do not agree with her. She nudges Everett to slow him down, as he tears into his lettuce like a man who hasn't eaten in weeks.

Everett puts down his fork. "Do you think Liebowitz will get renewed?" he asks.

"No shop talk," Grete commands. "How are the children?" she asks Evelyn.

Evelyn twists her napkin in her hands. "They're well," she says, "as far as I can tell. Mark doesn't write."

"He called last week," Max reminds her.

"It's not the same," Evelyn says stubbornly. "I can't reread a phone call. I can't hold a phone call. The grandchildren don't know any better, but Mark was brought up differently. He has no excuse. He has a secretary. He could dictate."

Evelyn gets up to refill the wineglasses. She skips her husband. Max looks flushed.

"In the forties," Grete tells Betsy sternly, "on the base in Hawaii, there wasn't any underwater cable connected. We used telegrams."

"I used to write from the ship." Max laughs as if this were an absurd occurrence. "I was in the navy, you know. I wrote three letters a week. One to my wife, Marjorie, one to my brother, and one to my girlfriend. Once I mailed them together, and I was awfully upset because I couldn't remember which letter I'd sealed in which envelope. Because . . ." He trails off and realizes he hadn't meant to tell the story quite that way. He hadn't really meant to tell it at all.

Betsy laughs gaily into the hushed room. "Evelyn, did Max ever tell you all this before?"

Evelyn shakes her head, bewildered. Later, after services, she feels embarrassed for Max. He brings in the dirty tablecloth to throw in the wash. "I never knew that about you," Evelyn says.

Max smiles dreamily. "Oh, goodness." He sighs. "I haven't thought about it in years. I was so young. We all had no idea whether we'd make it through the war. You have to admit it was a funny thing with those envelopes. Anyhow, it shows I always was absentminded." In the past few years Max has had a small problem with his eyes, and he can't control their tearing. He looks as unconcerned as a man chopping onions, with his radiant smile and the tears gathering in his eyes.

∾∾

Because the Philippine mahogany conference table was taken from the MBT library during remodeling, the board meets in a religious-school classroom. Before the scandal, Gottlieb had chaired the meetings, flanked by Max and the social vice-president, Gary Roth. Gary is a real-estate developer and owns a world-class shrimp farm out on Molokini Island. He bought the farm as a tax loss, but profits doubled when accidental overfeeding produced super-jumbo-size shrimp. Gary received a governor's citation for his contribution to Hawaiian aquaculture. After the Gottlieb scandal, he was voted in by the temple board as acting MBT president.

"Old business," Gary announces.

The newly divorced divorce lawyer, Phil Lieber, rises. "I'm still concerned about the treasurer's report on dues," he says. "The collections situation is out of control, and we need to exert some kind of pressure. I'd like to propose public posting of all dues offenders. It works at my club, and it should work here. There's no reason why MBT can't run as smoothly as the Pacific Club."

"Is that a motion?" asks Ruth Katz as she takes minutes.

"Um, yeah, okay," says Phil.

"Yes or no?" Ruth demands.

"Yes."

"Seconded."

Ruth records the motion and then says, "Okay, I have an objection to the motion on the floor."

"Wait," the chair says. "You weren't recognized by the chair."

Ruth shoots back, "Don't try to shut me up, Gary. I've been a member of this temple for twenty-eight years. Okay, this is what I'm trying to say. I personally am not offended by public posting of dues violators, but there are people who might not have the funds to pay because of financial difficulty, and I think they might be embarrassed if they were posted. I mean, we all know who they are, but posting would be a little blatant."

Phil stands up. "Amendment to my motion," he announces. "Those persons who the board feels may be unable to pay will not be posted. They will be called in for a private session with the subcommittee on finances, and we will determine the nature of the financial problem and how much the individual can afford to pay."

The amendment is seconded, but the motion is tabled for further discussion. "Time is at a premium," Gary reminds the board. "We move on now to my report on the remodeling problem. I've called several contractors for estimates, and nobody will touch the sanctuary because of the height and the kind of wood used. Also, the brass fixtures came from the mainland, and they can't be repaired locally. We've had to conclude that George Kugel's firm is our only chance if we want to get this renovation done. Now, apparently George has some problems with coming to work on the building because of some things that happened years ago. I wasn't here at that time, but from what George tells me, the temple didn't strike him as a very welcoming place at that time. I think what we need to do is make George feel needed here at MBT, since obviously he is needed. The Executive Committee did some brainstorming on this, and we think the best thing to do is invite him as guest of honor to the annual dinner dance, where we will present him with a lifetime MBT membership and some suitably inscribed gift."

"That's beautiful," murmurs Betsy Sugarman.

"All right," Gary says. "Moving right along. In new business, Rabbi Liebowitz's contract renewal. And I'll have to ask for a three-minute limit on individual comments. Also, please remember that our recommendation is subject to a vote of the full membership."

Betsy Sugarman begins. "I find that the rabbi is too inexperienced for the needs of mature people like my husband and myself. Most of you know how strongly I feel about what happened at Yizkor." Her voice trembles. "I don't think I can talk about it now. It was—" She stops. "Well, you know what I'm trying to say."

"Thank you, Betsy," Gary says. "Just to put in my own two cents. I'd like to comment that I enjoy the Hebrew Liebowitz is introducing into the service."

"Now, that's just what I find offensive," Phil cuts in. "This temple is not chartered to serve Israelis. This is an American temple in the American tradition. I'm deeply disturbed by this movement to Hebraize all the prayers until we're muttering by rote. Vatican Two got over this sacred-language fetish; so can we."

The room hushes as Rabbi Siegel stands to speak. Gary taps his watch and shows him three fingers before he even starts. "As an ex officio member of the board," Siegel begins, "I rarely make an appearance. But I feel moved to say a few words about the character of the young man we are considering as a possible spiritual leader of this community. Barry Liebowitz has many fine qualities. The boy has a sweet nature. A gentle manner. But I fear he has also shown many weaknesses in the past year. When we choose a leader of Martin Buber Temple, we choose a Jewish representative and ambassador to the community at large. This was the position I filled in Hawaii for twenty-five years—thirty-one, if we include my time as military chaplain on base during the war, when there were so many hardships and shortages. You remember, Evelyn. I like to think that during my time here I gave a little that was unique to Hawaii. After all, few of you remember how different these islands were without—"

Gary taps his watch again.

Siegel rolls on. "I like to think that I never brought shame to this community. I am deeply distressed when I think that my proposed successor might have even a tangential connection with any kind of dealing based on principles of dubious probity."

Ruth Katz rattles the minutes furiously. Liebowitz loses his savings, and they're using *that* against him? She feels a sudden sympathy for Barry. Sympathy mixed with guilt. Maybe she shouldn't have said anything to Grete at the foundation sale. Poor Barry. Such a victim. And married to such a cat. Linda didn't come through for Rachel after the engagement fizzled, and she didn't come through for her own husband either. Ruth always had a feeling Linda wouldn't make it in Hawaii.

Siegel continues. "At first I dismissed as vicious rumor the very hint that our young rabbi was involved in a shoddy get-rich scheme. . . ."

"I hope everyone's listening," Ruth snaps, "because

I'm not taking this down. With all due respect, Everett, I think this kind of assassination is—"

Gary thumps his gavel. "Everybody just cool down," he says. "Rabbi, I think your time is up, but I know we all thank you for your input. I think right now we need to get back to the bottom-line issues. What was the rabbi *hired* for? The young people. This is his forte, and I think we all agree that he's made the new confirmation class the best attended in years."

∾∾∾

Three days later, after the votes are counted, Siegel mopes in his apartment. He looks out the window and watches the after-school canoe teams race down the Ala Wai.

"Grete," he says, "what am I to do with my final years? They've all turned against me. They voted Liebowitz in, and I'm resigning."

Grete throws her arms heavenward. "Thank God!" she exclaims. "They would have killed you if they had the chance. You were never meant for a pulpit. You're a genius. You need to write. Beautiful prose like yours, and you wasted it on people who never listened. I've told you a thousand times to finish your article. Listen, no one in the world understands Buber like you. Don't give me that about your final days. You have four grandchildren to visit. My God," Grete breathes, "this is the happiest day of my life."

She picks up the car keys and goes out to look for hazelnuts for a Linzer torte.

Retrospective

*H*enny's just hung up the phone when she sees it in the paper. And it's not the best time, to begin with, because she's worrying about Annette alone with three sick kids on her hands in the dead of winter in Michigan, and Jacob says another trip to the mainland is out of the question. So it's not the best time when she sees her sister's name in the "Arts Spectrum." It jumps out at her the way names do when you know them. Lillian Pressman. And she only passed away one month ago.

"Jacob." She gasps. "The University of Hawaii is having a retrospective show of Lillian!"

"Let me see that." Jack folds back the newspaper and creases it in half. "They can't do that," he pronounces.

"But they are," she says. "Is it legal? Don't they need my permission or something, as her only surviving sister?"

Jack leans back in his chair and doesn't answer.

The fact is, Lillian wasn't an artist, though she worked in the Art Department at UH. Henny never really told people more specifically what her sister did. She didn't lie about it; she just chose to put it very vaguely. That her sister assisted art professors. That she worked as a civil servant, which was perfectly true, because she worked for the state university and had the same medical plan as any secretary. It's just that Henny never mentioned Lillian was an artist's model. It's one of those jobs that never come up by themselves in conversation. The vocation is honest, but a little awkward.

" 'In the retrospective,' " Jack reads from the paper, " 'the university will honor the contribution of a model who posed for generations of life drawing classes. Over one hundred studies of Lillian Pressman will be displayed at the Campus Center Gallery.' "

"Don't cry, Henny." Jack takes her hand. "I'm going to raise hell about this Monday morning. I'll call every office at the university. They can't do this to our family."

Henny looks at him for a moment. "They will," she says. "Just like the Helga pictures."

"Not like the Helga pictures," he reasons. "That was a great artist. No student ever did work like that. That was a sixty-dollar book."

But Henny shakes her head and clears the breakfast dishes. She half expects the phone to ring, with one of her friends asking questions. Honolulu is a small town when you've lived here as long as Henny. She and Jack moved to Hawaii just after the war. They've been at the temple from the beginning, and on the board. Two children through Oahu Prep. And Jack is Leading Knight at the Elks Club. Hundreds of people knew Lillian through Henny. She lived with them almost thirty years; she was part of every party, every function. Everyone will know. And they'll talk about it. Henny couldn't bear that. To have it reflected back on her. It's a position you have in the community. After all, she and Jacob were the first kosher family in Hawaii. They made the first arrangements with the butcher in Long Beach. You have a kind of pride built up over the years. When you've lived here longer than everyone you know who wasn't born here. When you *saw* statehood. When you remember exactly where you were on Kalakaua, 1959, with the newsboys screaming and the traffic stopped. Even the tourists rising up on their elbows on the sand, forgetting about their own *pupiks* for a minute. When you've lived here that long, people will talk about your sister. The only person Henny knows who came before she did is the old lawyer Farber, who came out to settle the water rights case fifty-two years ago, and he's still working on it in his eighties— "I'll lick it before it licks me!" he yelled when they toasted him at the Elks testimonial. And what will they say, the Elks, when they find out about Henny's sister? You work up to knowing everyone in the lodge. Your husband is the Leading Knight. And then that such a revelation should appear! They'll never let her hear the end of it. It's their motto: An Elk is never forsaken, never forgotten. They remember everything about everybody. It's their creed.

She marches through the house, collecting the wastebaskets from each room. It's a small house with small rooms. She wouldn't take Lillian's money for rent when she moved from Detroit. Not after she'd cared for their parents for so long. Lillian was in her forties by the time she came to Henny, and she never again took up with men. She earned extra money as an Avon Lady. She gave away her samples to Henny's grandchildren.

Picking up the blue plastic wastebasket, Henny pauses in the front bathroom. The cabinets are still full of Lillian's Avon inventory. Rosebud soap and sample perfumes and air fresheners in little Hummel-figure pumps. Would the company want these back? Henny wonders. She's packed up her sister's clothes and given them away, as Lillian would have wanted. But everywhere she looks, more of her sister's things appear. *Peklach* you don't even notice after so many years. There is a crocheted doll, for example, that stands on the lid of the toilet tank. It's got a blue crocheted skirt designed to fit over an extra roll of toilet paper. And there are little things like Lillian's cotton makeup applicators. Hundreds of them. She loved makeup. She had a complete Clairol display with a three-way mirror you could light up for daytime, night, and fluorescent office light. Henny should clear out the cabinets; she should do it today. On the middle shelf Lillian left bottles of nail polish, maybe fifty, in every shade. And a pink flowered traveling case with unbreakable containers for hair spray, powders, perfumes, eye shadows, rouges. Henny shudders. She must have brought that along to work.

Why did Lillian choose that profession? Henny has asked herself the question hundreds of times. What is a professional model, after all? A kind of exhibitionist. Henny has always thought that. But her sister was no exhibitionist. Not Lillian. You would think, really, that the models would be the young ones, the pretty ones, with smooth skin, taut bodies. That's what the artists want, isn't it? They want to make something ideal. And Lillian modeled when she was old. When she was sick with cancer. It breaks Henny's heart to think of that. Lillian almost seventy and cancerous inside, though it wasn't diagnosed yet. Her sister with her creased face and breasts hanging. And still under scrutiny. Still ruthlessly looked at, without a robe to cover her. With age should come a little dignity! Henny even asked Lillian to stop. "I don't understand," she told her sister. "Why do you model like this? Why did you even get started with this? And now when you're so old?"

Lillian smiled at this and said, "It's what I do." In Detroit she lived with an artist. He taught her how— started her off. And then when she came to Hawaii and Henny wanted her to settle down, it was too late. Lillian just said, "It's good work. You never get too old. The artists like the older bodies. They're much more interesting. If you asked a life-drawing teacher, he would tell you. They don't want Greek gods in their classrooms."

Henny was appalled by this. She had known vaguely that her sister lived with a painter, but studiously, for thirty years, she'd chosen to forget it. It's what you owe your sister. To think of her at her best. To try to ignore the times she acted reprehensibly. And Lillian herself helped maintain that better image in Henny's mind. In Hawaii she acted as sedate as anyone could have asked. The fact of her profession was the only vestige of her wilder youth, her love affair—the only one in their family, to Henny's knowledge. In her years in Henny's house, Lillian never once spoke about her work. She was the shyest, most discreet person in the world. She was a respectable woman.

The exhibit, of course, cannot be forgotten. There it is in the newspaper. Lillian on the walls for the neighbors. After all the years Henny and Jacob worked and entertained, became public figures in the community. Now the tables turn; now all the people they befriended will stop and look at them. It's like a magnifying glass that turns on you. It's no good imagining it can reverse. No one forgets humiliations in Honolulu. They remember clear as day, sometimes better. It's because the more people you know, the more witnesses. There were a thousand witnesses on Rosh Hashanah, 1970, when Rabbi Braverman, the stand-in, forgot to turn off his cordless microphone for his trip to the bathroom during silent meditation. There isn't a child who doesn't know about Steven Gottlieb and the imaginary condominium. And such glee, the way they tell it! Henny clenches her fist. When it comes to Lillian, she won't give them a chance.

～～～

She leans over Jack as he phones the university, Office of the President. "Is it ringing?" she asks.

"They put me on hold." He rattles the box of paper clips on his desk. The desk is at the back of the store, where they sell wallpapers. Jack used to do installation work as well, but now it's too hard on his back. Anxiously Henny watches his face. He has a terrible temper. He'll bawl out anyone on the phone; he doesn't care two bits for their feelings on the other end. And she can see he's in that kind of mood, pacing around with his fingers hooked under the body of the old black phone as if it were a bowling ball. A short man, but he never seems that way. He thrusts out his chin, and in arguments he rocks forward on the balls of his feet, hands clasped behind him.

"Did they answer it yet?" she asks.

"If they answered, wouldn't I be talking to them?" he snaps. They wait a little longer, and then he slams down the phone and tries again.

The door jangles and Henny runs to the front to help a young couple, the Chongs. She generally does the customer side, matching colors and explaining about the pastes. The Chongs want to cover only one wall of their kitchen. They're painting the rest, they tell her. And she sighs because she and Jacob haven't had a whole house or a restaurant since the Clambaker, three months ago, and that was only a neutral grass-weave matting. She and Jack had three years when they made real money. The first was 1952, when they got the contract for the Royal Hawaiian. That was the house. The second was 1972, when the Japanese Kikaida Robot TV shows first came to Hawaii, and she and Jack were the first to bring in the Kikaida Action Wallpaper series. That was the new car. Then the other year was 1979, with the foil, mirror-inset, wallpaper. That was the refrigerator and the enclosed lanai, and that was the trip to Europe without Lillian. And even on that trip Henny would have taken her, except Jack said it was going to be their second honeymoon.

"The president is in conference," Jack announces after the Chongs leave. "I left my number with the secretary, and in the meantime I spoke to the Art Department. We have an appointment tomorrow with Mohanty."

∾

Krishna Mohanty is a stocky Indian professor with a beaming face. He shakes hands jovially with Henny and Jack Seligman as if nothing were wrong and ushers them into his gray office on the eighth floor of Porteus Hall.

"They say in the administration these save electricity," he tells them, pointing to the flat ceiling fixture flickering above. Leaning back in his swivel chair, he clasps his hands over his stomach.

"Dr. Mohanty," Jacob says sharply. "I'll get right to the point. We want this exhibit canceled."

"But why?" asks Mohanty with his gentle accent. "It's beautiful, these works of art."

"That is my sister!" Henny blurts out. She hadn't meant to be so direct. "My sister, who passed away one month ago in pain, suffering with cancer of the stomach!"

"We planned the show one year ago, with her full knowledge," Mohanty answers serenely.

This stuns the Seligmans for a second. "I need written proof of that—that she would consent," Jack says finally.

"It's all in her release papers in Personnel. Please don't be upset," says Mohanty. "My idea is perhaps we could go look at the studies together."

"I will not go see pinups of my sister-in-law!" Jack explodes.

But Krishna continues, unperturbed. "It was really a notion of my students, not mine. They revered Lillian; I am not exaggerating. She practiced meditation when she posed; she never spoke. It was a very mystical body she had. Especially as she got older. There was a yoga instructor in the class who said she had the most complete inner focus he'd ever seen in a mainland haole. You see, she brought much to the department, and we want to pay tribute to her. Lillian was the perfect illustration of the mind at rest. It was her gift to stand or sit for hours, relaxed and yet centered in her pose. Her face became so impassive, so clear, you would hardly notice that she, a person, was there at all. She was like those horoscopes in the newspaper—for each artist she could mean a different thing. For me, she was the best model I ever had. She illustrated every lesson I had to teach. Look, I would tell my advanced students, this is a woman who has erased all the noise from her mind. Draw her and try to become like her so that no noise comes in your mind. Just the line and your paper. That's all I need. And for my intermediate class, I said, Look at the whole body and the way no one part calls attention. And now draw the whole body as a whole so no one part stands out. And for my beginners, I said, Look at the stillness of the model and try to capture that stillness in you, so all your lines are clear without erasing."

Henny looks at her husband. What is the man talking about?

"Her gift was she was so unexpressive," Mohanty muses. "She was a blank sign, open for interpretation."

"She wasn't any signpost for you to hang your pictures on," cries Jack, his face reddening. "Come on, Henny. We're wasting our time."

"Come see the exhibit!" Jack fumes in the elevator. "I'd tear every last one of them off the wall."

Henny puts a restraining hand on his arm, but all the same she asks fiercely, "Can we fight it, Jacob?"

He looks at her. "I'm sorry, honey; I don't see how. Here we are Tuesday, and the show opens Friday."

And Henny feels it now: They have lost. If Jacob gives up, there's good reason. Henny's husband can get all his money back in cash on refunds; he can spot a false ad a mile away. He's won two small-claims suits. He even won against the city when Henny broke the axle of the old car, driving over a pothole. The corporation counsel of

Honolulu himself said Jack put together the best pothole suit he'd ever seen—that no one else had thought to photograph the pothole with a yardstick in it. So if Jacob can't go on against the university, there isn't any way to go. Besides, Henny realizes despairingly, the damage is already done, what with the newspaper article. Everyone in Honolulu reads the joint Sunday issue, the *Advertiser* and *Star-Bulletin* combined. Even the ones who would never attend a nude picture show would have seen the article, with "Lillian Pressman" in boldface.

Just as she knew and feared, Betsy Sugarman accosts her that night, shopping in Foodland. "Oh, hello, Henny," says Betsy. "Did you see that article about Lillian in the paper Sunday? The doctor and I were so surprised and interested. . . ." She lets her voice trail off, all innocence, while Henny wheels her shopping cart away, unable to reply. She doesn't know what to say, she feels so humiliated. The cereal boxes on the shelves blur together, and she has to force herself to push on toward the liquid detergent, and even there she can only stare at the bottles arrayed by size, from pint samples on the top shelf to the Survivor Specials on the bottom. Every brand in columns: Cheer, Bold, Surf, Tide. And as the colors surge before her, all she can think of is Lillian hung up in different sizes on the wall. Her naked body reproduced small, medium, and large.

In the shopping center outside, wheeling past the liquor store, she stares at the magazine racks with half-naked women on the covers, glimpses of black lace and cleavage and even worse. And to think Lillian should be displayed like this, and when she covered herself in long bathrobes at the beach and bathing suits with skirts.

Henny has to catch her breath. And then she has an idea. She will go for help to Rabbi Siegel.

She doesn't tell Jacob, because he hasn't gotten along at the temple in recent years. He served as treasurer two terms, and then when Steven Gottlieb first appeared and everyone thought the Meshiach had come, they told Jacob his time was up, without so much as a thank you. Just because Gottlieb was the big developer come to town and remodeled the old religious-school buildings—guilt money for his shady dealings, Henny believed even then. Of course, when Gottlieb absconded in the middle of the night, the board at MBT changed its tune. But the damage was done. Jacob told Henny he wouldn't volunteer anymore, even if they asked him. He'd come to services, and he would leave. That's all. He'd have nothing to do with the president and the rabbis; they knew what he thought of them already.

But Henny can't forget Siegel's goodness about the funeral. She went to him distraught because Lillian had told her she wanted cremation and the ashes scattered out to sea from a catamaran. Henny couldn't bear that. Her parents would suffer in their graves at the thought of such a *hurban*. Henny herself had been to one of those nonburials, and it was a disgrace, a trauma. They stood on the boat with the urn to scatter poor Samuel Miller out to sea, but the wind was blowing the wrong way and the ashes blew back in their faces, as if the Pacific was spitting him back. And it made you shiver there in the catamaran to feel Samuel floating in the air around you, drifting into your hair. So she went to Siegel, guilty that she wanted to deny Lillian's wish, not knowing what to do. Though Jacob denies it, there are some moments when Siegel reaches a very high plane of insight. He told

Henny, "You know, in this day and age, Jewish law is not something to cling to. But I will say this about cremation. There were enough Jews burned in the Holocaust." Because of that, Lillian got a proper burial. That comment of Siegel's is what she thinks of now. That despite Jacob's opinions about the temple, Siegel has some moments on a very high plane. So the next day Henny goes to see Rabbi Siegel herself.

∾⃝∾

Everett Siegel's office is much smaller now that he is an emeritus rabbi. His books crowd the shelves, and there is less space between the photos on the wall behind his desk. In the center, black and white, the rabbi shakes hands with JFK. In other photos, Siegel meets with Senators Matsunaga, Hiram Fong, Daniel Inouye. Siegel looks up after Henny tells him about Lillian. "I'm sorry," he tells her. "I can't think of a way to block this, even under Jewish law."

Henny protests. "But I thought there must be some ordinance in the laws about the dead. If it was only a month ago that she died." Her voice trembles. "Aren't there rules concerning the treatment of the body after death?"

"Yes, there are," answers Siegel. "But they have to do with burial. You are talking about the body in a more philosophical sense."

Henny looks down at the white wicker purse on her lap.

"The truth is," Siegel tells her, "we try to preserve a bit of dignity during our lifetime, and the jackals strip it away after death. This is what it comes to."

Henny nods fervently, feeling this is exactly what she has been thinking.

᠙᠙᠙

"This is what it comes to," she murmurs that night, sorting through the bathroom cabinets, opening Lillian's desk drawers. You try to earn a living, support your temple, entertain your friends, and finally what's left? Some talcum powder, some envelopes, a booklet of eighteen-cent stamps. There was a time when she and Lillian would entertain—fifty people at a dinner. They would really serve. None of this pot luck. They made roasts and capons. It was all kosher, from California. Once Henny bought smoked salmon mail order from Scotland. They had kugels, two kinds, and potatoes—no mashed-potato mix. They would work a whole day. They would spend their money on it, because that was what was important to them—to make for the community. To gather together. They remembered their parents' house in Detroit. That was what they tried to create in Hawaii. Of course, no one under Henny's age cooks like that. They get the catering service with the little white dresses and the bite-size food—filler for drinks. Or they go spend on themselves at John Dominis or Bagwells or the Third Floor. They go the two of them and leave the kids. Henny had a children's table at every dinner party; they set up the card table at Pesach, and at Rosh Hashanah, so the children were included. They're big now, some of them. Geoffrey and Alyssa Fifer—must be twenty, twenty-three. Or they were, last time she had the Fifers. It was surprising when they sat down at the card table and it lifted up on Geoffrey's knees. She hasn't seen them in a while. It's been some years, because Lillian was ill, and Henny had a harder time alone.

Not that Lillian ever cooked like Henny, but she would sit in the kitchen and peel the potatoes like a sous-chef. And she was patient, more than Henny ever was. So that for the twelve-egg sponge cake Henny made on Pesach, it was Lillian who sat whipping the egg whites until they stood up in the bowl—up to the rim. When Henny brought out that cake, standing ten inches high, there was a gasp. "Not since Mama Linzer was there such a cake in Honolulu." And that was the highest praise. After all, Mama Linzer founded the Sisterhood with her bare hands when she came during the war and made dinner for the servicemen.

You try to entertain and give your sister a chance to meet people, and in the end she's up on the gallery walls for ogling. Never once did Lillian try to get married, Henny thinks, rattling the desk drawers. Never once did she try to leave Henny's house. True, she was six years older than Henny and thirty-four when she first visited Hawaii, but thirty-four is not so old if you make some effort. Rochelle Lazar married for the first time at thirty-eight—with her shrieking voice and her purse full of Mace. There would have been more chances for Lillian in Detroit; she could have married there. Maybe she was worried about her reputation after living with the artist. She said she was depressed by the weather. But who knows? She was depressed sometimes in Honolulu too. It was, Henny thinks, because she didn't have a family of her own. That was the tragedy. That she never had children. Her life would have been different. She would have gone into a different line of work. She did take courses at the university. But only painting and pottery.

Henny opens the bottom drawer and shakes out some empty penny rolls. She feels as if there ought to be a diary or love letters. Some happier or at least more noble secret about her sister. She did read Harlequin romances, but she checked them out from Aina Haina Library and always returned them on time. She never bought them. Apart from those books, she didn't do anything romantic. She wouldn't leave a will. In the hospital, Lillian would only tell Henny, "When I'm gone, I'm leaving the insurance policies to the girls"—she called Henny's grandchildren the girls. "And the rest," she would say, "I'm leaving to the temple. Except I want to give twenty-five dollars to Hadassah." And then the next time Henny visited, she would say "And I'd like to leave fifty dollars for trees in Israel." Henny begged her to write it down, but she wouldn't do it. Even now, Henny can't remember if it was fifty dollars for the Humane Society or for the Elks Piggy Bank Fund.

ᔓᔕᔕ

Henny sings in the choir Friday nights at the temple. Jacob says he wouldn't go at all on Friday nights if Henny didn't sing. There was a time when the choir was Jewish, and now Henny's is the only Jewish voice left. The board hires the rest—ringers from the Honolulu Opera chorus. Henny helps the conductor teach the Hebrew pronunciation. On the night of Lillian's opening, she sits stiffly during Rabbi Liebowitz's sermon, tense under her white billowing robe. Let them stare at her. She'll stare them back. Her friends and supposed friends. Let them dare confront her or sidle up with snide questions. Betsy Sugarman is beneath contempt in her pink double-knit

suit and her colored hair. At least Lillian's hair was originally auburn. More than Betsy could say for herself. And
Grete Siegel in her reserved chair at the back: Well, let
her look. She isn't worthy of her husband. She doesn't
have half the mind of the rabbi.

And Hermione Gross, with her long press-on nails, as
if she were half her seventy years. As if she were slender
instead of only skeletal, with her leathery tanned skin.
What could she give the temple that Lillian didn't give in
her life? She saw with her own eyes when the rabbi recognized Lillian and Henny for donating the Torah. That
was Lillian's idea. She told Henny during Yizkor on Yom
Kippur, "I want to give a Torah to the temple in memory
of Mama and Papa." Henny never understood why Lillian called their parents Mama and Papa. She started doing it when she was about forty-eight years old. That was
also when she began going to Saturday-morning services
as well as Friday night. Often she just stood with her
book open to one page and read it aloud to herself over
and over—in English. This distracted Henny, but Lillian
said she liked to pray one page at a time; she didn't like
rushing through the book. They bought the Torah, and as
Hermione Gross can see, it's embroidered with Lillian
and Henny's names—though naturally Henny and Jacob
gave the bulk of the money and Lillian gave what she
could afford. Lillian also embroidered the curtain for the
ark, and everyone knows full well who did the work when
Hadassah installed the needlepoint miniatures of Chagall's twelve windows. Lillian did Reuven and Dan, and
Hermione did only half of Levi.

Henny sighs, exhausted with ignoring these people.
There is no escaping it. The civil ones, the more refined,
will make a point of not saying anything. But they know.

They know. Even Evelyn in her fawn silk dress. Evelyn would never say an unkind word, but she thinks them all the time.

The worst comes when Henny turns to her prayer book, and it opens to one of the places Lillian marked. The temple is full of prayer books Lillian kissed open-faced. Over the years she used nearly every book. Her lipstick stain appears in each of them. And now it makes Henny shiver to think of her sister's lips kissing all those pages during her long illness. It's morbid; it's like kissing some relic. And what good did it do? What sacred words rubbed off on Lillian? It was Lillian who rubbed off. In pinks and reds, rose blushes, sugared oranges.

In the social hall after services, Henny makes Jack wait and take some *kiddush*. She won't run away. She strides through the hall, where the congregation gathers for lemon squares under the mural of Solomon's judgment. French doors open to the front courtyard, where a fountain flickers orange in the night. The blue light Ephie Tawil installed is broken. It's supposed to look Mediterranean, but all Henny can see is a big cement planter sprouting water, aspergeni trailing down the sides. Hermione and her newly married niece pour at either end of the long table. They sit before the silver tea and coffee urns with stacks of gold-rimmed cups and saucers. "Oh, hello, dear," says Hermione. "Isn't that lovely about Lillian. Such a tribute to her." Henny steadies her cup and glares, but the line surges forward and Hermione is already pouring for Irene. That is the only comment anyone makes all evening.

Henny admits it to herself that night. She's disappointed. Brushing her teeth, she feels disappointed she didn't have a chance to defend her sister. They acted as if they knew about Lillian's work all along. She stops brushing, with her mouth full of toothpaste, and gasps at herself in the mirror, blurred with mascara and frosted hair. Quickly she finishes washing up. "Jacob," she calls. He's already reading *Wanderings* in bed. "Jacob, she must have told them all behind my back."

"Lillian?" he asks vaguely. "Why would she do that?"

"I don't know why," Henny snaps. "But she must have. I could see they all knew about it."

"It was in the paper."

"No." Henny gets into bed and sits there propped up on her pillow. "They all knew except for Betsy Sugarman." She sits silently for several minutes, fingering the long satin bow on the front of her nightgown. She tried to shield her sister so Lillian could hold up her head in the community. She tried to protect her memory. And Lillian hadn't cared at all. She'd gone off and told them— God knows what. "Well," Henny says finally, "she did what she wanted." Then Henny turns over and falls asleep.

And Also Much Cattle

"*H*ell-o." Mark has an empty voice, and he welcomes guests mockingly, as if they were the first victims in a horror film. He rolls his eyes and holds open the torn screen door with two fingers. "Mom! The Sugarmans are here," Mark yells at the kitchen.

"Oh, it's so good to see you!" Gail Schick calls out. She is smoothing foil over all the kitchen counters, because the Contact paper is curled up and won't stick anymore. "MmmMUH! MmmMUH!" She kisses each of them. "Betsy, you look wonderful! I was so worried you couldn't make it! You're the first ones here! Listen, you two, just make yourselves at home, and I'll finish cleaning up in here."

"I didn't think we were early," says Betsy. "At the temple we started at six."

"Oh," says Gail. "We start when it gets dark. *HaShem* ends every day at sunset. I'm so excited! I tell you, Yom Kippur is my favorite holiday. No cooking tomorrow! And Yom Kippur in Hawaii! This was my dream!"

Betsy moves tentatively into the living room and looks at the house with a practiced eye. She notices the dust on the piano immediately, for although she married at the age of fifty-three, Betsy had a practiced eye long before she met the doctor. She is a career housewife, though she started late. A reentering woman.

The carpet needs vacuuming. In front of the couch is a green Marbelite coffee table such as Betsy has never seen. Not in a private home. Betsy looks resignedly at her husband. It was the doctor's idea to come here for services. He had told her last night. "I can't go to the temple," he said. "Not with that Gary what's-his-name president with the shiksa wife. We're going to the traditional Orthodox services."

The sofa alone confirms Betsy's suspicions about these traditional, Orthodox Schicks. She told the doctor last night that it wouldn't be clean, but he dismissed this. "They just moved in," he said. "They're still unpacking."

"After four months?" Betsy countered. But in the end she conceded to the doctor. She hates to argue with him, and it's true the new temple president doesn't appreciate the doctor. Besides which, after Rabbi Liebowitz was renewed, Betsy was not reelected as Sisterhood president. But despite these problems with the temple, Betsy regrets not warning the doctor about the Schicks' reputation. Everyone at the temple is talking about the Schicks' crazy plans for Hawaii. They want to start a permanent Orthodox synagogue in their own house, with services every week. They've already borrowed a Torah from the black-hat Lubavitchers in New York. But meanwhile their house leaks and they're living out of cartons. Betsy has even heard that Hawaii is only a resting place and the Shicks are really on their way to Australia.

Over the couch hang two bar mitzvah portraits— twenty-two-by-twenty-three-inch color glossies, oak-framed. "These are my sons!" Gail tells Betsy. "This is Elliott on the right. He looks like his father, with the brown hair. Tiny, he was. But now he's sixteen, and he's getting chased all over by girls. It's crazy. He was this little boy with no self-esteem, and I signed him up for a class in Silva Mind Control. He started lifting weights; he started getting confident. Pretty soon he has these huge muscles, this unbelievable chest. Girls started phoning every night. I created a monster! All the girls in his class were crying when we left New York. And already there's a girl chasing him in Hawaii! But look on the left. This is Mark. Look at that face! Blue eyes. Blond hair. My oldest, Pearl, also had the most beautiful blond hair. She never dyed it; she just rinsed it with a lemon rinse. She goes away to college, and it comes out brown. I don't understand. Brown hair."

"Has Pearl graduated yet?" Betsy asks politely.

"She graduated in June. Mark is between Pearl and Elliott. He's going to start college. Last year he learned in Israel. That was what nearly killed me. A year without Mark. It was the worst year of my life. But now he's back home," Gail cries happily. "I had to drag him away from his yeshiva, but I got him back. You can imagine how I was. Ecstatic. I made him his favorite cake. Chocolate with chocolate icing with chocolate chips. We're all together in *Hawaii*! It's a dream come true! What can I tell you? I dreamed about this night and day in New York. You know, meeting you on that second trip out here was definitely a decisive factor. You remember. It was at the temple dinner dance! It was this beautiful evening at the Kahala Hilton. Your husband spoke about the Jewish community in Hawaii. So eloquent. He was so convincing! B.J. and I just went out on the dance floor and I said: We're coming out here. It was that speech that did it! *That* was the reason we came to Hawaii!"

Passing through the room, Mark slams out into the yard. Gail doesn't notice. Even with Mark directly in front of her, Gail sees his bar mitzvah picture. His radiant smile. Mark blurs for her, too close to come in focus.

Pearl's blow dryer screams in one bathroom and Elliott in the other, "Whereza frickin' hot water?"

"B.J.!" Gail calls to her husband. "B.J., you're going to blow a fuse!"

B.J. holds up his newspaper. "No plugs on this," he says.

"Show what you built to the Sugarmans," Gail orders proudly.

B.J. leads the Sugarmans out to the enclosed lanai. "What I did," he says in his placid voice, "I glassed it all in, but I used louvers for ventilation."

Gail dances into the room through the broad opening of the sliding-glass patio doors. "This is the new Hawaiian synagogue!" she sings out. "Look, B.J. built separate seating!"

Betsy ventures in mistrustfully. The synagogue is a narrow room taken up by a long table. The roof is rough with splintering boards, but a rose plush carpet covers the concrete floor. At opposite ends stand the ark and the dark, hot women's section. The cooling radius of the ceiling fan does not extend that far.

"Such a builder!" Gail says. "B.J. built this, and he added on a bedroom for Pearl. A beautiful room."

"Beautiful," echoes the doctor magnanimously.

"Very nice," agrees Betsy. She speaks carefully, as if she held a bunch of straight pins in her pursed lips.

"This is just for now," B.J. tells them. "When I get this place really fixed up, I'm going to sell, and then we'll get something really big on the beach. Then we can expand the shul."

"Can you imagine?" Gail sighs. "An oceanfront synagogue."

"When are the other people coming?" Betsy looks at her watch.

ᔕᵔᔕ

Pearl is applying eyeliner in her room, though there certainly isn't anyone out there to impress. At Sarah Lawrence, Pearl was premed, so she didn't go out much. Not seriously. She went out three times with Mike Rosen. The third time wasn't exactly a date. Mike gave Pearl a ride to the train station because she was going to Westport to visit her roommate's family, and Pearl left her overnight bag in the car. Mike let Pearl's jewelry get stolen.

After Mike Rosen was Todd Sherwin. He might still be serious. It's hard to tell. In senior year, Pearl and Gail came out to Hawaii on a mother-daughter package tour. Their guide turned out to be a Jewish Hawaiian just back from Brandeis. Todd is tall and dark. He refrigerated the tour bus with his cynical humor. Not only that; he had ideas for the Jewish community here. A Hillel at the university, a better Jewish paper, a community Hebrew school. After Pearl went home to Long Beach, Todd wrote her ten-page letters filled with plans and ideas. He was giving Hebrew lessons. He was organizing a Shabbaton for teenagers out on the North Shore. Pearl was thrilled when they moved to Hawaii. She wanted to help Todd and see him all the time. He said he needed her. With her yeshiva education, Pearl could teach Hebrew and *tanach*. But when she got to Hawaii, Todd had only one student, so Pearl didn't have to teach. Gail thinks Pearl will marry Todd yet. But meanwhile he never calls. They went out once to Hanauma Bay with Todd's tour group. And they went once to the dress rehearsal for the Fort Ruger military production of *Patience*. But just last weekend the Japanese students at Kansai Gaidai English College put on *The Sound of Music* right down the street, and Todd pretended he didn't even know. He doesn't even seem to care that Arnold Bogner is chasing after her. Not that Bogner is the type to incite jealousy. Elliott calls him Bald Booger. It's hopeless. Todd used to come to services all the time, but now he claims he's been sleeping late. Pearl blinks off a blob of mascara. Maybe he'll come tonight.

By now the living room is crowded with people damp with sweat and humid September heat. A man the doctor knows by face rushes over to the Sugarmans. "Hello, Ben," Betsy says, remembering his name. Ben has narrow eyes and bulging teeth. He turns to the startled doctor and asks rapidly, "Do you forgive me for all the wrongs and insults I did to you the whole year?"

Ben's wife, Sonya, has just finished vacuuming the room. Sonya wears a lace mantilla on her head. She is a Filipina convert and takes her new religion very seriously.

"She loves to vacuum," Ben announces.

Betsy stiffens. "I hope you appreciate her."

"You saw that dress she was wearing? That was for her birthday."

Gail's mother has been sleeping all this time in the corner chair by the vacuum cleaner plug. When Sonya unplugs the vacuum, Grandma bends her head down farther from her stooped shoulders and cries softly, "Where are you?"

Gail points at her mother and throws up her hands. "Crazy!" she tells Betsy. "Now that she's back from the hospital, she's making me as crazy as she is! I can't give her that kind of service. I try to explain it to her—she's not sick anymore; it's time to stay home. But she wants round-the-clock; food on trays; she wants to see TV above the bed. We aren't clean enough for her, she says!"

"Where are you?" Grandma repeats. Kneeling at her feet with the tangled vacuum cord, Sonya smooths down Grandma's skirt so it won't climb farther above her knees.

The doorbell rings. "Don't get up, Pearl," Mark warns in a stage whisper. "It's not Todd, it's Booger." Pearl retreats into the kitchen, but even here she can see Arnold's truck looming up outside the window. Arnold makes lawn furniture. His truck is painted: "Make Lawns Fit for Loafing—Arnold Bogner Associates." Flat, Pearl thinks. A typically flat slogan.

Outside, in the living room, Gail greets Arnold. "Did you see the baby rabbis?" she asks him. "Listen, I was promised these would be good. They came straight from the Rebbe, with fifteen pounds of whitefish."

Arnold looks respectfully at the young rabbis in their black coats and hats. Arnold committed himself to Judaism only last year. He built the shul's ark in his shop, and he's trying to grow a beard. He rubs his face; the stubble is scratchy in the heat. "They going to hold out in those heavy jackets?" Arnold asks Gail with sudden concern.

"Believe me, they'll hold out. I was promised these would be good."

The baby rabbis are nineteen. They aren't quite rabbis yet, but they will be next year. They've finished their schooling and begun traveling with white shirts from home and food in plastic bags. They carry candlesticks, tefillin, *tanachs*, and press releases. They plan to get in touch with Jewish college students at the University of Hawaii, the local newspapers and radio. But tonight they look small and young as they sit together on the piano bench, backs to the keyboard, covered for the holiday. Dovidl has a dark, curly beard, but Moshe's beard is red and wispy. Moshe looks wide-eyed at the crowded room with its sagging white couch smudged into brown hollows by dirty feet. The long dining table still stands covered with sticky clear plastic. A dark woman reads the *Jewish Post,* and in the doorway to the kitchen Mrs. Schick waves her arms as she talks. She has pulled her sleeves up above her elbows.

"Pretty weird, huh?" Mark says to Moshe. "God, I wish I were still in Israel."

Moshe answers, "God willing, we'll all be there soon."

And Dovidl puts in, "Your parents are doing a great mitzvah."

"No, they're just getting flaky," Mark retorts scornfully. "They've always had this thing about Hawaii, with the picture books and the trips to see the volcano. So for their midlife crisis they decided to become the young pioneers. They drag me out here away from my friends, where there's no kosher pizza and no one to learn with. First they send me to Israel to learn Talmud, and then they bring me out here to be a Jew by myself in the middle of the Pacific Ocean."

"You're never by yourself," Moshe reasons. "And you can learn now to shed some light on people who maybe know less."

Mark raises his voice. "I am not a rabbi! That's not my job."

"Let me tell you something that the Rebbe said," Moshe begins.

But Mark cuts him off. "Hey, do you think your Rebbe is the Messiah? Is he going to like save the world—headquarters in Borough Park?"

Moshe answers in a lilting Talmudic voice. "No one says the Rebbe is the Messiah. We think only that in every generation there is one man who could be the Messiah. And our Rebbe is a good candidate for the job."

∽

The service is about to start, but Arnold lingers in the living room, hoping to see Pearl. He always tries to get another glimpse. For the past week, even during reserve-duty drill, Arnold has been thinking about Saturday night with Pearl at the Elks Club. They danced all alone on the dance floor to soft music. Outside, the waves smoothed themselves over the sand.

Leaving the kitchen, Pearl rushes past Arnold and enters the shul. All week she's tried to block him from her mind. That hole! That bar! The Elks baseball team leered at her over bulging T-shirts that read: "Win or lose, we booze." She went there out of pure destructive frustration because Todd didn't call. It was the most humiliating night of her life. Dancing with Arnold! No one else on the floor but a white-haired couple standing stock still and vibrating a little in the shoulders. "Hey," Arnold said as they danced. "This is fun. We should get together sometime."

"What do you call this?" Pearl asked. Sarcasm was wasted on him.

"We should get together again," he answered.

"I like to be alone," Pearl snapped.

Then he tried to snow her. "A girl like you? I bet you're never alone. I hate being alone. I have to keep busy. Work out at the club. Go train in the reserves. I mean, I never stop. I gotta grow—keep growing, otherwise you die."

⌀

Dovidl puts on his white *kittel* and begins chanting Kol Nidre. But Moshe can't help staring at the strange, narrow room. Behind him in the women's section, the timer on the lights isn't working, so Gail, Pearl, Betsy, and the others lean forward with sweating, pale faces. Through the window the streetlight flickers with the dark black bodies of swarming termites. Outside on the highway, cars rush speeding past between the houses and the dark beach. The sand at night: Is it still hot? And do they still swim in the dark? Men and women together. Strange dark place with speeding shadow people. While inside the house, Dovidl sings the same words sung at home.

⌀

Overnight, the wind and a stray cat tear open the Schicks' trash bags. When the Sugarmans return for services, they have to pick their way through scattered plastic forks and plates and past a billowing plastic tablecloth stuck with bits of lasagna. Betsy swallows. Fasting makes her nauseous, and this house is too much for her. She wanted to stay home, but this is such a hard day for the doctor. He must say Kaddish for his first wife. Betsy promised when she married the doctor that she would always stay at his side. Still, she cannot understand the doctor's sudden love of tradition. The house is filthy, the Schick boys insolent. The prayers are sung in weird foreign tunes. Betsy tries to follow in the English, but she can't help missing the temple, with its soft chairs and tropical stained glass, its harmonious organ music.

No one greets them at the door. The rabbis sit at the dining table, bent over the great leather-bound book between them. The page edges are marbelized pink and purple. Gail is screaming at Mark.

"Don't do this to me!" she cries.

"Well, why should I have to?" Mark shouts back. "You've got a dog running in and out of the shul. If you can't keep Whiskey out, it's not a place to pray. I am *not* going to throw him out every time. We're closing the sliding door."

"We are not," B.J. countermands his son. "It's too hot to close the door."

"Right, Dad, let the air in. Let the dog in. Let's cool down the room. Get comfortable. First one thing, then another. What's left of Yom Kippur?" Mark flings off his shirt. "Let's go to the beach already!" He stamps out of the room.

Gail turns tearfully to Betsy. "Oh, Betsy, he's so angry with me for making him leave Israel. This isn't kosher enough, that isn't *frum* enough. Not everyone in the minyan is *shomer shabbos*. He hates it here already, he told me. Can you believe that? This is not him—my son I sent away. This is his yeshiva talking.''

Gail's face looks swollen. Her radiant makeup has run together, and she looks like a doll left out in the rain. Betsy tries to sympathize. "I can imagine how you feel," she says. "But you know, things usually turn out well in the end. The doctor had a son who was a real rebel in the sixties. Now he lives in Santa Barbara, and he has a beautiful family." Gail doesn't seem comforted by this. At her feet, Whiskey scratches with his hind leg. "I know just the thing to get for heat rash," Betsy says. "If you put a little farina powder on the rump, he'll stop scratching right away. I have a terrier too, who gets just miserable in the heat, and this powder works every time."

"Really?" says Gail, brightening. "That's good to know. Farina powder. I've got to try that. I'm telling you I do everything for this dog. Whiskey is the hero of this family. Whiskey is why we're all together now. Whiskey saved Pearl's life in Long Beach. No, no, it's true. She was just napping in her room, and a rapist got in through the window; shinnied up the drainpipe and got in. God knows what kind of weapon he had. Knives. Guns. But Whiskey saw him. This *little* dog ran and *attacked*. Not only did he wake Pearl in time; he jumped through a plate-glass window and warned B.J. Like Lassie, he was."

"That is something else," murmurs Betsy.

"But wait," says Gail. "A year to the day after that, we found two pigeons on the doorstep with their necks wrung. You would not believe how sick New York is. It's just sick. Even in Long Beach."

"I know," says Betsy. "When I married the doctor, he

said he wanted to retire out here, and I couldn't have been happier. I left real estate and never regretted it."

"But you know," Gail muses, "it wasn't just the crime and violence and worrying the boys would get killed out in those neighborhoods at night, where all you can see is eyes and knives. We had a good business, after all. We had friends. Actually, we moved because we had this dream of starting an Orthodox community in Hawaii." Gail offers Betsy a babushka for her hair, and Betsy politely refuses.

In the shul, Mark and Elliott are scrolling through the Torah to find the place for today's reading. "Goddammit, Elliott, hold your end steady!" Mark yells at his younger brother. Neither of them is wearing a shirt, and neither notices Ben and Sonya enter as they bend over the table, pulling and rolling and cursing. Pale from the fast, Sonya adjusts her mantilla and settles into a corner of the women's section.

Gail runs out of her bedroom, pinning a stained babushka to her hair with a plastic orchid. B.J. promised Gail a flower every day in Hawaii.

"All right, Grandma, up you go." Gail grasps her mother, nails snagging her orange polyester muumuu. Slowly, doubled over on her cane, Grandma keels onto her feet. Gail lifts her mother from behind, and for a moment, Grandma's white orthopedic shoes tread the air, barely reaching the ground. Then Gail lets go, and Grandma doubles over onto her cane. They walk together to the women's section. Gail eases Grandma onto a straight-backed chair and takes a seat between Betsy and Sonya.

Moshe begins the morning service, chanting the opening psalm. He leans forward in prayer, heels to-

gether, poised on his toes like a diver ready to spring into
the air.

Pearl drags in a folding chair and sets it up in front of
the older women. "Would you look at that white dress?"
Gail whispers to Betsy proudly. "She looks like a bride.
You know, I had a dream Pearl got married. Right here in
the shul. You were there, Sonya. And the Felds. They're
from Long Beach. It was a beautiful wedding. Today
you'll meet the boy she's been seeing. He comes for services. Todd Sherwin. A beautiful, religious boy."

"Sherwin," says Betsy. "That must be Estelle's
grandson."

"That's right. Such a tan. And such a kidder! One in a
million. He came to the door with these beautiful flowers,
and he looks around like he can't find Pearl. Then he
says, 'Oh, there you are! What's a nice Jewish girl like you
doing in a place like this?' It's not just what he says, it's
the way he says it. Such a sense of humor. He has us on
the floor all the time, until the tears are streaming down
my face."

Betsy shakes her head gravely. "Maybe Pearl should
get an apartment," she suggests.

"Well," Gail says, "she's been job hunting. She's
looking for a medical job, because that will help her get
into medical school next time."

Pearl turns around and glares at her mother. "Mom,"
she warns. "I hope you're not too fond of that dress. Because after *yontif* that thing goes."

"But I wike this dress." Mrs. Schick pouts and droops
and looks wall-eyed.

"I'm sorry; it makes you look like a blimp."

Gail sulks down at her electric-blue size fourteen with
gold embroidered pineapples. "I *am* a bwimp. Look at

this!" She sticks a small arm in front of her and bats at the flesh with her free hand. "I was so good in New York. I used to go tone up every day. Now I don't spend any time at all on myself. I have to cook and clean three separate times for each person in this house. So naturally I'm fat. That was the first thing Mark said to me when he got off the plane. I put a double pikake lei around his neck. I was crying so hard I couldn't see—it's been a whole *year*—and as soon as I let go, he looked at me and said, 'Mom, you're so fat.' I could have cried, but I already was crying. He's right, you know. Now that he's back, I'll have to get in shape. See, he remembers me when I was really gorgeous, when Pearl and I went on this mother-daughter diet and lost thirty pounds together. You know, that diet where you eat only pizza for a week—as much as you want. And then you eat only ice cream. It was fabulous. The idea is, you get so sick of that one particular food you're allowed to eat, you stop eating altogether."

"Mom, will you shut *up*?" Mark whispers over the *mechitzah*. He rolls his pale-blue eyes. "If you aren't going to pray, just leave. Show a little respect."

"Sh, Mark. All right. Just calm down," his sister hushes him.

"Oh, yes, Pearl, let's be calm. It's only God." Mark turns and leans against the louvered window. The yard is a tangle of weeds and dead branches on the highway. He stands scowling as he watches the cars rush by.

"G-a-i-l! Gail, I can't move." Grandma has slipped down in her chair and can't pull herself up. On the men's side of the *mechitzah*, Arnold rises, but Sonya is there first, and he can only give Pearl a longing look as he sinks back into his chair.

Elliott bends down thoughtfully over his open *machzor*. He rolls his right sleeve higher and checks his left to see if it's the same length. Then he looks back at his right arm; it bulges satisfactorily from his shirt. He's as strong as Mark, even if he isn't as tall. He feels as big, anyway. Mark used to hit Elliott for being smaller and stupider. But while Mark was in Israel, Elliott worked out. Then, when he got to Hawaii, he got a girlfriend, Susan Finberg. When Mark came back, he was so impressed he looked at Susan and said, "Nice piece."

"Elliott?" It's Greg, a squeaky thirteen-year-old with braces.

"Yeah?" Elliott squints with concentration, because he is too vain to wear glasses and Greg is puny.

"Elliott, will the baseball hot line be open after *yontif*?"

"Yeah," Elliott replies. "Yeah, it'll be open."

"But, El-liott. It's such a long time to wait. It's not fair."

"Yes, it is fair." Elliott playfully knocks Greg over. "Listen, Hashem planned it this way."

"No way. What does God care about the pennant?"

"Greg, Hashem knew I would be in agony if I had to watch the Mets lose, and so he made the game on *yontif*."

A long-faced young man who goes by the name of Avi gets up from his seat, annoyed. "Hey, guys, cool it. This is heavy-duty praying here." His beard makes his jaw seem even longer and narrower. He has bright, vacant eyes, the eyes of a veteran worshiper—Tantric meditation, Kabbalistic texts, imported drugs, and Hawaii-grown, all-natural marijuana. "And another thing," he adds. "If it were any team but the Cubs, they would have rescheduled the game."

Elliott screws up his eyes and wrinkles his nose, squinting at the words that float down. "No," he contradicts. "That's beside the point."

In the women's section, Betsy looks in horror at Avi's tall figure, now in view above the line of the *mechitzah*. He bends over Elliott and Greg in cut-off shorts and a green T-shirt. His head is covered with a homemade hat woven of hala leaves. "Gail." Betsy gasps. "There's a lunatic in the house!"

Gail looks around her. "Where?" she asks.

"That man with the hat! He's talking to your son!"

"Oh, that's Avi!" Gail says. "I didn't introduce you. He's a sweetheart. A gem. I met him swimming at the beach. We started talking about religion. You know, he had a bar mitzvah in Rhode Island. I saved him from the cult on Ewa Beach! Psychiatrists and lawyers. They howl at the moon the first of every month. I found him howling at the moon. How could I leave him there? I took him to our Torah Understanding sessions. He's terrific! He's getting really involved. He just came to one session and—"

"He never left," Pearl finishes. "Mom, I'm sorry, there's no reason to keep a grown man in the house."

"Oh, my." Betsy breathes, near panic. "He's living in the house." She looks desperately for her husband. She wants to go home. But the doctor stands near the ark, swaying, singing tunelessly, engrossed in prayer.

"Mom," Pearl presses. "It's either me or him."

"Pearl, Avi needs us. He picks up Grandma from the kitchen floor."

"He stinks up the whole house."

"He helps your father."

"Like hell he does. Mom! He does everything so slowly. It's painful to watch him. Mrs. Sugarman, you see that piece of wood behind you? No, not that one—the little two-inch strip above your head. He took a week, a solid week, to paint that. Three days to take it outside and paint it the wrong color. And then hours to redo it. And then there were little cracks he had to caulk up. I wanted to pick that thing up and hit him over the head with it."

"He's a perfectionist. If he didn't live here, how could he learn *Yiddishkeit*?"

～

Moshe nods to Dovidl, who is standing in front of Bogner's ark. The laminated koa doors shine behind Dovidl's black coat as he speaks in his lilting Hasidic voice: "We thought that before we go on, we might tell a little story which could maybe set the tone of the service, perhaps. In a little town in Poland there was a farmer who went to shul only once a year for the holidays, and this farmer had a little boy. . . ."

Elliott's girlfriend walks in with her mother, Fan. "Gail, I'm sorry we're late," whispers Fan Finberg. Fan started coming to services when Susan got interested in Elliott. Her older daughter married a Mormon and moved out to Laie. Fan takes a seat next to Betsy. Sixteen-year-old Susan squats on the floor and flips back her streaky blond hair. "We had such trouble getting out of the house," Fan explains. "Mother told me she is going to die today, and Horace had to watch the game."

". . . And so," Dovidl continues, "the boy told his father, I have to go with you to shul. That's it, no questions about it, I'm going. . . ."

"Oh, Gail." Fan shakes her cropped iron-gray head.

"Gail, she wants me to bathe her every day. What she needs is a nurse, but it's so expensive."

"Bring her over here." Gail points at Grandma, sleeping bent over in the high-backed chair. "Just bring her over; I'll bathe them together."

". . . So what was the little boy to do in this great temple? He didn't know any Hebrew. Didn't know how to *daven*. And yet he felt in his heart the need to pray. What was the way to express the true sincerity of his heart? He went to the altar and said the only Hebrew he knew, the *aleph bes*. . . ."

Ignoring the story, Mark stands in a corner with his *tikkun*, practicing the *laiin*ing. Elliott whispers, "You don't have to *laiin* today. Pearl said Todd Sherwin was coming to do it."

"I'll believe it when I see it."

"Mark." Elliott jostles his brother. "Why can't you believe *me*?" Mark's book falls facedown on the rose carpet.

"Now look what you've done, idiot!"

"And so you see," Dovidl concludes, "it doesn't matter with what words we pray. It was the boy's sincerity that God heard."

"Fuck off, Elliott!"

"My G-d, they're fighting in front of the Torah." Gail rises up from behind the *mechitzah*. "Mark! Elliott! Stop it! Doesn't this holiday mean anything to you?" Gail shrieks forward and pulls Elliott back. "Go to your rooms! You are both leaving this house instantly!"

"Good!"

"But, El-liott"—Greg squeaks in awe—"you share a room with Mark; how can you go to your own room?"

"Elliott, you go to your room. Mark, you go to Pearl's."

"My room? Wonderful. He's going to pack in my room," mutters Pearl.

"Mom, I wasn't the one who wanted to come to Hawaii," Mark spits back. "You should've let me stay in Israel. Let me tell you something. In Israel there aren't any cars at all on Yom Kippur." Mark slams the door to Pearl's room, and B.J.'s add-on walls shake.

Elliott turns to the two rabbis, motionless in the stifling room. "Sorry, guys," Elliott says, turning to go. Susan Finberg rises to go after him, but Fan holds her back. Little Greg follows Elliott out, wide-eyed.

"B.J.!" Gail sobs to her husband. "B.J., go talk to them. Tell them I'll never forgive them for what they've done in front of the whole congregation."

"I'll try and convince them to come back." B.J. starts for the door.

"They're never coming back! Do you hear me, B.J.?"

Grandma wakes up with a start. "G-a-i-l? Gail, I'm hungry."

Gail points at her mother's bent head. "B.J., do it for her sake. These may be her last holidays."

"Do what, Gail?"

"They're never coming back!"

"Listen, people," Arnold Bogner reasons. "We don't have a *minyan* at the moment. So they'll have to come back, at least to finish the service. I mean, we're all hungry, kind a thing, but we can get through it if we pick up the pace."

"Oh, shut up, Arnold," Pearl says with feeling.

"Wait awhile," Dovidl advises Moshe in a low voice, "then go in and talk to Mark."

Sonya staggers as Gail sinks back into her arms.

"Well." Susan chirps, unfazed. "Todd Sherwin is coming, right? Then we'll have nine people."

"I hear he has a beautiful voice," Fan tells Pearl. "When did you two start going out?"

Pearl turns away, near tears. "I don't believe this," she mutters. "They broke up the whole service. We should have a women's service; we'd be done by now. Men are such animals."

"Oh, I know." Susan giggles from the floor. "Let's go to The Wave tonight; I feel like dancing."

Betsy pulls herself off her chair and walks stiffly into the living room. Her stockings itch, and the fabric of her aqua striped dress sticks to her back. She makes her way to the doctor. She will insist he take her home. But the doctor's concern for her makes this impossible. "Betsy, you look terrible," he exclaims. "Why don't you go home and lie down? This may take a while, before the service starts up again. I'll come home later, after Yizkor."

"No, no, I can't leave you here alone," Betsy feels compelled to demur. "It's just a little headache."

"A headache! Don't stay on my account, dear. I think you're overdoing with the fast."

"Don't worry." Betsy purses her lips with a trouper smile. "I'll sit right here by the bookcase with Sonya, and she can tell me all about the Philippines. I just have to sit down; I'll be fine."

"All right, dear," says the doctor, taking this at face value. He is a fine man, but he has cultivated a literal mind.

⌒⌒⌒

Elliott flops facedown on the olive-green army blanket on his bed. An enormous Disneyland panda sleeps on a pile of clothes in the middle of the room, and at the very top of all this, Greg perches on the panda's belly. "Elliott, you'll kick through the wall."

"Who cares? I don't live here anymore."

"Where are you going to live now?"

"I'll get an apartment in Waikiki—I'll get someone to share the rent."

"Could I share the rent?"

"No, stupid, you're not old enough."

"Don't call me stupid."

"Look, Greg, just go away. I don't feel like talking to you."

"If you go, what will happen to the shul?"

"Who cares about the shul? They do everything wrong anyway. I'm not going out there again to get insulted."

"But if you leave, the Finbergs will stop coming. The only reason Susan comes is because of you."

Elliott gets up and examines the crack he has made in the uninsulated wall. He kicks at it one last time, smiling through his tears.

∾

In the living room, Gail massages her temples. "I worked my whole life for those boys," she tells Pearl. "I was just a girl when they were born; all my friends were out dancing when I had them. First one, and then the other. And what do we tell Todd when he comes?"

"Mom," Pearl begs, "will you stop? He's not coming." Pearl looks at her mother's puffy eyes and jokes bitterly, "The wedding is off, okay?"

"Just don't make the same mistake I did," Gail says. "You shouldn't marry the first person who asks you. When you get older and you just think of all the different things you could have done! I tell you, if I were young I would do it so differently. One year more; if I'd waited one year more I would've married a rabbi, and that's what I've always wanted. If I didn't have you kids, I would marry our Long Beach rabbi in a minute. Either him or Paul Newman I would marry. Just to get out of the house. But I'm too fat. I have to go work out and get really gorgeous. *Then* I'll leave. But listen, Pearl, don't get yourself upset. I predict Todd will come. You'll see."

❧

Still sitting in the shul, Arnold Bogner gazes at Pearl, sulking in the living room. "I definitely love her. Definitely," Arnold tells Sonya's husband, Ben. "I think about her all the time. Like during bowling, and everything. I mean, you saw my game Thursday."

"Did you tell her?" Ben asks.

Arnold slumps down in his chair. "What can I do? She's really young. She's got everything. She's beautiful; she's got brains. Boy, does she have a brain! Some people don't like the smart ones, but I've got like a thing about it. I can't just have this physical kinda thing. I go for the intellectuals every time. It's like a need I have. I have to have this mental relationship. Aw, Jesus, I need a Coke. I mean, if this thing with Pearl happens, it has to be a relationship. See what I'm saying?"

"Yeah." Ben stretches and cracks his knuckles.

"What do you think I should do?" Arnold pleads.

Ben stares at his trim fingernails. "You gotta give it time," he says philosophically. "Look at me and Sonya. I didn't want just a face from the book. I wrote letters every day to the Philippines. I wrote to more than one girl, and I read all the letters to see how good the English was; what kind of person she was; how old; what kind of family background. It took a long time. But if you want a real relationship you've got to do it right. They get older, you know. There are a lot of questions: what kind of cooking? what kind of mother? what skills for work?"

"But, Ben, I don't care about that. She doesn't have to do anything. I'm not so modern like you. I want romance."

Ben looks at him. "So go to a movie."

Arnold sighs. The shul is empty except for the rabbis, who read quietly from their leather *Tanya*. "I know one thing," Arnold tells Ben. "If those boys think they're going to stop Yom Kippur, they've got another thing coming."

∾

There is hardly space in Pearl's room for Arnold to berate Mark. Arnold stands pinned between the bed and Pearl's new rolltop desk. The desk is completely empty. Only a single piece of white paper lies on the shining wood surface. The paper is a list, beginning:

1. Wash hair
2. Paint nails

Mark wriggles his toes in the pink shag carpet. "I'd rather die," he tells Arnold.

Arnold turns on him, furious. "You look at me when I'm talking to you! It takes a lot to get me angry. But when I get angry, people listen. What you've done to your mother—to your whole family! And not just today. When Pearl needed a rug, did you help? No, you let your father do the whole thing. You and Elliott never cook or clean; you let Pearl do everything, and you treat her worse than dirt."

Mark laughs—a coughing, smoker's laugh. "Face it, Arnold. Pearl's a dog. She's ugly and she's got a terrible personality."

"Watch it, Mark. I am twice your age."

"Congratulations, Mr. Bogner." Mark pumps Arnold's hand with a hollow-eyed smile. "You're also twice as old as Pearl."

〜〜〜

Betsy's headache is getting worse, but Sonya makes her a cold compress. "You're a doll," Betsy says gratefully. "You know, I want to tell you, the American Yom Kippur isn't as much of an ordeal as this. At an American temple, you come, and you stay for as much as you can stand, and then you go home."

"Someone's at the door!" Gail cries. "It's Todd. Pearl, go answer it."

Pearl opens the door, and a wiry-bearded man in a bottle-green suit appears. "*Hu*llo," he exclaims in his Oxford accent. "I am Jonathan Collins. I walked from Bet Ha Knesset. I'm the one they brought in to lead services, but they decided to knock off early, so I thought I'd walk

over to catch the rest of your service. Todd Sherwin gave
me directions. He said you needed a *baal koreh*." Jonathan
flashes Pearl a smile and walks on into the shul. He looks
all around him and exclaims, "Why, what a charming little synagogue! This is quite extraordinary!"

The baby rabbis watch circumspectly, and Dovidl
rises to greet him. Gail really would have done it, but she
is still not herself. "Mr. Collins," Dovidl asks timidly. "Is
it your *minhag* to carry a handkerchief?"

"Oh, well, I don't think of it as carrying. This is really
an ornament. It's quite usual to adorn oneself with a
pocket handkerchief—even on *yontif*."

"But you are carrying something."

"Well, you see, I have no intention of using this handkerchief. This is not a functional handkerchief; it is a
ritual handkerchief. I may wear it on *yontif* because it is
part of my costume."

"Costume?!"

Ben looks up from his *machzor*. "He means it's not for
blow, it's for show."

"He's cute," Susan comments to Pearl in the living
room.

"Such an accent!" says Gail in her still-quavering
voice. "Like *Masterpiece Theatre*. Strangers come to pray,
but my own sons insult God to my face!"

"You know what?" Susan tugs up the front of her
sundress. "I think the rabbis are kind of cute too. Especially the one with the red beard. Where are they staying
this week?"

"I don't know. Mom, where are the rabbis staying?"

"They'll just have to fend for themselves. They'll
just have to scrounge. I'm not doing another load of laun-

dry. Pounds of clothes I've done. Wash it and dry it and fold it . . ."

Betsy refuses to take part in this hysteria. "Fan," she says, trying to make polite conversation. "I've heard wonderful things about your writing."

"Mom, the rabbis. Where are they staying? What hotel?"

Gail looks up vaguely. "They're staying at the Tahitian Beachcomber. Arnold and Avi reserved the room. They're the ones that care about me. . . ."

"The Tahitian Beachcomber? Mom, that's on Kauai!"

Fan answers Betsy, ignoring the crisis. "I belong to a small writing group—mainly retired English instructors from the university. I set up my word processor in the corner of the TV room. But I have so much trouble finding time to write. My mother came to live with us, and then the baseball season started. Horace won't move from the TV room during the season. I can't come in at all, except to take out the empty Perrier bottles. And then there's the problem of subject matter. It's so hard to find appealing ideas. As an academic, I've been trained to a very formal and elegant kind of writing. My prose is so . . . intellectual."

"Those idiots!" Pearl screams. "We are on Oahu, and they reserve a hotel for the rabbis on a different island! Where are they supposed to spend the night? Great, they'll probably end up in my room. I told you, Mom, Avi goes. I should have known he and Arnold would get together and mess this thing up. But what can you expect when you give men a job? Of course it's a disaster with those two morons at the helm."

In the shul, Jonathan counts nine men, including himself. Mark and Arnold are still absent, though Elliott and Greg have returned. The boys sit leaning against the sliding doors separating the shul from the living room; they have one foot each in the shul. The two rabbis are talking softly at the end of the table.

"Tell me, B.J.," Jonathan says to Mr. Schick, "do you always have a hiatus between Shacharis and Musaf? No, no, I am fascinated by this, I truly am. Perhaps this is a tropical phenomenon—a religious form of siesta. Yes, a spiritual siesta, a rest from unworldly concentration."

"I don't know," B.J. replies. "Look, Arnold's back. Ask the rabbis."

"Ten men," Jonathan announces. "Shall we?"

"Wait," says Moshe. It is time, he decides, to talk to Mark. He walks into Pearl's room and he says simply, "Come back."

"Rabbi, I'm sorry," Mark says. "I was obnoxious, but this service is totally screwed. I mean, it's insane. It's surreal. Yom Kippur used to mean something. What's going on here? Is this the same holiday? Is this the same book as in Long Beach? Who is this guy with the hat *living* in my house? What happened to my family? The hell with this. I don't need to be a part of this charade."

"Yes. Yes," Moshe says, pulling his red beard. "This is a charade. That is a very good word, because truthfully, in this whole world there is nothing here except *HaShem*. Just *HaShem*."

Mark scowls. "You want me to go back for *HaShem*'s sake."

"No," Moshe answers. "I want you to go back for your sake. *HaShem* is real. *HaShem* doesn't need to pray. You do. You come back and pray; and maybe if you pray with all your heart, then for just one second you'll be real too."

"Well," Mark says. "I can't leave until after *yontif* anyway." He follows Moshe out.

∽ℰ∽

Jonathan turns to Moshe and Dovidl as they unroll the Torah. "Would you like a Sephardic or an Ashkenazic melody? Actually, I rather fancy Sephardic. I picked up a lovely *niggun* in Turkey." Jonathan bends over the scroll and begins the *laiin*ing in his light, springy head tone.

"M-o-r-r-i-s? *M-o-r-r-i-s?*" Grandma's voice is surprisingly loud.

"No, Grandma, this isn't Yizkor." Gail turns tearfully to Fan. "You know, at the hospital they wanted to pull out the plug, but I wouldn't let them. I brought her with me all the way to Hawaii. And now my sons abandon me."

"She brought me here to die," Grandma confides to Susan, at her feet. "I'm no fool. First she poisoned Morris. But I'm too smart for her. I wouldn't eat that honeydew, even cut up into little pieces on toothpicks. Even from a spoon into my mouth." Grandma begins to cry and then forgets about crying and falls asleep.

∽ℰ∽

"Look at this." Avi thumbs his *machzor*. "Elliott," he calls downwind, "it says here that Jonah was bummed because God killed the gourd shading Jonah's head. But look at what God says!" Avi points a dirty fingernail at the passage: " 'Then the Lord said: You would spare the gourd, though you spent no work upon it, though you did not make it grow; it sprang up in a night and perished in a night. Should I not then spare the great city of Nineveh with more than a hundred and twenty thousand human beings, who do not know their right hand from their left, and also much cattle?'

"Elliott, that would be so great for a peace rally. It's like, if you hate people, at least don't nuke the animals."

⟋⟍

Betsy is appalled by the black-hat rabbis. They ask all nonmourners to leave during Yizkor! This has never happened to Betsy before. At the temple, she stands at the doctor's side. She waited all this time to stand with the doctor, and now she is asked to leave. Betsy is exhausted; the heat has made her ill. She excuses herself to lie down on the Schicks' queen-size bed. Just as she suspected, cartons of clothes and books line the walls. On the bureau stands a wedding picture of a handsome young couple.

⟋⟍

Pearl's spirits begin to recover in the break for nonmourning during Yizkor. Jonathan is delightful. "What does one do at night in Honolulu?" he asks.

"I wouldn't know," Pearl says half jokingly.

"Well," Jonathan says, "perhaps we can find out together. I wanted to go hiking, but that didn't prove feasible. Perhaps we could go to Waikiki and look for something vegetarian. Dinner, perhaps. Shall we be adventurous?"

"I'll think about it," says Pearl.

After Yizkor, when she returns to the women's section, Pearl tells Susan with happy relief, "It looks like I will be going out tonight, after all!"

✑✑✑

Dovidl stands next to Moshe during the evening service. "In closing the day, we want to give you one small story," he begins. "There was a king with a beautiful daughter, but she didn't want to get married. So, okay, it's all right, she doesn't have to get married. It's good to have her around the castle. But after a time the king grew worried. The princess was older. . . ."

"Yeah, at least twenty," Pearl says.

". . . So the king swore that the next person he met would marry his daughter. Well, the next person who walked in just happened to be the town water carrier. But an oath is an oath. What could the king do? The princess and the water carrier were married. Now, when the princess saw her new home, she was very upset. Cleaning and cooking—she was not accommodated to all this. And also all the villagers hated the girl. They said, 'Oh, she thinks she's a princess!' And they all avoided her. So the water carrier sees how upset his wife is. The water carrier is a good man, and he wants his wife to be happy. What does he do? He sends for the king; he convinces the king to come for urgent help. Now, when the king comes, all the town is friendly and the house is clean and the princess is happy. But in his heart, the water carrier knows that as soon as the king leaves, everything will go back to the way it was before.

"And this is the way we are today. Today is the High Holiday. The house is clean, we wear our best clothes. Everyone is praying. But how will we act when the King

is not here? We have to think about all the ordinary
days. . . ."

◠◡◠

"Gail," says Fan, "it was a beautiful service, such a treat.
And you know, every year the fast gets easier. I'll leave
Susan with Elliott, but I'd better get home and feed Horace. He's probably starving. And my mother too. With the
pennant on, I'm sure he hasn't left the TV room. Gosh,
you know, I hope he hears me at the door. I left my keys.
But listen, thanks again for everything."

"And I thank you too," the doctor adds. "That Yizkor
service was absolutely moving. With the Hasidic chanting—it was like something from my childhood."

Betsy throws up her hands, out of patience. "What
are you *talking* about?" she implores him. "You grew up at
Temple Emanuel in Cleveland, Ohio. Since when are
these people your childhood?"

"Betsy," the doctor says, "I can't explain it—the
Yizkor. I felt so close to her memory. It wasn't a physical
or emotional presence. It was just an absolutely compelling feeling of continuity through the ages. Beautiful."

Hurt, Betsy retorts, "I'm sorry. But I cannot call anything in this house compelling or beautiful."

"Well," reasons the doctor, "she wasn't your wife."

"Elliott." Avi carries a bowl of tofu–bean-sprout
salad. "Hey, Elliott, could you pass this around?"

"No way, Avi. I'm history. You live here."

"Elliott! Mark!" Gail still has a sob in her voice.
"Boys, you can't leave the house. You couldn't live alone
in Waikiki. The cults and the *treife* food—what could you
eat? I can't let you become born-again pedicab drivers.

You have to stay here. But you have to understand. I can't ever forgive you!"

"Oh, Mom, why?"

"After what you've done? Why can't I forgive you?"

"No, why do we have to stay here?"

⌒∽⌒

Moshe and Dovidl sit tired and happy, sipping from paper cups of ginger ale. "Let me tell you, Mr. Schick," says Moshe. "We have been to many Jewish communities. And yet we have never seen one quite like this. A small group of people in Hawaii learning and praying, spreading *Yiddishkeit* from this home. It is remarkable, and I mean that in a very positive sense."

"Here, Grandma, apples and honey for a sweet new year!" Mark dips a slice of brown apple and dribbles it over the plastic tablecloth.

"El-liott, what if the hot line doesn't answer?"

"Then phone all the radio stations. Greg, it just hit me. We're so far west that we'll probably be the last Jews in the world to find out who won the pennant."

Jonathan looks at Pearl brightly. "The most remarkable thing!" he says. "I will be hiking this week, after all. It seems that the rabbis have mistakenly reserved a room on Kauai, and I can stay there for the week. I'll be taking a flight out this evening. I am sorry about our dinner. Perhaps we can go next weekend."

"Yes, well, I don't think I can make it next weekend," Pearl says in a brittle voice.

"Oh, dear. I suppose we'll see each other next Rosh Hashanah." Jonathan kisses Pearl lightly on the cheek. "But I will give you my forwarding address in Albania.

I'm doing fieldwork there this winter. Have you given much thought to the Jewish community in Albania? It's brilliant. Really. The average age of a congregation is seventy, but they're terrific fun. You must look me up. I'm quite serious."

Mark and Elliott wrestle on the couch. "Elliott, you are *not* going to Waikiki with me tonight."

"Ow!"

"Get off the couch!"

"No!"

"You're not even eighteen!"

"No one's going to card me. I'm taking Susan."

"So. I'm taking the car."

Gail sighs with exhaustion. "Pearl, dear," she asks, "would you clear the table?"

"No! Mom, I'm not a slave. I won't! No one else lifts a finger around here. Look at Avi and Arnold—eating like pigs, and they never help."

Arnold hears his name. "What's wrong, Pearl?"

"Oh, forget it." Pearl locks herself in the bathroom, and Sonya begins to clear the table.

Mark turns to Arnold. "See what I mean? Terrible personality. She turns off the charm the minute Jonathan leaves. And I'm also leaving!" Mark adds, for his brother's benefit. "I don't want to see you anywhere near the Pink Cadillac."

"We'll be there!" Elliott yells after his brother. "Thanks for telling us where to be!"

"He's trying to fool you," says Susan.

Elliott considers this for a minute and then concludes, "Nah, he's too dumb."

While Elliott changes in his room, Susan tries to shake hands with the embarrassed rabbis. "Hi! I'm Sue

Finberg," she says. "I heard you guys didn't have a place to stay, and I thought, why don't you stay with us? Mom and Dad aren't kosher and stuff, but I'm into soybeans and whole-wheat kernels."

The rabbis look at each other in surprise and then look back to the top of Susan's head.

"If it isn't an imposition," Dovidl replies uncertainly.

"Hey, no problem. You can stay in the TV room!"

Further Ceremony

"*M*argaret McCrae," she announces to the receptionist. Then Margaret takes a burlap-covered chair in the doctor's waiting room. She unfolds a new handkerchief and dabs gingerly at her nose. World hunger brochures cover the end table. Margaret met her doctor, Annie, in the seventies at a Hawaii hunger march in Thomas Square. Annie was returning to med school, and Margaret was leaving her second husband.

"Hey!" Annie cries from the doorway. Annie still wears loose Indian clothes. She is ideologically and aesthetically consistent. Margaret likes that. She can count on the fact that Annie will never shave her legs.

Annie sits with her patient on the examining table. "So," she says, peering into Margaret's throat. "Looks like you've got a cold."

Margaret groans. "I know that. I want an antibiotic."

Shaking her head, Annie takes a packet of salt pills from the cabinet. "You'll just have to sweat this thing out," she admonishes. "You're going to have to slow down and rest."

"I can't." Margaret sniffles. "My mother is coming in from Maui. I'm putting on a party, remember?"

"What's more important?" demands Annie. "Your one and only body or some dinner party? You just want me to give you a wonder drug that'll knock you out for twenty-four hours so you can wake up when it's all over."

"Yes." Margaret's eyes brighten. "That's exactly it."

"No wonder drugs here," Annie declares.

Margaret looks imploringly at the prescription pad. But Annie stands unmoved under her notice: THIS IS A NUCLEAR-FREE ZONE. "You are a priss." Margaret pouts.

Yes, she thinks as she leaves the office, Annie shows consistent commitment to all the good causes. But sometimes a little flexibility is called for. Sometimes there are emergencies.

When she gets to the door, the phone is ringing. "Bruce!" she screams hoarsely into the converted garage–game room. "Someone answer it." The dog, Shi-shi, runs to the door, barking ferociously. When she sees Margaret, she returns with a wet tennis ball in her mouth. She loves to fetch and carry the ball but has trouble dropping it. The phone stops ringing, and Margaret sinks into a chair, exhausted. Her long straight hair slips down her back.

A dim figure moves in the kitchen. "Bruce, my boy," Margaret calls, with vestiges of crisp maternal authority. Bruce appears with a Bud Light in his hand. "Bruce," she tells him. "You may pick up your grandmother at the airport, Hawaiian Airlines Flight Fifteen."

"Oh, God," Bruce says.

Margaret continues smoothly. "I am now going to take a shot of Jack Daniel's, which you may find in the lower left kitchen cabinet. And I will go to sleep in the game room until I wake up. You may tell your grandmother I am lying down and will see her at the condominium tomorrow."

Margaret takes her drink and shuffles into the dark game room she set up when the kids were in high school and she wanted to know where they were. She lies down queasily on the furry water bed. The pachinko game glows in the corner as she drifts to sleep amid these relics of her children's adolescence. Stacks of *Playboy*, a foosball machine. Margaret lined the walls with mattresses to contain the sounds of Bruce's band, Lethal Dose. Classic. It will become a Smithsonian exhibit. Or perhaps even be reassembled in a gallery. The Hideout, 1972–75, mixed media. Margaret McCrae, b. 1935.

∾

It is evening when Margaret gets up and throws away her pile of used Kleenex. She makes her way into the dark living room. It's filled with her collections. Behind and underneath the couch, chairs, and coffee table, Margaret stores her miniatures, along with boxes of Victorian paper dolls. The bell of her antique gramophone swings out from the bookcase like a gilded trumpet flower. Under the baby grand lie the tracks of an HO-gauge diesel train set with real locomotives that must be repaired at a specialist New York train repair shop and require parts that must be sent for from the German manufacturer. These things were acquired during Margaret's antique-toys period, when the children were small and she lived in Scarsdale.

Margaret decided when Hal left her that she wouldn't

collect for herself anymore; she would become an interior designer and collect for other people. When she moved home to Hawaii, she planned to cull her things to essentials; live in a spare and spartan unit near Oahu Prep. But instead, she found this shambling project, miraculously priced, on old missionary land. This house has an appetite. It sprawls its length around the garden, demanding furniture. Ironically, even as her own house filled, Margaret found work weeding out the clutter in hotel reception rooms, making space in lobbies with mirrors and one well-placed floral focus. Her second husband was a hotel manager and commissioned earth-tone hotel rooms and beige bridal suites. Even after she left him and began remodeling private homes, Margaret could not realize the country kitchens and Edwardian armoires she envisioned. She was asked to oversee the installation of stainless-steel gas ranges and high-gloss white wall systems. No commission for a dream house has come her way. She is still waiting for a white Victorian on the North Shore. A villa on Molokai. A jewellike setting for a collection of antiques. Meanwhile clients come for the "clean, contemporary lines" praised in the remodeling issue of *Honolulu* magazine.

Margaret's boyfriend, Charles Yim, pads down the hall. "You look terrible," he says. "Should you be up?"

"I am up," Margaret states. "I am worrying about the party on Thursday."

"Cancel." Charles turns on the light in the kitchen and riffles through a bag of potato chips. "You're sick. You're tired. I'm tired too. I forget why you planned this thing in the first place."

"My mother," Margaret reminds him. "She hasn't met you, remember?"

"Mm." Charles munches. "She wants to see if my intentions are honorable. I just don't see the need for the big production."

Margaret looks at him. What an age for ritual, she thinks. Epithalamiums are dead. She studied them at Smith. Where are the gifts, the feasts, the portraits? She imagines a latter-day Van Eyck. The two of them standing as they are now under the kitchen light. Pale reflection of the artist in the bowl of the Kitchenaid. Where are the records of occasions? Are there occasions anymore? Parades, circuses, royal weddings. The pageantry is all on television. The ceremonies are all only ceremonial. The big productions are for the tourists. Courtship is for soap operas—suspense to hold the viewers through commercials. Why should she watch other people's lives? "I want to see some people!" Margaret explodes. "I want a big production. I want to entertain once in a while."

"Fine," Charles eases. "Why don't we take her out to the Swiss Inn?"

"Charles, you don't take your family to a restaurant. I'm talking about all my friends."

"We'll put it on VISA." Charles pats Margaret's shoulder. "You're going to get all worked up about this and go into a cleaning frenzy. And you won't like the way it works out. You're setting yourself up for some kind of confrontation with your mother, your sister."

"Shut up," Margaret begins to say, but she sneezes. "What you don't seem to understand is the invitations are out; the RSVPs are in. I'm really making this party. In this house. I happen to like entertaining."

"You keep saying that," Charles observes.

"And I happen to think my mother should meet you after two years. I don't see why we should coop up here with the VCR as if we were some kind of sting operation. Have you thought about the way we live? We go to work. We come home. No one sees us."

Charles looks up, puzzled. "But why do we need to be seen?"

∾

The next morning Margaret rolls over in bed and phones in sick to her assistant.

"How's the cold?" Charles asks at her side.

"Just fine. Marvelous. Blooming." Margaret steps into the shower and feels her nose clear under the steaming water. She pours her hair over one shoulder and examines the gray streaks. She is going to dye it next time she goes in for a haircut.

She finds a box of chocolate doughnut holes in the fridge and eats a couple cautiously. She has not yet regained her appetite. Margaret has always been a rail-thin voracious eater. She was teased in school on Maui and envied later on at Smith. Her weight never seemed to catch up with her. Her thighs are big, but the rest of her body stays lean and bony. She leaves Charles a note to go buy milk and then drives into Honolulu to meet her mother.

∾

Elizabeth McCrae is staying in one of Margaret's sample units at the Waikiki Vista. Margaret's assignment was to create a unified space with a muted color scheme. "Good morning," says Elizabeth. "Have some coffee."

Margaret takes a cup and surveys the white kitchen. "Think it will sell?" she asks her mother.

"Well, I don't know," Elizabeth says. "I certainly wouldn't buy such a place. I wouldn't want my dishes picked out for me and my furniture planned. But I suppose it would appeal to people with a limited imagination or to newlyweds with no taste of their own."

"It's a sample," explains Margaret. "It doesn't come fully furnished. These are accessories to give people the idea."

"Oh, I see. Is the bed here a sample too? I like a firm bed, but what you have here is a rock."

"Well, it doesn't matter," Margaret says. "The owners won't really live here. Most of these units are investments or time-sharing arrangements."

"That's what I thought," says Elizabeth. "It's a beautiful design for that sort of thing. Very pretty. You've been working hard, I can see. You have those pouches under your eyes. Your father had them too."

"Well, I've been busy. I'm working on the party for Thursday night."

"And I'm sure it will be beautiful," Elizabeth declares reassuringly. "I'm looking forward to meeting your fiancé. Now tell me, exactly what sort of affair are you planning?"

Margaret pours herself another cup. "I couldn't tell you," she says. "I mean, I'm really in the midst of the planning stages right now."

"Of course," Elizabeth says with the breezy cosmopolitan air she cultivated in the thirties as a Maui plantation wife.

Margaret looks at her nervously. "I mean, I've invited

the whole design firm and the architect and chief contractor for this building. . . ."

"Are you going to tell him?" Elizabeth says in a low voice.

"Tell him what?"

"About the tile here on the floor."

Margaret looks down at the white ceramic tile.

"You didn't see the cracks," says Elizabeth. "I moved a chair across the floor and the tiles simply cracked underfoot." She points to a web of hairline cracks across the tile floor.

"My God," cries Margaret. "What did you do to the floor?"

"I walked on it," Elizabeth says.

Margaret stands and stamps her foot. The gesture chips a tile, her spike heel grinding the corner into powder.

"You're right." She moans.

"Of course I am," Elizabeth tells her. "They're defective. Don't knit your brow. You don't want wrinkles."

"Onaga, the bastard. He cheated me." Margaret fumes. "I'll sue the pants off of him. I'll make Brown sue him; that'll be even better." She picks up the phone, then realizes she called in sick. "God damn it." She slams down the receiver. "Well, when I see him . . ."

"You invited him for Thursday," Elizabeth reminds her.

"Mother," Margaret says. "Just stop gloating."

Elizabeth raises hurt eyes. "I'm not gloating. I was stating a fact, Margaret. How can you accuse me of gloating over such a botch?"

"You did it again." Margaret splutters. "You don't even pretend to feel any sympathy."

"I certainly do," retorts Elizabeth. "Now sit down and pull yourself together. You can't do anything now, so you'll have to wait. No patience whatsoever. You remind me of your father. I sometimes think if he had learned to wait a little longer, if he had been less quick to anger, he would be here now."

"Don't worry about me," Margaret snaps.

"I hardly ever do," Elizabeth reassures her. "You've got a temper, but you know how to take care of yourself. It's really Emily Ann I'm concerned about. She is so easily hurt. Such a child, really. I just want her to get that degree."

Margaret snorts. "Maybe by the time she's fifty."

"In any case," Elizabeth says, "I've decided to leave her the house and property on Maui for after I'm gone."

∽

"Such a child," Margaret mutters the next day as she fights the traffic on Nimitz. Poor sensitive Emily Ann. Delicate flower. She grimaces. Emily was the problem child at the plantation school on Maui. The adults were convinced she suffered acute allergies to mold spores in the schoolroom. Margaret knew this was a lot of malarkey. Emily's allergies clearly grew worse when she was exposed to such subjects as algebra and geography. Margaret pointed this out to her mother, who did not speak to her for a day. Later Margaret was taken aside by her Sunday school teacher and told about the Indian who learned to walk ten miles in another man's moccasins. She was also given the wash as a weekly penance and had to stand over the violent white washing machine stewing the clothes, wringing them through its two rollers. She

pinned the water-heavy sheets to the line and ran to un-
pin them during the quick mountain showers. Margaret
did not grow more sympathetic to sensitive Emily Ann.
Naturally, Margaret became the harsh one, the uncaring
one. Emily Ann was the shy one, to be chided softly or
not at all. Naturally, Mother concludes that as the pos-
sessor of more feelings, Emily Ann should inherit the
plantation house.

Margaret believes Emily Ann chose to be useless and
ineffectual. She does not know when Emily took up this
strategy, but it has been effective, in its perverse way,
from the time of her eighth-grade graduation, when she
cried so hard she was excused from reciting Lady Mac-
beth's sleepwalking speech and comforted with a dress
ordered from Saks on the mainland. Margaret knows
there is nothing inherently wrong with her sister. Emily
Ann would have grown up if she wanted to. She still
could, if she would simply finish her thesis and apply for a
job. But Emily Ann would rather live under cover, doing
fieldwork. She is studying the Hawaiian family structure
in Waianae. However, she did promise to help out with
the party. Margaret must of course drive out and pick
her up.

Out in the Hawaiian homelands, the road roughens
and the volcano slopes down to the sea in green ridges
threaded with faint waterfalls. Emily has lived here for
two years with the Ilohelani family, the subjects of her
thesis. A mule raises its head as Margaret parks. Farther
up the road, two small children are screaming at each
other in pidgin. *"Hana! Hana!"* the little girl warns. Then
she chants tauntingly, *"Hana okolele;* they're gonna get
you."

"Bye, Auntie Em," the little girl calls, as Emily Ann

emerges from the house. It's a small frame house with a big garage, set up with picnic tables for family gatherings. Around the back, Mrs. Ilohelani grows plumerias, orchids, roses, and ferns for the family lei stand at the airport and for sale to florists in Chinatown and Waikiki.

"You know, those children in the yard aren't Ilohelanis," Emily explains as Margaret drives. "It's been two years, but I think I'm really breaking into background kinship structure. The little girl you saw is one of the grandchildren; she's the daughter of Pi'ikea's youngest son, the one who moved away to California. Apparently he had a girlfriend, who lived with him at home, but when he left her, she stayed on as part of the Ilohelani family. Then she had the little boy, Kimo, by another man. But the boy lives with the Ilohelanis too, even though he's no kin. I only found this out last week, because everyone calls this boy cousin. But right now it looks like he isn't a real cousin at all. I got this all on tape from the neighbors."

"That's nice," Margaret says tensely. "Isn't it convenient not to write this up? It saves you all those revisions."

"Mother bought me a computer," Emily answers, "so when I start, I don't have to retype. I'm reading the manual."

"Good, good," says Margaret.

"But I'm very excited about the genealogy," Emily continues. "Dr. Lloyd said I'm making real progress, because I'm observing the whole extended family. Not just blood relations but also unrelated members. I have here, in my own focus household, a mother, father, and four children, along with three grandchildren, the two children of Randall, and his girlfriend I mentioned. And then there

is the grandmother, who holds everyone together. Lately
I've been following her around. She is the most dynamic
woman I have ever seen! She never gets tired; she's always cooking, taking care of the children, breaking up the
fights, picking the flowers. She does all the shopping. She
makes everyone go to church. And for the luaus! She
roasts the pig, she teaches the children to wrap *lau laus*. I
asked her, 'Do you ever have a day when it doesn't seem
worth it? When you just feel you can't go on? Can't get
out of bed?' And she looked at me, and then she said, 'I
go stay sleep, no one wake up da family.' Imagine! She's
only forty-six years old! Two years younger than me!"

"Than I, dammit," Margaret corrects.

"Oh, Meg, don't be so hostile. If you could see the
way this family lives together. Such generosity! On top of
all the other people I mentioned, there's Uncle Bradley, a
Chinese gentleman who used to rent next door. His wife
died and he couldn't live alone anymore, so he just
moved in. So at my latest count there are ten people in
this house, some completely unrelated."

"You forgot to count yourself," Margaret reminds her.
"You're also unrelated, and you've been living there without any questions asked for two solid years."

⌒⌒⌒

At home, the sisters sit at the kitchen table, and Emily
Ann takes down *The Joy of Cooking* and an old *McCall's
Cookbook* from the cabinet. "This is beautiful," she says,
pointing to a picture of duck a l'orange. "Why don't you
make this?"

Margaret slaps shut the dusty book and Emily begins
to sneeze. "Emily," Margaret says with clenched teeth,

"where are you from? You don't pick out a dinner party like a dress in a catalogue. Let's get some statistics straight. One duckling is a meal for one person. Maybe two, if they're close friends. We are having thirty, forty people at this house. We are not talking about a candle-light dinner for two. We need a buffet, and we need it in two days. That's a lot of food. Not to mention cleaning, borrowing chairs—"

"Stop it! Stop it!" says Emily. "Why do you talk to me like that? You know I can't bear it. I came to help you, not to bear the brunt. You know I don't cook. You know what cooking did to me."

Margaret tilts back her chair against the wall. "Cooking didn't *do* anything to you."

"It was the Thanksgiving dinner when I ran away," Emily reminds her. "Don't you remember that? I made cranberry sauce and I ran away. I have a fear of cooking."

"You had a fear of your husband."

Emily considers this. "No," she says. "I wasn't afraid of him. I was afraid of the role he put me in. He put me in a kitchen filled with implements. Knives, mashers, choppers." Her voice quivers.

"Snap out of it," orders Margaret. "That was twenty-five years ago, for God's sake. Will you consider the problem at hand? Look, can I trust you to take care of the cleaning?"

Emily Ann dries her eyes. "All right," she says. "I can do that. But don't make me feel—"

Margaret won't wait for the end of this. "Fine," she says. "Go to it."

"Where are you going?" Emily calls after her.

"Work," Margaret screams back. "Believe it or not, I have a job!"

ᴀᴜᴏ

Despite this pronouncement, Margaret has trouble concentrating on the cabinetmaker's estimates. "A thousand dollars in one room will get you nowhere," Ephraim Tawil shouts above the band saw grinding in his shop. Margaret nods vaguely. She can't really afford to take off a whole day to cook. She'll have to make a ham. But who eats ham in July? Turkey is out of the question. "I can't hear you," Ephrie shouts.

"What?" she screams back. Her throat still hurts from Monday.

Ephrie beckons her outside. Her ears ring with the silence of the parking lot. "Two thousand, each room," he says.

"I don't know," Margaret answers. "Look, I'll get back to you. I'm throwing a party on Thursday. I've got a lot on my mind."

"You worry about the cooking," Ephrie divines. "You have a lot of people. Important people. Listen, I have got the caterer for you. My own brother and his wife. Let me tell you this, they could own a restaurant. That's the kind of food Ruti can make. Exotic food. Six hundred dollars cash, they do it all. Shop, cook, clean up."

"What kind of food?" Margaret asks.

"Like I said, exotic food. Have you tasted the Yemenite palate? You have not seen anything like it. You will be the first in the trend. There was French, Chinese, Thai—those are old by now. Yemenite is new. I can tell what you need. You need the ethnic family-style dinner. This will bring tears to your eyes. And quantity. Food for the hordes. That's what you get with Ruti. She's visiting me right now. I can send her over. Your problems are solved from this moment on."

"Interesting," says Margaret. "But listen, I can't spend more than three hundred. I've only got thirty-six people coming. I don't need a lot of leftovers."

"No leftovers with Ruti," Ephrie declares. "Four hundred you get a dinner. Six hundred you get a feast. Watchyoucallem—an experience. Six hundred and I throw in my best friend and his wife. Strong workers. You need some tables set up? The yard cleaned out? They also for a little extra can bring tablecloths. They work in the portable dry-cleaning business. They're in restaurants all the time. Michele's, the Kahala Hilton."

"My God," says Margaret. "Listen, I'll take it all for four-fifty. Tell them to come on over. This is a concept I can work with."

∽∽∽

When Margaret gets home, she finds Emily Ann rubbing a corner of the piano with a small cloth. "What the hell are you doing?" she asks.

"I'm waxing the piano," Emily says.

"I told you the whole *house* needs cleaning."

"I know," retorts Emily. "I'm starting with the piano."

"Never mind," says Margaret. "You don't have to finish. I've hired a very expensive Yemenite caterer. She'll do everything. We're having a traditional family-style dinner outside."

"Oh, lovely," says Emily. "Should I unpack my things now?"

"No, no," decides Margaret. "You can stay with Mother at the condominium. Bruce will drive you."

∽∾∽

"Crazy!" Margaret explodes that night, watching the cable news on the couch with Charles.

"She's just a little confused and oversensitive."

Margaret flips off the TV. "Mad as a hatter," she insists. "Look I'm too upset for you to watch the goddamn news. Did you see her? She was pushing around the dust on top of the piano. She does that only to infuriate me."

Charles yawns and pulls his Polo jersey down over his belly.

"It's true, you know," Margaret muses. "She did have a bastard for a husband. But, I mean, is that an excuse? Okay, she went through hell. Okay, she escaped from Bellevue in her nightgown in the snow. But I had bad marriages too. I'm not denying she had problems. It's just that she got so much attention for it. She loves the attention. Father came for her and took her back to Maui. He arranged for the whole divorce, and they didn't trouble her with the details, of course. She's never done any work in her life. She's spent her life shuttling back and forth between men."

"It sounds like a fifties' movie," says Charles.

"Do you say things like that to your patients?" Margaret asks. "Is this what they pay you for?"

∽∾∽

Shi-shi jumps on the caterers as they burst through the door with their bags of groceries. Margaret shoos the dog into the yard and then leads Ruti into the kitchen. Ruti dumps her load onto the table. "My God, you're pregnant," says Margaret. "You shouldn't carry things like that. When are you due?"

"Thank you," Ruti answers. "I am due any day, no problem. I have three already." Ruti's three children trail after her husband like the magi, each carrying one light thing. A bunch of bananas for the oldest, a bag of grapes for the next, and for the smallest child a pack of three hundred paper napkins. Outside, Ephrie's friends are banging together folding tables, unstacking chairs, and shaking out their snowy restaurant tablecloths. "Those are Uri and Efrat," Ruti tells Margaret. "And this," she says, pointing, "my husband, Natan. Where may I find the dishes?"

"What are we serving?" Margaret takes down the china with a twinge of uneasiness.

"Wait and see." Ruti winks. "We have found everything we need at the Foodland. Israeli ice cream for dessert. You go, and I will cook up the surprises."

The kitchen is like a hothouse by the time the guests arrive. Sweating, Ruti stirs something in a huge pot while Efrat mashes eggplant. The men smoke outside, and Ruti's children run in a pack with Shi-shi to open the door. Margaret feels frazzled just watching pregnant Ruti in the steaming kitchen. She walks out to the living room with a tray of cut cucumbers, pita slices, and *baba ganough*. The Falks, old car-pool friends from Oahu Prep days, are telling of their last conference in Fiji. "So one after another," Kate Falk says, "these women stood up and talked about the equal gender roles in their societies. And then finally one woman stands up. Big woman. Talking three hundred pounds, but with the little brittle English accent. And she says, 'You know, in Truk, I'm not sure things really are so equal.' Shock, commotion, uproar in the audience. But then she starts explaining how in Truk, she and her arthritic mother have to serve dinner on their hands and knees and then crawl out the door to let the men eat alone.''

Onaga the contractor is holding forth next to the piano. "Hi, Margaret," he calls out.

"What did you do to my white kitchen tile?" she answers.

"In the Waikiki Vista? I just laid it down."

"Really?" Margaret's eyes narrow. "How'd you like to lay it down again?"

"You don't like it?"

"I love it," Margaret says sweetly. "But I'm just wondering how a future owner might feel when she drops a teacup on the kitchen floor and the tile cracks. You're going to do it over, starting Monday."

"No, I did my job," Onaga snaps. "I can't help it if the floors weren't laid properly."

"What's that?" asks Larry Brown. "Don't you try that one again. My floors are completely level."

"Look, you are all my guests, and I couldn't care less whose fault it is. I want it redone now." Margaret's voice rises. Ruti appears, carrying her thick beef stew in Margaret's antique crystal punch bowl. "The first food," Ruti announces. And the overheated glass shatters in her arms.

"Christ!" Margaret groans, as Onaga's wife runs to get paper towels. "Get that off the floor before Mother comes."

Ruti crouches down, wiping the floor with wet rags.

"Ruti," Margaret begs, "please come sit down. Pregnant people can't do that. Do you want to give birth?"

"Of course," Ruti says. "No problem, the baby will come. Good luck to break the dish."

Charles greets Margaret's sister and mother at the door.

"Charles," says Elizabeth. "At last. Come tell me who all these other people are, and then you must sit down and tell me all about yourself."

Margaret's doctor, Annie, arrives in her violet-and-gold caftan, and Margaret takes her aside. "Listen," she says, "my caterer is pregnant. I want you to promise me, whatever happens, we call an ambulance; we go to the hospital. No birthings on the water bed, okay?"

"No shit," says Annie. "I wouldn't touch it. You think I pay that kind of insurance?"

Circulating through the guests, Elizabeth pauses to observe Ruti's children. "Just look at those black eyes," she murmurs to Charles. "Those gypsy eyes."

By dinnertime, everyone has arrived. Even Margaret's daughter, Holly, turns up. She doesn't come to visit much. She lives with her boyfriend out in Lanikai. "Hi, Mom," she calls to Margaret as she walks in the door. "Can I help with anything?"

"Where's Buzz?" Margaret asks.

"Night shift. Listen, can we talk?"

Margaret glances at the room filled with guests, children, the fumes of roasting food. "Ridiculous child," she says.

"Really," says Holly. "This is serious. Buzz has like made up his mind he wants to marry me."

"Holly," Margaret warns. "This will have to wait until we don't have thirty-six other people in the room."

Outside, at the white tables, Efrat serves the kebabs Natan and Uri are broiling on the hibachi. Elizabeth coughs politely as the smoke drifts over her table. "Columbia," she says to Charles. "How could you bear it after the islands? That city and that climate! Emily Ann had a terrible time at Wellesley. She became ill, poor thing, wearing her sandals in the snow."

Margaret stares at Emily Ann across the table in her *tapa*-pattern muumuu. She is picking at her food. Margaret's mother seems to be enjoying herself, however, good-humoredly eating her kebab. She doesn't know the other guests, of course.

One of the caterers comes over and offers Emily Ann some kebabs. "You want more?" Natan asks her.

"No, no," she says. "I don't eat meat."

Natan nods vehemently. "I would not either. Personally I am strictly kosher. I told Uri originally we shouldn't feed unkosher meat."

"Oh, no," Emily explains. "I don't eat any kind of meat. I'm not Jewish; I'm vegetarian."

Margaret's doctor waves from a distant table. Annie has found a can of insect repellent, and she is table-hopping with it, meeting new people as she sprays their legs. At her first table she meets Margaret's architect, Fred Chung. He is complaining about his children to the Falks. "Oldest son works all day for his Ph.D. Never takes his nose from the grindstone. All I want is grandchildren. Does he listen to me? No. Second son at Yale never works at all. Straight As and doesn't study. Yale lets him get away with this! Why? I don't know. Then my daughter, Vickie. All I ask is that she marry and settle down. She gets full scholarship to MIT and studies math! Useless, I tell her. Still the companies are all offering jobs! Why? I don't know."

"C'mon," says Annie, missing Chung's point. "You're not seriously upset, are you?"

"All I want is grandchildren," Chung repeats. "And this is what I get."

"My heart is bleeding for you," says Richard Falk.

Chung nods. "So that's it," he concludes proudly. "My children. One worse than the next."

At her table, Elizabeth takes a fork and knife and cuts her beef away from the kebab stick. "Well," she says, "I suppose you're planning an August wedding."

Charles looks at Margaret.

"We're not marrying just yet, Mother," says Margaret.

"What are you waiting for?"

Charles answers, "For one thing, my divorce."

Annie comes up behind Margaret. "I looked over the pregnant one," she whispers. "This girl is gonna pop anytime. I'm telling you, this baby is imminent."

"Thanks," says Margaret.

"Don't worry." Annie laughs. "I've got her sitting down by the phone."

Holly sits with Ruti in the kitchen. Ruti hands Holly the check Margaret has made out. "Please, give this to your mother for cash instead." She winks. "We need cash; we have no work cards for this country."

"Wow," says Holly. "You're pretty far from home, huh?"

Ruti smiles. "In Israel, *I* have a cook."

"So what's the deal?" asks Holly. "Are you going back?"

"Of course. When my husband finds enough American dollars. I myself could have stayed in Israel, but the men like to come here, so I come with my husband and the children. When you're a married woman, you go when your husband says go; you stay when he says stay."

Holly looks at Ruti's glowing face, her keen eyes. "That's what I'm trying to figure out," she says. "My boyfriend wants me to stay in Hawaii and marry him, and my mom wants me to take a job in Silicon Valley."

"Ah!" Ruti says.

"What's that supposed to mean?"

Ruti smiles. "How old are you?"

"Twenty-three."

"That's why I say 'Ah.' I am twenty-seven. I have three, almost four children. How much time can you have? Do you want children?"

Holly shakes her straight blond hair. "Well, I mean, eventually, but I'm not sure this is it. I mean, I'm not sure about Buzz. You know, we fight. This is not a perfect relationship."

"He hits you a lot?"

"Of course not!"

"Ah! What are you waiting for?"

"Well, also, Mom says he isn't going anywhere. He packs meat for Matson."

"What are you waiting for?" Ruti repeats. "He will be a rich man. Meat packing in America—he will be promoted every year if he likes it or not. Then he can strike and make even more."

Holly laughs.

"I'm not joking," Ruti says. "Take my advice. Marry him. Later, if he hits you, hit him back."

∽∾

"Israeli ice cream," Efrat tells Margaret.

"But this isn't ice cream," Margaret protests. "This is Tofutti. This is made out of soybeans."

"Traditional in Israel," Efrat explains.

Holly leans over Margaret's chair. "Mom," she says, "the caterers need cash. They don't want a check."

"Well," says Charles, "I could use the fresh air. I'll go to the cash machine in Kahala Mall. Let me get my shoes."

"I'm taking off too," says Holly. "Mom, I was in there with Ruti in the kitchen, and I got this incredible domestic urge. I feel like I've got to get back and cook Buzz dinner before he gets home, or do the laundry or something."

Margaret and Elizabeth sit alone at their table. They look at each other in silence. Citronella candles from the other tables flicker in the dark.

"Well, what do you think?" Margaret says at last.

"Of what?" asks Elizabeth.

"Of the party. Of Charles," her daughter explodes.

"Well, you aren't getting married," Elizabeth points out pragmatically. "Why should I say anything?"

"Mother, this wasn't advertised as a betrothal banquet. I never said this was a rehearsal dinner."

"No," Elizabeth allows. "Nor did you say that Charles is a married man and has no intention of marrying you."

Margaret reddens. "That's not true."

"I fail to see," says Elizabeth, "how two years' homesteading in your house can make Charles feel any need for further ceremony. And I certainly don't see why you insisted I come from Maui to meet a man who is married to someone else. It's childish, Margaret." Elizabeth turns to her other daughter. "Emily," she says, "I'm very tired. Please ask Bruce to drive us home."

"Great dinner. And listen, no hard feelings about the tile," Onaga says hopefully to Margaret.

Margaret walks him to the door with a tight smile. "No hard feelings," she replies. "Just a slight adjustment in your bill."

The last guests leave; the last dishes are washed. Charles counts four hundred fifty dollars cash into Ruti's hand. The caterers bustle out the door, waving good-bye. Ruti walks like a dancer, balancing a sleeping child over her shoulder, with the unborn child within her.

"Now I feel like celebrating," says Charles, closing the door. He pours himself a drink in the empty kitchen.

Suddenly the house feels so quiet and dark, Margaret runs and turns on the light outside the front door to show the neighbors she and Charles are still home.

Fait'

Ginnie lifts her heavy black hair from her neck. As always, when she first arrives, she feels the moist heat mixed with the scent of flowers. She puts her lei into a plastic bag and pushes it into the refrigerator. Mom's inspirational quotes are still taped on the fridge door: Make a Joyful Noise to the Lord! Jesus Is Our Salvation! Bible study, Kaimuki Y. PTL! Also stuck to the fridge door: Quik Bake Lattice Crust Pie—foolproof recipe. "Eh, Ginnie," Dad calls from the garage. She goes to help him with her suitcases.

The steps are steep on the pole house. The whole street is steep. Even the driveways look like sheer drops. Most people park on the street. The roofs of the houses are sharply angled, built like ski chalets, as if they had to shed snow. It's not a street for roller skating or bikes. You can burn out your brakes just going down the hill. Ten years ago Ginnie's paper route ruined the transmission on Mom's car.

Dad groans as they reach the lanai. "What do you have in here? Rocks?"

"Books." Ginnie pushes open the sliding door.

"You going to study at your sister's wedding?"

"Dad, it wasn't my idea to have it on spring break. I've got finals coming up. I have to finish *Mein Kampf.*"

Dad heaves the bag across the living room. "That's crazy, girl. What course is that?"

"Modern Political Ideologies."

"You help your mother."

"I know, I know. But I have to study too. I'm only up to Mussolini."

"Read it on the plane."

Ginnie doesn't intend to catch up with Mussolini. Her suitcase is filled with heavy books from Comp Lit. She has finished them already, but she's reading them again. Baudelaire, Mallarmé, Proust, Borges, German war poetry. She had to pack all the dictionaries that went with them, of course. She loves these books because they are strange and frightening. The language of Proust is far more exciting, more dangerous than Mussolini's, because it's beautiful.

She started German and Spanish together in high school, and then added French. These were the only classes she liked. With each language, she learned again to speak and read. Each was like a new birth and child-hood, a retreat into the blurry world of half-understood sentences: an escape from Oahu Prep, with its balanced curriculum and well-rounded students. Everything her teachers taught was diagrammed and organized: proofs and sentences outlined on the board. Ginnie ignored the teachers' summaries and felt her way through unanno-tated books. Her Spanish teacher warned against more languages; Ginnie would confuse herself. But the tangle of words was what attracted her: the convergence of roots, the joining and diverging of dark cognates. She tried to translate Cummings into Spanish with her friend Vivian Wong. She organized an after-school poetry group and attracted rebellious freshmen with long Möbius earrings and white-streaked hair. They read Dylan Thomas and hid behind mock-orange hedges to smoke clove cigarettes while waiting for their parents to come to take them home. A group of local girls: Chinese and Japanese and Ginnie, Filipino. On her own, Ginnie began Italian lessons with the oldest French teacher. He had a cane and a Santa Claus beard. He asked Ginnie to call him Grand-père. But one day she saw Dale Carnegie on his desk and was so embarrassed for him she stopped the lessons.

In the living room, Ginnie pushes a stack of magazines off the couch and sits down. Her father sinks into a chair with a sweating beer. He looks fierce in his undershirt and close-cropped hair.

"You look tired, Dad," Ginnie says.

"It's a big job," he answers shortly. "Your mother's been sewing for three months. Six bridesmaids. You're not the only one with deadlines. I've got two tile jobs and a chattahoochee deck for April tenth. All week I've been driving to the airport. I don't get time off to do that."

"God," says Ginnie. "You're killing yourself for one day. I don't want a wedding."

Her father chooses to ignore this.

~

"I made you chicken long rice," Mom tells Ginnie at dinner. "They don't have this up at Berkeley, huh?"

Mom smiles behind her round glasses. She is still wearing her tennis skirt. Those are the things Mom does: tennis at Kapiolani Park, Bible study at the Y, Chicken long rice. When Mom was young, she left Manila to work as a missionary north of Baguo. She tried to pray with animists. Now she reads the Bible with concerned mothers vying to show how much they agree with each other. This Bible study seems to Ginnie nothing like prayer. All reassurance; nothing desperate. Ginnie is a secret agnostic, but when she thinks of prayer, she imagines Mom pleading with the animists under poisonous trees.

She had forgotten how hungry she was and spoons up her food quickly. The long transparent noodles and slivers of chicken dissolve on her tongue. On the other side of the table, Teri sits with her fiancé, Earl. They talk to each other in low voices about place settings.

❧

The next day Teri insists that Ginnie help choose her bouquet. Teri never could decide on anything. In high school she didn't pick out what she thought would appear on tests; she studied everything. Ginnie would find her late at night, memorizing textbook chapters in order. Ginnie is just the opposite. She gambles that whole books won't appear on tests. When she guesses wrong, she writes fanciful essays, fabricating detailed illustrations of reversible arguments. For Poli Sci 104, Ginnie dreams of writing an essay that reads like a holograph—melting into whatever shape the prof is looking for.

They meet Earl in front of Jr. & Lou on King Street. Ginnie can't believe it's the same place. Just last summer, this was a tattered bucket shop with a green shredded awning. For years Christmas, Halloween, Easter, and St. Patrick's Day decorations hung side by side above bulletin boards of old prom pictures. Farrington High couples decked with *ilima* and *pikake*, or *haku* leis woven with rosebuds. Now the multiseasonal decorations are gone. The shop is clean and painted candy pink, accented with blue neon lights. It makes Ginnie feel she's been away not months but years. She looks at her sister critically. Teri has a flat local nose, and she speaks pidgin. She isn't stuck-up like Ginnie and never fought the habit. Teri never planned to leave Hawaii. She stayed at home and went to nursing school. Now she is working at Shriners Hospital. For her honeymoon, she's taking a twenty-five-minute flight to Maui, where all her cousins are.

"Nice, yeah?" Teri asks. She holds four white orchids, each ruffled at the edges, then curving deeply to reveal pale-yellow centers. Ginnie nods vaguely and watches Earl check on the order for the centerpieces and bridesmaids' bouquets. Teri wants more stephanotis.

"How much is this going to cost?" she asks Teri.

Teri stares. "You care about me, or what?"

"I'm just asking. I mean, can we afford all this?"

Embarrassed in the busy shop, Teri whispers fiercely. "I never heard you ask that question before. When Dad sent you to Oahu Prep, you never asked could we afford this. If it's for you, it's important. If it's for me, it's a waste of money, right?"

"No," protests Ginnie. "You deserve whatever you want. But why do you want flowers? You're putting Earl through chiropractor school. Wouldn't you rather have the cash?"

"It's for the family." Teri rubs her nose impatiently. "They came all this way."

Ginnie groans. "You are such a saint. It's your beatifi-
cation ceremony is what it is."

"It's my wedding. It's the bride's day, right?"

"I thought it was Mom's day."

"Oh, shut up, Ginnie."

⤳

Five cousins are coloring by the television. Ginnie
brought the coloring books as presents from Berkeley.
Her boyfriend, Noam, helped pick them out. *Great Civil
Rights Leaders, World Feminists from Lesbos to NOW, Polit-
buro Paperdolls, Whales of the World,* and *The Jumbo Book of
Protest Leaders.* Michael scribbles crayon over Malcolm X
in his own design. It was fun buying them anyway. Noam
said, "Look, in Hawaii you get Hawaiian stuff. You're at
Berkeley; you have to get Berkeley stuff. Come on, radical coloring books. This is it."

They started going out in December, when Ginnie
needed help on the Poli Sci take-home final. Noam has
read all of *Das Kapital.* That was in his Marxist phase. He
reads bulimically. He says he read *The Rise and Fall of the
Third Reich* three times in fifth grade. Then he got obsessed with military history and assassination. Now he is
obsessed with Ginnie. He makes her laugh. He doesn't
seem real to her. He's stocky and nervous, brilliant in a
completely shallow way. After a string of mean, effete
boyfriends, Noam was just what Ginnie needed. He hates
poetry. He yawned through Kurosawa's *Ran* and leaned
forward only to watch the blood spray at the decapitation
of the avenging princess. During the titles, while people
wiped tears from their eyes, Noam cracked, "Whoa, that
princess was a total bitch." Ginnie isn't upset about leav-

ing Noam for spring break. She both enjoys and scorns his lack of feeling for art. She has come near treating him as if he had no feelings at all.

❧❧❧

Mom circles Ginnie, pinning the hem of the pink brides-maid's dress. Even Ginnie's store-bought dresses have to be hemmed; she wears a size two. She could probably pass as a child at movies, but she purposely wears spike heels and dark lipstick. "Mom, I look dumb," she whispers so Teri won't hear. "I'm twenty years old. This thing makes me look like Little Miss Muffet."

"No!" her mother protests. The dress has a pink bow and lace pinafore-style sleeves. It looks like the prom dress Mom sewed her. What a night. Ginnie sprained her ankle coming down the stairs and fought with her date, a suicidal army brat. They made up in the back of his truck.

"This is such a gross color, Mommy."

Mom finishes pinning and sits back on her heels. "It's the theme of the wedding. Teri picked it. Pink rose-buds."

"I hate it!" Ginnie wriggles out, bursting unseen stitches.

Mom starts to cry. "Why are you so angry? Don't you want Teri to be happy?"

"This what they teach you at Berkeley?" Dad calls from the other room. "Make your mother cry?"

"I'm sorry! I'm sorry!" Ginnie screams, and puts on her Walkman to drown out the voices. Mom pries loose the earphones, sobbing. "What music is this? What is this you listen to?"

"Ginnie! Telephone!" A cousin screams from the kitchen.

"Hello?" she says, wiping her eyes.

"Hello, Ginnie? This is Noam."

"What?"

"This is Noam. Guess where I am."

"Hi. No clue. How're you doing?"

"Great! I'm at the airport."

"Yeah? I wish I was. Where are you going?"

"Not my airport, *your* airport. I'm *here*. In Hawaii!"

"Oh, God." Ginnie groans.

"What? Isn't this amazing? The thing is, my sister got a trip for two as a bonus from the bank. She sold the most loans in write-your-own-loan month. Ginnie?"

"Yeah, I'm here. Wow. So she took you. Isn't this the one with the tennis boyfriend?"

"Ginnie," Noam whispers. "She's right here, okay? She took me."

"Oh. Where are you staying?"

"Well, all we got was free tickets. It's a cheapo bank. We spent all our money renting a car."

This sinks in slowly. Ginnie stares at the kitchen table, covered with toys, magazines, bags of groceries. "Noam, you can't stay here! We're having a wedding."

"Oh, yeah, I forgot about that. Is that your sister?"

"My parents are going to kill me!"

"We'll sleep on the floor. You can work it out. Give us some directions."

Ginnie peeks into her mother's room. Maria is still hemming. She sits in bed, glancing up at *Mystery* with wide, surprised eyes. "Mommy?" Ginnie crawls onto the bed. "I'm sorry about what I said. It's a beautiful dress. It just felt weird at first."

Mom smiles. "Teri's getting married," she says. "It's hard to get used to. She's growing up. Soon you'll be grown up too."

Ginnie lets this pass and says, "Remember Noam, that guy I told you about? He's coming here to visit with his sister. It's really awful, but they don't have any money, and there's nowhere they can stay. I wouldn't ask, but he helped me a lot when I was in trouble in Poli Sci. He'll sleep down in the den, and his sister can sleep on the cot in my room."

Mom leans forward and tries to tune the TV. The murderer's face turns green, then orange. "He's Jewish, yeah?"

"He says he's an atheist."

"Well, you try be a witness to him."

Ginnie slides off the bed, relieved.

"When are they coming?" Mom asks.

"Now." Ginnie slips out the door.

◦⚬◦

The coloring books are stacked on the table. Mom is basting the ring bearer's pillow, while Teri tells Grandma again which grandchildren are coming. Grandma hasn't even seen some of the youngest. She flew all the way from Manila. "And there will be a mass at the church," she says in her clear, barely accented English.

"No, Grandma," Teri explains. "No mass. It's a Protestant service, at Oahu Prep chapel."

"Oahu Prep chapel." Grandma recites the words as if they had to be repeated to be believed.

"We were going to have it in Kaimuki Bible Church," Mom explains, "but the chapel looks prettier. You have to book way in advance, but we got in because Ginnie went to school there."

"Before the wedding," announces Grandma, "I will go to an early mass."

Grandma, Teri, and Mom look up curiously when Noam arrives with his older sister, Lee. Lee has Noam's sandy brown hair, but she is tall and big-boned. In college she was a discus thrower.

"Where you folks from?" Mom inquires.

Lee answers, "King of Prussia, Pennsylvania."

"That's a place?" asks Teri.

Lee is annoyed. "Yes, it's a place. It's got one of the biggest contiguous shopping malls in the world."

"I can't believe it's a place," Teri repeats.

Ginnie is glad for the wedding preparations and even for Lee. Noam was a good thing at Berkeley. He was like a good, numbing mentholated cough drop. He provided temporary relief. The trouble is, Ginnie now realizes, Noam doesn't know he's temporary. At home he's all wrong, embarrassing. She flinches from his touch. "We'll go to the beach tomorrow," she tells him that night. She closes her bedroom door and climbs into bed. Lee snores gently on the cot.

∽∾∾∽

Ginnie stares out the window as Lee drives the rented car along Kalanianaole Highway. "We just passed Hanauma Bay," she says vaguely.

Lee swerves and starts looking for a U-turn. "Look, you've got to tell me where, Ginnie. I just keep going until you tell me." Sweating, she plucks at her purple bathing suit for air. Her thighs spread out on the vinyl. When they finally get to the beach and shake out the towels, Lee sinks down to sleep on the sand.

Noam splashes Ginnie, who stands waist deep, feeding frozen peas to the fish. "I'll teach you." He gurgles, blowing water out of his snorkle.

"No."

"Come on. You live in Hawaii and you can't swim? That's so weird. How can you avoid it?"

"I don't know." Ginnie looks down at the bright water.

"This place is wasted on you!"

Beyond the blue-green bay, the ocean deepens to a colder blue. "I don't know," Ginnie says again. "I've always wanted to be somewhere else."

"Like where?"

"Spain, Germany."

Noam shrugs. "So go."

"I don't have any money," Ginnie reproaches him.

"Well," Noam says comfortingly, "Europe's not what it's cracked up to be. I went to Oxford one summer with my friend's family, and I was bored out of my mind. Warwick Castle was cool. I really got into the torture implements. But most of the time we just hung out in the country, and there wasn't anything to do."

Ginnie looks away, impatient. Lee sleeps in the sun near a tanning Japanese tour group. "Your sister is going to roast," she says.

Noam dunks himself in the water. "Sorry she had to come. Do your parents really mind?"

"No. She's just another haole."

"What's that?"

"Someone white like you."

∽

Mom is waiting for Ginnie on the lanai when they get home. "I missed you at Bible study today," she says. "Teri was worried."

"I don't go anymore," Ginnie announces recklessly. "I don't believe in it." Her heart races as if she were running. No place is far enough to run to. She turns from Mom's wide eyes and escapes down the hall, only to find her hemmed bridesmaid's dress floating in the doorway of her room.

∽

"Tough!" her father yells that night in the kitchen. "No way Berkeley next year. You go to Berkeley one year, and you lose sight of all your values."

Ginnie is crying too hard to argue. She can see Noam listening in the living room. Lee is rubbing lotion on her sunburn as she watches TV.

"Daddy"—Ginnie sobs—"I have to learn Italian."

"You learn here at UH." Dad turns away, and Mom comes and puts her hand on Ginnie's shoulder.

"Ginnie," Mom cries in her tearful voice. "I prayed, Ginnie, and I got the message you have to come home for next year. It's too far."

"It's too satanic," Ginnie adds sarcastically.

Mom nods. "Amen. Drugs and bad men, Ginnie. I don't know what else. You get sick all the time. It's too cold for you, and dirty. I read about the pollution in the paper."

"But, Mom," Ginnie whispers painfully. "I have to go. Don't you want me to achieve something? I want to go to grad school. I want to do research."

"You want to bum around Europe is all," says Dad. "You don't know what work is. You don't know what a family is. You're too selfish to see that your family is the only thing that's out to help you in this world. You stay here for a year and straighten out before I send you back to Berkeley."

"No!" cries Ginnie.

"Ginnie!" Mom pleads. "We love you! Jesus loves you!"

Yes, I know, Ginnie thinks automatically. 'Cause the Bible tells me so. She breaks away from her mother. "I don't have friends here anymore. There's nothing to do here. I can't work here."

"You will, you will," Mom pleads. "Where's your faith? There's the Fellowship; help me with Bible study. They're bringing French films at the Art Academy. You'll make new friends. There's the job at Pioneer Chicken. Teri is so happy; look at Teri."

"No! She's nothing! She makes herself stupid. She can hardly talk." Ginnie runs downstairs to the street before Dad can catch her.

It's night, but the sky is only ink blue behind lighter clouds. Across the street, Mr. Loo is playing a rumba on his Fun Machine. Ginnie can see him, framed in the picture window, picking out the tune with his right hand, while the machine thumps an automatic bass. Ginnie sinks down on the curb. Above, on the lanai, Grandma sleeps in a straight-backed chair. Grandma does not approve of Praise the Lord bumper stickers and Protestant weddings. She is Ginnie's silent ally. She prays in another language. In the Philippines, she reveres the icons brought from Catholic Spain. There is no enthusiasm in her piety. Her prayers are ancient, nothing improvised. Her church rings with music; its windows and its walls are jeweled with art.

The stairs creak, and Noam appears with the car keys.

"Sorry, Noam, you can't have the car," Lee announces from the lanai. "I signed for it, I paid for it, and I'm driving it." Lee drives them to Waikiki and then goes to pick up her film at ABC.

Noam and Ginnie trudge down to the beach. "I'm never going anywhere with her again," Noam says. They walk barefoot at the edge of the water.

"Well, she gave you the other ticket," Ginnie points out.

"She didn't have anyone else."

The sand still feels warm from the day. The beach is blank, except for the best-fortified sand castles and some kids drinking. The lifeguard perch looks like an empty throne. They walk past the hotels, and from the beach they can see the back of each hula show. Tahitian dancers at the Royal Hawaiian; next door, a hula demonstration. Red-faced men come up onstage. "All right! Let's give these guys a big hand!" Farther down, a man announces "what we call the mosquito dance." The men jump on the stage with their grass bracelets and anklets, slapping their bare bodies. Hula shows light the beach all the way down the bay, and in the distance they seem to bend closer, like beads of light.

"Ginnie," says Noam, "why don't you get a job at Berkeley and move in with me?"

"No," Ginnie says bleakly. "But thanks anyway. If I work here for a year, I can earn enough for rent. I have to find out about transfer credits."

"Oh, come on," says Noam. "What about tuition? If you stay here a year, you won't have residence. You'll never earn enough for out-of-state tuition."

"But Dad will pay," argues Ginnie. "You don't know my dad. I mean, you're not exactly seeing him at a good time."

Lee thumps across the sand with her pictures of that morning's Kodak Hula Show. "You guys, aren't these great? Actually, mine didn't come out, and I was so bummed. But they sold all these professional shots right there in the store. You can just go buy these. You don't even have to go to the show!"

∾

Teri takes Ginnie aside during the rehearsal. The cousins mill around with their flower baskets, posing for the photographer.

"Ginnie," Teri says, "be happy. I want you to be happy at the wedding."

"I am happy," Ginnie snaps. "You think I'm going to ruin the pictures?"

"I prayed for you last night with Mommy."

Ginnie shifts her weight uncomfortably in the pink dress as Teri puts her arm around her waist. "You wait for yours, Gin."

"I don't want a wedding. Or a goddamn dinner dance. I just want to go back to Berkeley!"

Teri stares. "But didn't they tell you? We don't have the money."

"What do you mean? They spent it on *this*?" Ginnie turns and looks at the chapel, covered with orchids and lace, pink roses. *Maile* leis for each usher. And Teri all dressed for the pictures in satin and ruffles. "They spent my tuition money on *this*?"

"It's not your money, it's theirs, and they wanted to," Teri retorts with wet eyes. Then she whispers, "They can't send you back; they took a second mortgage on the house."

Ginnie feels a sudden shame, embarrassment for her parents, as if she saw them overtipping at a restaurant or on television as the smiling losers of a game show. "What's the show for, Teri, who's it for? Who are you pretending to be?"

"I'm the bride," Teri flares. "You got some better idea? Who are you? You think the mainland's cool?" She flips into angry pidgin. "You like be some kine haole?"

Ginnie lets out a long, shuddering breath. Finally she says softly, "At least they could have split the cost with Earl's dad."

Teri looks down at her bouquet. "They did."

✧

At the Oahu Prep chapel, Ginnie sits down with Noam, but she pulls her hand away from his. Even after the sanctuary fills and the service starts, she can think only of the required chapels she sat through at school. Trying to sleep in the front row, rolling marbles down the aisle, erasing parts of the letters on paperback copies of *The Good Earth* so the title would read *The Cool Fart*. Once at fellowship after school, she thought she was born again. They sat behind the altar and she told her friend Carol that she felt the spirit of Christ in her. Carol cried with joy and gave her a birthday card signed "Your sister in Christ." It proved a false alarm for Ginnie, but Carol went away and became a missionary in the Philippines. Ginnie closes her eyes and pictures Carol preaching to the animists in her angora sweaters.

At the altar, Earl kisses Teri. Mom's glasses shine with happiness and green light from the stained glass. Of all the family and Teri's nurse friends, no one is crying. Only Lee cries. Her face is wet with tears.

∽∾∽

"So what do we do now?" Lee asks that night after the dinner dance. Ginnie's parents are in bed, and Ginnie and Noam slump together on the couch, exhausted. "Ginnie, what do you do on Saturday nights?"

"You could go to a club." Ginnie yawns.

"No," says Lee, "I don't need music and stuff. Isn't there someplace you can just go and drink?"

"Why don't you drink here?" Noam suggests.

Ginnie grimaces. "Not in this house. Beer's as far as it gets. My mother was the third immaculate conception, remember? Teri was the fourth, and I was number five."

"What a fun bunch of people." Lee groans.

"I'll play you a record." Ginnie pulls herself off the couch and rummages through the record cabinet. "Okay, this is local comedy. This one was really popular when I was about eleven."

Lee puts down her beer. "Oh, good-ee."

"No, it's funny." Ginnie puts on Rap Replinger's "Poi Dog."

"What is this?" asks Noam.

Ginnie explains. "In this song, Replinger is impersonating a local guy drowning, and he's singing about his girlfriend, Faith Inaya, only since he speaks pidgin, he says Fait' Inaya."

Noam cracks his gum. "What's so funny about that?"

"Guess you had to be there," says Lee.

Ginnie walks out to the lanai and swings in Dad's basket chair. The city shines far below St. Louis Heights, and the farthest lights ripple up and down against the lanai railing. As Ginnie swings, the chain suspending the chair creaks, and for a long time this is the only sound outside, except for Replinger singing "Please tell her, 'I love you, Fait' Inaya.'" Ginnie wonders how they did it in the studio, the gurgling song drowning in the waves.

Total Immersion

"*H*eavenly Father," the chaplain begins. The students hush at the outdoor assembly. They bow their heads and only a slight rustling can be heard among all the children marshaled in a standing wave—first graders at one goalpost, rising seniors at the other. "On this first day of school we thank you for your many blessings," the voice intones from the speakers rigged up on palm trees. "We thank you for Hawaii, for this campus of ours, filled with flowers. We thank you for the lovely buildings of Oahu Prep. The new swimming pool, the Cochran Gym. These are gifts of people who care for us and for the beauty of our learning environment. We thank you for our parents, who give so much to us, for the men and women who clean the campus and tend the grounds. And for the teachers, who work so hard to prepare us for the future. In Jesus Christ our prayer, amen."

A sudden flood of students pushes Dr. Lefkowitz from behind. Her homeroom diffuses into the crowd, and she is left to teach her first class. Sandra grasps her teacher's manual tightly. It's not that she hasn't taught before. At Georgetown she was head teaching fellow for Molière and the Comic Muse. She taught two sections a week. The only difference was, those students already knew French. Looking out into the courtyard, Sandra tries to remember where they said her first class was.

The chair of the French Department emerges from behind an oleander bush. A tall, heavy woman, she moves with the proprietary magnificence of twenty years' teaching experience. "Hilda," Sandra calls. "Where is Dole Hall Annex?"

"En français. Toujours en français," Hilda cautions jovially. *"L'entrée de Dole? C'est ici."* And she rolls on, stately in her platform shoes and green print muumuu. *"Bon chance,* Sandra," she calls back.

"Bonjour, mes élèves." Sandra greets her class of small, frightened freshmen. *"Je m'appelle Dr. Lefkowitz. Je suis votre professeur de français. Comprenez-vous?"*

The class stares. "Is this French One?" asks a girl with a bleached shock of hair over one eye. Sandra takes a deep breath.

❧

Sandra's husband rushes to the door when she gets home. "Sandy!" Alan cries. "How was it? How did the dress go over?" Sandra sinks into his arms, exhausted. She had completely forgotten the new dress, a tropical shirtwaist they had picked out for the first day of school.

"Oh, Alan." Sandra moans. "That woman. Hilda. What a concept! Apparently all French teachers have to speak French to each other at all times. She's the self-appointed guardian of the oral-aural method. She goes around telling us *'Nous ne comprenons pas l'anglais.'* She's also informed me that next week it's my turn to write up the French One test on Unit One, but my class refuses to understand what I say, so I really don't know how I'm going to *finish* Unit One."

Alan pours Sandra a Coke. "Don't you think for one minute that woman teaches in French," he says. "She's probably from Iowa. You just go ahead and teach in English. You didn't notice the bookshelves," he adds. "They were only a hundred dollars each. And would you believe the guy who sold them to me is Israeli? Ephraim Tawil. He runs the whole business. Importing, manufacturing, and selling. He grew up in Rechovot, married an American, and came out here in the teak-import business. And he gave me the name of a kosher butcher in California who can ship a quarter steer frozen—you write in the order. He's *baal koreh* for a traditional group that broke away from the temple, and he wants us to come for dinner tonight."

"Oh, lovely," says Sandra. "But I can't stay out too late. I have to be at school by seven-thirty tomorrow morning."

Alan stares. "What for?"

"Well, I was told unofficially that homeroom teachers are actually supposed to come half an hour early in case any of the kids want to talk."

"Jesus," says Alan, who had got through med school swapping schedules to avoid early-morning shifts.

"I mean, the school was founded by Congregationalist missionaries," Sandra explains.

Alan rolls his eyes. "*We're* not missionaries."

"But I really want to make a good impression," Sandra says in a small voice.

✧

The Lefkowitzes drive their new Ford to the Tawils' house. Sandra navigates, with a map of Oahu spread over her knees. They married last year and moved to Hawaii only a month ago. They still feel the newness like the stiff sizing in new clothes. New car, new bookshelves, new bed. New apartment walking distance from Sandra's school and a short drive to Alan's hospital. They still have to buy chairs and a table, but that will have to wait until the first paychecks come. Their pots and pans and dishes just arrived from Washington. At Georgetown, Sandra planned to enter the diplomatic service and travel around the world. She married Alan and got halfway.

"Alan," says Sandra, "I think we're lost."

Alan pulls over on Waialae Avenue. Together they study the map. "We got off the freeway too soon," Alan says.

"Should we ask?"

"No, no. I know where to go." Alan starts the car.

Sandra's map blows in her face. "I never asked you about *your* day," she says.

"Couple of well babies, lots of school checkups." Alan changes lanes. "A Korean kid with a broken arm. His parents were hysterical. Somehow his friend's truck rolled over it. Lucky he wasn't killed."

"Now I think we overshot," says Sandra. "Get off here and try that thing. Wilhelmina Rise."

The transmission purrs as they climb the steep road. Below them the city stretches out to the shore. The ocean rises, a thin band broadening as they climb the hill. Deep and startling blue, it circles and overwhelms the view.

The Tawils live near the crest of the rise. Their stilt house tilts rakishly over the cliff. In front of the house, Tawil's truck stands parked on the sloping road. It looks ready to roll into the sea. A blond woman answers the door and stares at them wordlessly, taking in Alan's sports coat and the basket of roses Sandra holds in her arms.

"Is this the Tawils' house?" Alan asks.

"Yes. Who are you?"

"We're the Lefkowitzes. Ephraim invited us to dinner."

"He did? Oh, my God, this is *it*. This is *it*!" She screams into the house. Then, to Alan and Sandra: "Come in, come in. Listen, unfortunately I wasn't told anything about this." She leads them to a fuzzy beige sofa and intercepts Ephraim as he emerges, beaming welcome, from the shower.

"That must be Judy, Ephrie's wife," Alan tells Sandra. They can hear Judy clattering pans in the kitchen. "Why do you do this?" She screams. "Why can't you *tell* me you're bringing people home? After what happened today. I can't believe it. I just can't."

"It's a surprise," Ephrie says smoothly. "Like I always tell you: Relax or you'll never enjoy yourself." He returns to the living room as if no time has passed and repeats his welcome.

"Maybe we should come a different night," Sandra ventures.

"No." Ephrie waves the thought away. "This is the perfect night. Timing could not make it better." He takes the roses into the kitchen and tells Judy, "Here, have some flowers. You have to—watchyoucallem—smell the roses, or they'll pass you by. You scream all the time, you'll get a heart attack."

"Can I help?" Sandra calls to Judy. She looks in through the kitchen's open pass-through.

"Thank you, no," Judy answers. "I'm not really cooking. I think I'll just put up some hot dogs. You wouldn't believe what I went through today. And I got a forty-dollar ticket on top of everything, because my son released the brake in the truck and rolled over his friend. *He* breaks the kid's arm and *I* get a ticket."

"That was the one Alan treated," exclaims Sandra. "You should be grateful. It could have been worse."

"That's right," Judy says in a tense voice. "Accidents every day. But you try to keep them in the house. They're boys. Chaos. You don't have kids? Enjoy it now. Later you watch as they tear up your house. And your husband will regress. You'll see. He'll become just like them."

"We love having people," Ephraim reassures Alan on the couch. "All the time people. In and out. That's what I love. In Rechovot I had nine brothers growing up. Always someone in the house to fight with. Someone to talk to. That's why, I come home to an empty house, I get lonely. One time they impounded an Israeli ship for debt in Honolulu harbor. I went and got permission to have the men here for dinner every night until they flew them out."

"My God," says Alan. "How many were there?"

"Judy," Ephrie hollers into the kitchen. "How many watchyoucallem on that boat?"

"You come here if you want to talk to me!" Judy screams back. Then, after a pause: "Twenty-four, I think, until they found girls."

Setting the table, Sandra asks Judy, "So, you're not Israeli?"

"God, no." Judy laughs. "I grew up in Chicago and went on a one-year program to Israel. My parents' worst fears were realized. It was the thrill of my life. I told them I was going to have the whole traditional Yemenite wedding. You know, with the veil with all the coins on it. Mom cried and cried. 'My daughter went and married a *schvartze*!' Of course, they all got their way in the end, and I wasn't consulted. We had the wedding in Chicago, and before I knew it, Ephrie decided we should stay in the U.S. In Israel I was a candidate for a degree in poultry science. I end up back where I started, training as a dental hygienist. You try and talk an Israeli into moving back to Israel. If I'd married an American, I'd be there now."

"Oh, I don't know," says Sandra. "I always said I'd live in France, but you can't predict what will happen—with whom you'll end up falling in love, who you'll become."

"What's love got to do with it?" Judy scoffs.

The two couples sit down at the table, and Judy calls out to the yard. "Hose down before you set foot in the house." Screams and spraying water last several minutes, and thirteen- and ten-year-old Lavi and Namir pound up the stairs and drip across the carpet. Each grabs a hot dog from the table, along with handfuls of chips. "You're wet," Judy snaps. "And you're behaving like animals. Dry off and then come back if you can behave like human beings." Namir takes a Coke and Lavi snatches another bunch of chips. Provisioned, they escape to watch TV.

"So," Ephrie announces. "We've got traditional services every other week."

"That's all?" Alan is disappointed. "How do you finish the Torah?"

"Every two years," Ephrie answers. "Listen, I don't ask questions, I just read."

"But that's absurd!" Alan protests.

"It's a hell of a lot better than the temple," Judy admonishes him. "You want to waste Friday night listening to Rabbi Liebowitz talk about himself?"

"Why is it called the Bet Knesset Connection?" asks Sandra. "It sounds so seventies."

"The Gluecks chose the name when they took over," says Judy. "They came from Miami. Terence teaches art history, and Pat is an orthodontist. Her children are ugly as sin, though."

ᴏᴜᴏ

After services at the Unitarian church, where Bet Knesset meets, the Lefkowitzes are formally introduced to the Gluecks. When Alan shakes hands, he feels the smooth band of Terence's oval carnelian ring. Pat wears a painted silk dress that falls in open cowl folds, exposing her chest. She is a tall woman, with a beak nose set off by a black lacquered straw hat with a spotted veil.

"Alan," says Terence, "I really enjoyed your comments during the discussion."

"Well," Alan says, "what I said wasn't actually so original. I mean, I don't think the notion that the serpent in Eden was a snake god is central to our tradition."

"Of course," Terence says soothingly. "Naturally this isn't the kind of thing you were taught in Sunday school. It's only when we leave Sunday school that we begin to see how subtle and subversive these texts really are. As a scholar, this kind of insight freed me to understand the Mannerist painters. I began to see the Mannerists not merely as descriptive trompe l'oeil technicians but as exponents of the seventeenth-century counterculture. Only then could I analyze Mannerism as a creative force."

Instinctively Alan bristles. There is something in Terence that makes Alan wary. He suspects Terence only half believes his own speeches. But at the same time he cannot stifle the horrible thought that Terence might actually trust in this swaying rhetorical structure. Terence confuses him. For Alan is the kind of doctor who decided to take up medicine not because he did so well in organic chemistry but because he read the memoirs of Albert Schweitzer in ninth grade.

"Does the discussion part of the service always last an hour?" Sandra asks Terence's wife.

Pat shakes off her children, who are trying to pull her toward the car. "Well," she answers, "it depends how much people want to say. Sometimes we have to cut *Musaf* in order to finish on time. Have you met Caroline?"

Caroline wears diamonds. Fleetingly, Sandra imagines her as a composite of designer names and concepts: Giorgio, Missoni, Dior, Ferragamo, Jaguar. Just as suddenly, Sandra sees herself through Caroline's eyes as some kind of nonsignature generic: unscented, hypoallergenic, better sportswear. The vision lasts only a moment, however. Caroline has two children at Oahu Prep, an overweight husband, and a faint New England accent.

"We must get together sometime," Caroline says, extending her long, cool fingers. "The thing is, we're doing some work on the house, and we've all been camping out for six months in four rooms. The banyan tree grew down into the plumbing and cracked the pool, and before we knew it, we had to open up the living room."

Alan walks over to Ephraim and shakes his hand. "*Yashar koach*, Ephrie. You did a beautiful job. Do you think we could convince people to hold services every week?"

"Listen." Ephrie claps his hand on Alan's shoulder. "Like I said before, I don't make waves, I just read. That's all. Everybody does their own thing. You can't change it. Some people don't even come to shul at all."

"Damn right," says Judy. "That's why we started Bet Knesset to begin with. There is no way I'll go to the temple on Friday night. Ask my kids: Friday night is my time."

Outside on the lawn stands a monkeypod with a tree house. Namir and Lavi climb from the tree house onto the church roof and won't let Caroline's daughter follow them. Six-year-old Jessica stamps in rage against the sturdy floorboards of the tree house. "My dad is richer than your dad." She screams.

"So," Lavi says, "my mom is richer than yours. Your mom doesn't do anything."

"Yes she does!" Jessica shrieks.

"What?"

While Jessica is thinking, her father calls from the ground that it's time to go home.

∽↶∽

Driving back to the apartment, Alan reasons, "Well, they're friendly people. You can't expect the community here to duplicate the one at home. Everyone has different needs. Ephrie understands that. He's very good at compromise. There are a lot of complications, living in Hawaii."

"And not so many options." Sandra sighs.

∾∾

All students at Oahu Prep attend mandatory ecumenical services. Thursdays at ten, Sandra has chapel duty. She must take attendance for three rows of students. During the organ prelude, she passes a clipboard, and each student signs opposite his Xeroxed signature. Sandra has the power to issue demerits if the students talk excessively, come to chapel barefoot, or slam their hymn books. The chapel looks like a theater in the round, with its egalitarian pews surrounding the altar. Chaplain Whitaker tries to speak to each person as an individual. He uses a cordless microphone and walks up and down the aisles, encouraging eye contact. Even as Sandra watches her quota of restless students, she herself feels watched.

Passing the clipboard, Sandra recognizes the girl next to her as a student in her French II class. *Ginnie Corpuz*, the girl writes, shaping the tiny letters with an extra-fine pen. "Nice name," whispers Sandra. "Are you Spanish?"

Ginnie looks up with her huge, black, ironic eyes. "Sometimes," she says.

She is a strange girl. During the hymn, Ginnie remains seated, writing a letter on an aerogram. Sandra hesitates to say anything. Finally, after the last chords, she whispers, "You know, it's so dark in here, and with your tiny writing you could ruin your eyes." As she puts her letter away, Sandra notices, surprised, that Ginnie has been writing in French. Ginnie shows little interest in class and rarely turns in homework. Last week, during a grammar review, she sat silently without taking any notes. Then, while someone was trying to conjugate *partir*, Ginnie gathered her books and walked to the door. "I have cramps," she said dramatically, and left.

"Dear friends," says Chaplain Whitaker. "When I was in junior high school I was in love. Yes, I was in love with a freckled girl with braces on her teeth and scratches on her knees." He waits for the appreciative laughter to die and then enunciates intensely, "Love is the most terrible thing in the world."

Ginnie puts her head down and closes her eyes. Sandra wishes she could do the same.

᠔᠊ᢐ

On their fifteenth anniversary, Ephrie and Judy Tawil invite everyone they know to an open house. The Tawils' hospitality makes for a strange assortment of guests: petite dental hygienists who work with Judy, tall Samoan carpenters who work for Ephrie, old friends from the Elks Club, a man Ephrie met jogging in Kapiolani Park. The entire Bet Knesset minyan is invited, and most of the couples come. Three years ago, in Miami, the Gluecks socialized primarily with academics and professionals, but life in Honolulu takes a different tone. Here they find the small dinner party replaced by the luau reunion of the extended family. As active and ambitious leaders, they find their large, stratified Coral Gables temple replaced by a tiny group in which each individual must be catered to as if he were a one-man party holding out on principle in the Knesset. And so, according to local custom, Pat Glueck leaves her spike heels at the door along with all the other pairs of shoes, ranging from size-15 Adidas to three-inch-long children's rubber thongs and pink plastic toddler boots with bells on them.

Ephrie never invites parents without kids. "I'm really touched by your hospitality," Stan Lamkin says, giving Ephrie a bottle of wine. "I can't remember the last time someone invited all seven of us."

"Like I always said," Ephrie replies, "at a party, the more watchyoucallem the better."

Guests overflow from the living room out to the lanai, where Ephrie has placed two aluminum kegs of beer. Below, in the yard, children shriek, pelting each other in a rotten-mango fight. Ephrie sits on the couch with three Samoan men. He looks especially small as he passes his homemade hummus.

"You make this? Very good for you," compliments Luke Oangalele.

Judy passes through to refill her drink. "Yeah," she says. "He doesn't know where the stove is, but he can make hummus." The men laugh uproariously.

When the Lefkowitzes arrive, Judy ushers Sandra into the den, where she is drinking with Pat and Caroline. "Isn't this a little medieval?" asks Sandra. "Separate feasts for men and women."

"Uh-huh," says Judy. "Have a drink. You've got a lot of catching up to do."

Bewildered, Sandra sits down next to Caroline, who wears a little teddy of a cocktail dress. Pat turns up the volume on the TV. "We're watching *The Way We Were*," she tells Sandra sternly. And then turns her back to the set.

"You know," Judy says, "I'm glad Alan finally broke down and got a few aloha shirts. The first time I saw him in that blazer . . ."

"Doesn't anyone wear jackets and ties here?" Sandra asks.

"Of course they do," says Caroline. "They wear them to work, if they work in banks—or at funerals. Not in real life."

"You're right," agrees Sandra. "Alan wore a suit to the clinic, and one of the residents asked who died."

Judy rattles the ice in her drink. "You watch what Hawaii does to him," she warns. "Ten years from now and you can't get him into shoes. Of course, Ephrie was like that to begin with. So he's found other ways to be disgusting. Someone told me he was good-looking. That's why I married him."

"There you are, Sandy." Alan walks in.

"Girl talk! Girl talk!" calls Caroline.

Alan backs away and Sandra rises to follow him, but Judy grips her arm. "We've got the cake in here," she says, cutting a piece of the white, frosted cake from Leonard's Bakery.

Sandra tries to eat the piece given to her, crumbling on a paper napkin.

"By the way, I brought you a present," Pat tells Judy. "I have here a letter from Barbara Ruth."

"Oh, my God, another one!" Judy squeals, and Caroline tries to snatch the envelope, but Pat waves it above her head with a tipsy flourish.

"Who is she?" asks Sandra.

"Barbara Ruth Bloom, you poor child." Pat giggles, as if the name explained everything. " 'Dear Pat,' " she reads, " '*Baruch HaShem* I am delivered of my sixth child, Barak.' "

"Jesus H. Christ," drawls Judy.

"Will you listen?" demands Pat. " 'I called my parents and asked them once again to come to Israel and see their grandchildren, but because they felt the trip would be too strenuous, they sent a gift instead, which I distributed to the needy of Me'ah She'arim.' "

Pat clutches herself with laughter. "You have to understand"—she gasps to Sandra—"what kind of people her parents are."

"Ira and Shirley Bloom," Judy explains, "live way up on Tantalus, and they're filthy rich. They each inherited. I forget what they did. I think Ira was a lawyer, but I mean, mainly they had this daughter they named Barbara Ruth."

"But wait," Caroline puts in. "You've got to tell about their house first. They have a house on the crest of the ridge. Spectacular. They spent a fortune. It was built for them by a New York architect and then redone to look lived in. The whole thing was a complete aggravation. Not only was it constantly remodeled—and they have my total sympathy on that—but it was always sliding down the mountain. Not sliding so you could see, but sort of inching down, sidling down, since they didn't use a local architect and it wasn't really entrenched in the rock. So after every rainstorm they have to spend thousands jacking the place up, redoing the retaining walls."

"Caroline," says Judy, "we're talking about Barbara Ruth."

"I know, I know," Caroline protests. "I was setting the scene."

"Listen, it's my letter; would you let me tell?" Pat orders. "Okay. They had one daughter, Barbara Ruth. And she worked for me as a hygienist in Miami. She was terrible, by the way. She could not be trusted to install braces without supervision. She didn't cement well; her brackets popped off within days. She soldered the wrong wires together. Unmitigated disaster."

"I'm confused," says Sandra. "How did she get to Miami from Hawaii?"

"Just listen." Judy shushes. "She grew up with these overprotective parents and then went off to the University of Miami, where she met and married a Sikh."

"Oh my God." Sandra laughs. "Did she convert?"

"Of course."

"What was he like?"

"How should I know?" asks Pat. "I never met him. This happened when she was about nineteen. She worked for me much later."

Caroline stretches out her legs and curls her toes. Unwatched on the TV, Barbra Streisand and Robert Redford meet again years later. "Well," says Caroline, "he was about six two, not counting his turban, and he rode a phallic black motorcycle."

"How do you know?" Judy demands.

"I'm guessing," says Caroline. "He made her feel for the first time like a whole woman."

Pat pours herself another drink. "That's antifeminist crap," she says. "We're talking about a young woman led into an exploitative relationship and losing her identity. Becoming a Sikh, for God's sake."

"Oh, come on," says Caroline. "She had a lot of fun. I lost mine to a British exchange student at Columbia. He was quite impressive. Went back and became an MP. I get all sentimental when I think about it. I feel like Nathan Hale. I only regret that I have but one—"

"Shut up, Caroline. The point is, the marriage didn't last."

"What did her parents do?" asks Sandra.

"Paid," says Pat. "They just kept paying. They bought her an apartment in Miami. They bought her beautiful clothes."

"She was really homely," adds Judy.

"But she had one beauty," Caroline amends. "Long, uncontrollable, flaming red hair."

"Oh, please." Pat grimaces. "Let's just say she had very lovely red hair, which she didn't really take care of. She never *did* anything with it."

Judy ruffles her own short peroxide-blond curls. "And her face didn't really live up to it."

"Anyway," Pat continues, "after her divorce she got the job with me. And she went into a deep depression. Most of my girls work for one or two years, get married, then carry on eight months into pregnancy and quit. But as they kept leaving, Barbara Ruth just stayed on and on. She never got any better at wiring either. Also, she was depressed by all these women big with child. She'd had a miscarriage by the Sikh. For which I told her she should be grateful. We'd gotten quite close by this time. Terence tried several times to fix her up with grad students at Coral Gables. In the end she decided to come back home."

"Was she still a Sikh?" asks Sandra.

"She was in therapy," answers Judy. "That's when I met her. We were cleaning teeth together at Kaiser Dental Clinic. She was very, very quiet. Almost stopped talking. She would work all day and then go home to her parents. They bought her a little white Alfa, and she drove it back and forth from home to work. Twenty-eight years old, and that was all she did."

"Then one Rosh Hashanah," Caroline interrupts, "I

was sitting at the temple—this was before Bet Knesset started—and Barbara Ruth walks in. Total shock."

"Will you let me talk?" Judy snaps. "It wasn't such a total shock. Her marriage was over. She wasn't *really* a Sikh. It was a phase. She'd had some kind of quickie conversion. But now she wanted to learn. So she studied for conversion to Judaism with Rabbi Siegel. He was incredible. He said she didn't need conversion, so they called it a confirmation ceremony, and since we don't have a *mikveh* here, she immersed herself out in the waves at Sandy Beach."

"Let me guess." Sandra tries to join in. "She began to talk again. Her parents forgave her."

"Wrong, wrong, wrong," declares Pat.

Judy shifts restlessly on the couch. "Just let me finish. She took a course in marine biology in the UH extension program. And there she met Brian Akimoto."

"He had the most beautiful body," says Caroline, "slim and muscular, but not brawny. He made her feel like a woman again."

"You never met him," Judy points out. "He had a good build, but he was short, like Ephrie. A real local type. He came from Kalihi, and he was studying kelp harvesting. He was the teaching assistant in Barbara Ruth's course. A real fisherman. He did it all: crab hunting, spear fishing. As a kid, he'd worked summers on a tuna boat."

"Meanwhile," Caroline breaks in, "Ira and Shirley Bloom, who had been paying and paying and jacking their house up, start to feel intimations of mortality. They have one daughter, Barbara Ruth. One source of grandchildren."

"Wait a minute," protests Sandra. "They aren't going to decide Brian Akimoto is suitable!"

"Of course not. I'm just trying to describe the extent of their aggravation. I mean, everyone knew they were the richest unaffiliated Jews on Oahu, and the temple couldn't get a cent from them. But the thought of inter-marriage and no grandchildren was driving them crazy."

Raising her voice, Judy reclaims her story. "Brian was definitely interested. He took Barbara Ruth hiking to Hau'ula. He took her to an all-pidgin review at the Waikiki Shell. I don't know what they saw in each other, but they fell in love."

"Respect and trust—that was their secret," suggests Pat.

"Loneliness. Hormones," Caroline volunteers.

"Anyway," Judy concludes, "she came to work every day more cheerful, more radiant. They weren't even sleeping together."

"How do you know?"

"I asked. She met his family. Then she forced poor Shirley and Ira to invite him to dinner. When Barbara Ruth told me how he came, I knew he was serious. He bought a whole new-caught *ulua*, twenty-eight inches from head to tail, wrapped in ti leaves. You've got to un-derstand, for local people this is it. Roses mean nothing. When you get a fish, you know it's real. I told Barbara she'd better get ready for the big one. Listen, let me tell you about this fish. Not only did he convert to marry her. This simple local boy left Hawaii, his family, everything. You see, after Barbara had emerged from therapy and the waves at Sandy Beach, she wanted a completely new life. I could see the change right away, because at the clinic she suddenly became a neat-freak. This was the girl who had received *warnings* about tying back her hair. Now she was sterilizing instruments every two minutes. She was vegetarian for a while, then macrobiotic. Just from one craziness to another, like she was looking for something to be compulsive about. And finally she settled on being Jewish. She evolved this dream—of living a totally Orthodox existence. And Brian went along. He converted here and then, would you believe, they moved to Me'ah She'arim. Brian reconverted under an Orthodox rabbi, learned Hebrew, and took the name Yehudah. Barbara Ruth cut off her hair. Right away they started having babies. Naturally Shirley and Ira are beside themselves. 'What have we done wrong? We gave her everything! Why did she do it? We never even sent her to Sunday school!' Here's their only daughter living with black-hats so black they burn bus stops and throw rocks at cars driving by on Shabbat. They are in agony, and they do the only thing they know how. They send huge, huge amounts of money."

" 'The children are well, *baruch HaShem,*' " Pat reads from the letter. " 'My oldest, Yael, is now nine years old. How blessed we are to see our children learn and grow. Yehudah is still working as a tour guide in Eilat. He is a gift to the tourist bureau, with his fluent Japanese and his golden *nefesh*. I often remember the day I first met him. I felt suddenly that his name, Akimoto, was an omen. The Japanese syllables spell out *HaShem*'s promise "and I will raise him up." *V'hakimoti*. How he has fulfilled this prophecy, raising up his family, elevating every act so that each is holy. For me, ours was the most beautiful seder in Me'ah She'arim because Yehudah led it with such love and understanding. And at Succoth, the four corners of our *succah* roof seemed to lift toward the sky in prayer.

Tears of joy fill my eyes when I think how every year on that holiday our children run in and out of the villa, carrying the silver and the platters of food. I feel such an indescribable peace and happiness in simple things—lighting the Sabbath candles, looking up at the stars through the thatch of the *succah*, baking bread, sending money to the Girls' Orphanage, ironing little shirts and dresses to give to the little needy children of Me'ah She'arim. Pat, look through the rummage sales and send me any used clothes or toys that you can find.

" 'I write this letter with a full heart, feeling that every day is a blessing, each new child a sign, one star in *HaShem*'s covenant. One day our people will be gathered up. *Im yirtzeh HaShem*, tomorrow we will welcome the Messiah.

" 'My love and prayers with you,

" 'Brochah-Ruchel Akimoto.' "

～～～

At Oahu Prep, Sandra has given up trying to teach in French. She finds that her French class does not pick up irregular verb conjugations from pure idiomatic dialogue. She types up grammar review sheets to supplement the green-and-purple "grammar tips" in the text. Sandra and her classes maintain only the thinnest shell of the oral approach. *"Maintenant,"* Sandra says, "we will study reflexive verbs." And the students ask, *"Pourquoi est-ce que le* verb over here instead of over there?" Sandra feels that she is cheating, but she finds that she cannot make herself understood in French. Sometimes, as she diagrams verb endings on the overhead projector or stops to replay a tape of market vendors hawking their wares, she worries that her booming department chair will enter and denounce her teaching with French obscenities. Sandra imagines herself dismissed, crushed by Hilda's platform shoes, smothered by the floral yardage in her idiomatic muumuu.

The Monday after the Tawils' party, Sandra's French II class struggles through *Eugénie Grandet*. Pacing the floor, Sandra listens to Candice read and translate from her heavily annotated *Graded French Reader*. " *'Il venait lui donner le bras pour descendre au déjeuner,'* " Candice reads. " *'Il la regardait d'un oeil presque bon.'* He looked at her with his one good eye."

"No, Candice." Sandra stifles laughter. "Both of his eyes were working fine. Try a less literal translation."

"His one good eye," Candice repeats.

"Consider the context. How does this old man feel toward the girl?"

"Je ne sais pas," says Candice.

"Class, can you help us out?" Sandra waits a moment, according to ritual. Then she answers her own question. "He felt benevolent. He cast upon her *un oeil presque bon*, a benevolent eye. You know, class, as we move on, we're going to be reading some great literature. This is Balzac, here. This is the language of Molière, Racine, Descartes, Sartre. Let's get out of the mind-set of those first-year textbooks that gave us such insight into contemporary French grocery lists."

The door swings open, and Hilda marches in, to pick up the skiing in Quebec filmstrip. *"En français, ma chère,"* she hisses.

That afternoon at the French teachers' meeting, Hilda stands and presents a reminder of the aims of the

Oahu Prep Modern Language Department. "We have an audiovisual-cultural approach," Hilda tells them patiently. As Sandra has learned, English is spoken at department meetings. Hilda warms to her subject. "Literature, formal constructions, all this is important. But learning a language boils down to one thing. Oral survival skills. Authentic pronunciation, current popular constructions are imperative. How are the kids going to manage in France if they are afraid to talk? We have to keep them talking. Make them live, breathe, and dream French. Total immersion is what we're after. Context will come. The fine points will come. I want them to sound French. I want them to go to Paris and order a beer and be mistaken for French kids."

Honestly puzzled, Sandra asks, "But whyever would they want to be mistaken like that?"

∽

"Alan," Sandra calls into the other room as she dumps her purse and books on the couch. "Alan, I said something terrible today at the meeting. Does that mean I could lose my job?"

"Can't hear you, hon." Alan emerges from the hall closet, carrying their folding luggage cart. "The meat came in!" he cries, out of breath. "Come down and give me a hand."

The car is crammed with frozen kosher meat wrapped in white paper packages. Each parcel is labeled with a grease pencil: LAMB. HAMBERG. CHIX. Sandra straps a turkey and packages of stew meat to the luggage cart. Alan follows, carrying the rib eye roast. Their neighbors stare as they ride the elevator up and down, carting their frozen meat to the tenth floor.

"Good thing we got the freezer," Alan says. They stand back and look proudly at their enormous Sears freezer. It's a bit out of scale for the apartment, and they had to put it outside the kitchen in the hall, but it does hold all the meat. "Well," Alan sings out, "just in time. I'm starving. What'll we have?"

"There isn't time to thaw something for tonight," Sandra reminds him. She flops down and unfolds the paper, careful to keep the newsprint away from the couch. "Alan," she says, "I don't think my students are ever going to sound French. In Paris, people will know they're spoiled American teenagers right away."

"Rich tourists," says Alan. "They'll get preferential treatment. Who cares if they sound French?"

"Well." Sandra sighs. "The other problem is they don't *know* any French. I wish Hilda would get off my back. I just want to teach them some *verbs*. I wish she'd cut this cultural crap."

"Sandy!" Alan laughs. "Is this the girl with Monet posters in her room, who went around singing because she got into the Proust seminar and was going to use quiet diplomacy to make France pro-Israel?"

"Well, I may yet," Sandra protests. "But really, Alan, do you think I'm going to lose my job?"

"No," Alan answers roundly. "I think you're wonderful. And I've always thought prep schools were fascist. You just keep your sense of humor. *Tournez l'autre chic.*"

"Hey, stop!" Sandra yelps. "No tickling."

"*Comment?*" asks Alan.

⌒⌒⌒

Sandra has some difficulty taking off time for both days of Rosh Hashanah. Her dean understood completely about the first day, but he thought a second day was a bit excessive. "You know," Dean Walker said, "we've had quite a few Jewish students, and none of them took two days. I guess the kids hate to miss anything here at school. Oahu Prep is a real twenty-four-hour experience. But use your own judgment."

Rosh Hashanah services run long because Bet Knesset has a translation policy. Terence stands next to Ephrie, and at intervals he reads aloud from the English.

Sandra sighs and estimates the pages left until the end. Judy glares at her sons and raises a threatening hand to Namir, who hangs upside down over his chair. " 'I remember your youthful devotion, the love of your bridal days,' " Terence reads. " 'How you followed me through the wilderness, through a land unsown.' "

Sandra looks at Judy and tries to imagine her raking chicken manure in Israel. "If I'd married an American, I'd be there now," Judy has said.

" *'V'hakimoti lach brit olam,'* " Ephrie continues, and he translates himself: "I will build up for you an eternal covenant."

"The omen." Caroline giggles, nudging Sandra. "Barbara Ruth's omen, *v'hakimoti.* See, my theory is she was lusting for Brian all along, but then she heard his name calling her in shul. 'Akimoto.' That was what did it. That's why they had to go and build the land. One word, and they forgot everything their parents tried to teach them."

Ephrie reads on: " *'Havain yakir li Ephraim.'* " His voice catches hoarsely.

"I'll take it," Terence says, and he declaims in the

accent he acquired at Oxford: " 'Is it because Ephraim is my favorite son, my beloved child? As often as I speak of him—' "

"I speak *to* him," Ephrie bursts out. "I speak—whatchyoucall—words, anger, to him."

Terence continues smoothly: " 'I will remember him yet. My heart yearns for him.' "

"Guts," Ephrie corrects, voice choking. "My guts are burning up for him, but I have pity."

Below, in the congregation, Pat leans forward and whispers to Sandra. "It's always an ego trip for Ephrie. He breaks up every year when he reads his name in that verse."

Ephrie catches Pat's stage whisper and looks up, eyes red with fierce tears. "It's not just because it's my name," he says.

⌒⌒⌒

Pat Glueck has become increasingly dissatisfied with the services at Bet Knesset. She calls for a meeting at the Shabbat Tshuvah new members wine-and-cheese *kiddush*. "This is the Sabbath of Repentance," she says, nibbling a sliver of goat cheese. "This is the last chance to change before Yom Kippur, right? So now maybe we should talk about where our group is heading. I think we have a quorum of concerned people."

The Tawils and the Lefkowitzes gather around, along with a few college students and a grizzled tramp who often stops by for the food after services. Pat faces the congregation and announces, "Terence and I have discussed this issue, and we want to share our views with you. I come to shul to pray, not to watch a male show. I want women counted in the minyan. I want women to lead the service, have *aliyahs*, and take a leadership role."

Ephrie smiles benignly. "Pat," he proclaims, "anything you want to lead you lead. As soon as you learn Hebrew—then I take a break."

"That's not the issue, Ephrie, and you know it." Pat huffs.

"Yes, it is the issue," snaps Judy. "My husband is trying to say that this group was chartered to run traditional services."

Terence Glueck knits his brows professorially as he reminds them, "Historically we often find that in time, traditions lose their psychological potency. Rituals become emotionally bankrupt."

"As far as I'm concerned," Pat breaks in, "egalitarianism is the moral crux of the Conservative movement in America."

"I don't think that's true," Sandra says. "And you're not speaking for all of us."

Caroline speaks up suddenly. "I'm for Pat," she says. "We need more group participation here."

"Wait a minute," Alan protests. "I grew up in a Conservative congregation, and gender wasn't an issue for us. I think I would be uncomfortable if—"

"Uncomfortable!" Pat's voice rises. "How do you think women feel, thrust into the audience? Always the echo in responsive readings. I want to lead. The Torah reading is the heart of the service. The *aliyah* is the heart of the reading. And that's just where I'm excluded! For three years I've sat here patiently. I'm not a new member. I've shown my commitment. Now I want this group to give a little back to me. Let's face it. What we've got here is a boys' club. This is my holy book too, and I want a piece of the action. I want to sing. I want to mourn. It's a crime to shut me out. You are negating me. You are denying me and relegating me to second class because you think that I'm impure."

Alan backs away from Pat's torrential words. Behind him, the tramp loads a basket of crackers into his bag. He sips delicately from a bottle of Manischewitz. "Pat," Alan says, "I don't think you're impure. I know we can resolve this. I've heard in some places couples go up together for *aliyahs*."

Pat scoffs. "Don't do me any favors. I don't want to make half a blessing. I'm not part of Terence. I'm my own person, and I want an individual leadership role. I'm telling you these services are patronizing, and I want *in*."

"Well, I'm going to say something dirty," Judy warns. "But you asked for it, Pat. You really did. If you want to be a man so badly, why don't you try and grow a penis?"

Pat turns on Judy. "And if you want to live like Brochah-Ruchel, move to Me'ah She'arim. You laugh at her, but I think her life is what you've always wanted. You pretend to be liberal. Inside, you're literal and rigid. You're afraid of change, and you want to climb into a paternalistic hole and get pregnant and follow orders every day because that's safe."

Judy doesn't answer.

At the wine-and-cheese table, the tramp puts down his bottle. "My dear," he confides to Pat. "I grew up in a small town." He loses his train of thought and wanders outdoors.

Alan breaks the silence. "Whatever happens," he

urges, "let's not break up the group we've got. We're such a small community and so fragmented already. It's so important to stay together. We can compromise—right, Ephrie?"

Ephrie sighs. "I couldn't have women up there with me," he says. "Not because of me—I wouldn't leave the shul for myself. But if I stayed, it would be shameful for my father's memory."

"If Ephrie leaves, I go too," says one of the college students.

"You're breaking up the minyan," Terence accuses Ephrie.

"And you don't care about the content of these services at all," adds Pat. "You're motivated by pure sentiment and emotion."

"So are you," Ephrie answers. "So are you."

○～○

Sandra's French classes make a poor showing on the departmental midterm that Hilda composed. As Sandra records her grades, she sees that her students' median score is several points lower than Hilda's. She looks miserably at the smiling photo of Alan on the wall of her office cubicle. She wants to phone him, but he is probably in the emergency room. In the next cubicle, she hears Liz whispering to Michael about the U.S. history lesson plan. The whole faculty thinks the two are having an affair.

Sandra pulls her lunch from her desk drawer. Though she doesn't eat the cafeteria meat, she usually takes her brown bag up to the teachers' dining hall to be sociable. Today she can't face the other French teachers with the midterm grades. She bites into her turkey sandwich.

They had opened up all the leaves on their drop-leaf table and invited the Tawils for Thanksgiving. Though it is hard to accept the schism in Bet Knesset, she and Alan now go to Ephrie's services on Saturday morning. Ephrie has trouble finding ten men for a minyan. The Gluecks count women. For some reason, the situation reminds Sandra of her mother's injunction: Don't take the last piece of cake; take half of what's left. She imagines Ephrie's new group splitting just as Bet Knesset had. Splitting like infinitely divisible cake. Scattering like crumbs.

"Mrs. Lefkowitz?" A student messenger from the office hands her a note. Heart pounding, Sandra puts down her half-eaten sandwich and walks to the dean's office. He can't know about the midterm grades yet, but Hilda must have complained. The courtyard seems unbearably bright. Students loll under the trees, reading and talking. The sky is a cloudless, searing blue.

"Sandra!" Tim Walker hails her as she enters his office. "How's it going?"

"Very well, thanks." Sandra takes a seat near the dean's Yale rolltop desk.

"Well, I know you're busy, and I've got to run, so I'll make it short. We've got the scores on the National Council of French Teachers exam, and they gave me a certificate of commendation to pass on to you as the teacher of Ginnie Corpuz, who won—uh, let's see—third place nationally. So here you are. It's just super, the job you're doing with the kids. Good going."

Sandra bounds into her next class. Smiling joyously, she passes back the heavily corrected midterms. She wants to congratulate the third-place national champion in front of all the students, but Ginnie is absent. Sandra contents herself with trying to encourage her depressed class. "Improvement counts," she reminds them. "You can all redeem yourselves on the final."

The Closet

When she got home from work, Evelyn realized that her sister was now living full time in the closet. It was a big closet that spread out under the eaves. The house was built in the old Hawaiian style, two stories and white, with a long porch in front and thick glass windows instead of louvres. There was even a cellar faced with stone—a rarity. Evelyn and her sister had a real old-fashioned mainland house dug into the ground. In the thirties there had been a terraced garden. What remained was a macadamia-nut tree that pressed against the second-story windows. All the plants pressed on the house, damp leaves against the glass. The Manoa rains bent and warped the wooden doors. That morning Evelyn had thought maybe her sister was stuck, that the closet door had jammed up there.

"Hit the top and pull the knob down at the same time," she called through the door. "Turn the knob and pull it down and hit the top above your head."

There was no answer.

That afternoon, when Evelyn walked in from the bus stop, the house was still. Lily's clothes and her books had been neatly cleared out of the rest of the house. Her toothbrush and even her old piano music were gone. The music rack and the piano bench were empty.

Lily had often gone up to the closet during the day. They were used to that. Lily was ill. Her illness had many shifting names and ambiguities. Her actions, however, seemed to become more pointed and specific every year. She would not drive. Then she would not leave the house. She would not cook or play the piano, pick up the telephone, or answer the door. Now, it seemed, she would not come downstairs.

Evelyn told her husband about it when he came home. "Should we call the doctor?" she asked him. "Should we call Roselva?" Roselva was Lily's case worker from the Hawaii Department of Human Services.

"Oh, for God's sake," Stan said.

"I'm sorry," Evelyn said, and she was sorry. It was hard on Stan, living with his sister-in-law in such a state.

"She's forty-nine years old," Stan said, and he paced around the living room.

Evelyn looked at him nervously. She was afraid Stan would blow his top. Lily had always been afraid of him. Stan came from a tall, meat-eating family in Providence, Rhode Island. He grew up wearing shoes in a dark house on a hill, a house rattling with storms and icicles. Evelyn, personally, had never seen it in winter, but the picture was there in her mind, the ice and snowdrifts.

Evelyn made spring rolls with fresh mint leaves for dinner. She steamed some rice and made mock duck and spicy vegetarian meatballs, which her sister loved. She set the table and opened the double doors between the living room and the dining room. Soon the scent would fill the house; it would drift up the stairs into every corner. She imagined somehow that the scent would drift up from her to Lily. It would be like the incense in their Chinese uncle's little temple in Kaimuki. She and Lily used to go there when they were children. They would smell the incense sticks and the candles in the shrine by the brown runoff canal trailing down to the ocean. Now a light haze of smoke drifted from the cooling wok in the kitchen.

Evelyn went to get Stan, and she found him in the basement. He was cracking a macadamia nut in the vise. It was the only way; they were so hard. "Dinner," she said.

They ate by themselves. Afterward, Evelyn took up spring rolls, mock duck, meatballs, rice, and a pitcher of iced tea on a tray for Lily. She left the tray by the closet door. The food was gone in the morning. Only a few rice grains were left.

She started leaving food out every night. Saimin on the hot plate, tofu-and-alfalfa sandwiches on sprouted-wheat rolls, vegetarian Manapua from work. Evelyn worked in Ala Moana Shopping Center at the Golden Apple—famous for selling vegetarian whole food. Evelyn had created a lot of the Golden Apple's recipes. She had been in the vegetarian-shiatsu-acupuncture community for years and had pioneered several techniques for taking the meat, fat, and cholesterol out of Hawaiian food. Admittedly, the vegetarian version often bore no resemblance to the original. Real Manapua—the kind kids bought after school—were big white dumplings, soft and glutinous, made of flour and lard, with a little pork in the center and a red mark on the round surface like the chop mark of a brush painter. Evelyn's whole-wheat-and-bean dumplings were nothing like this. Still, they had their following at the takeout counter. She brought extras home for her sister. She put out her homemade almond cookies and cold drinks. Each morning the food was gone. Lily didn't speak to her from inside the closet. She made no sign that she intended to move back into her own room.

When Lily had been living up in the closet for a week, Stan got nervous, because he needed to get an estimate from the exterminators. He had already scheduled the appointment. The termite-control team had to look at the whole house—and especially the closet. They had to get in there and assess the damage.

"Maybe it can wait," Evelyn suggested as they ate breakfast.

"It's waited thirty years," Stan said. "It's waiting that caused all this in the first place! We've got dry rot, mold, silverfish, beetles. They're talking about a tent job."

"If it's waited thirty years, I guess it can wait a little longer," Evelyn said.

"We've got some walls in the bathroom, they're only paint," Stan said, and he stared over Evelyn's head at the rotting part of the wall where he envisioned a gaping hole above the utility sink. He looked down at the worn wooden floor, which was damp and, he thought, chewed up.

"Don't be upset," Evelyn said.

She didn't know what else to say. Stan hadn't wanted to move into the old house in the first place. Evelyn thought maybe the mainland-style basement brought back unhappy memories for him. Maybe it reminded him of his father, whom he grew up disappointing. Stan's father was a famous theoretical physicist, a big professor at

Brown. He studied the structure of the universe and expected his only son to do the same. Stan was no good at it, and ran away to join the air force so he could be a pilot. He was going to fly fighter planes, screaming off into the sky from aircraft carriers, but in the end the air force decided to send him to Hawaii to be a meteorologist.

"Your parents just let this place rot away." Stan got up from the table.

As Evelyn washed the breakfast dishes, she looked out the window over the sink to where their fence had been. In a storm last winter the fence, hollowed out by termites, had floated up light as a glider and fallen softly into paint splinters in the neighbor's bougainvillea. But what did a fence matter? It was a good house. It was roomy. It had wood floors. How could it be rotten inside? Evelyn couldn't believe Stan when he said that. The place had ceilings high above even Stan's head.

Evelyn and Lily had come to their grandparents' house with some awe as children. It seemed ancient to them. The koa-wood floors were cool and smooth against their bare feet. Everything cool that way was old. Then, years later, when Evelyn and Lily inherited the place, Lily said she was glad Stan and Evelyn were going to live there with her. She said she would be afraid to live there alone. Five years ago Evelyn and Stan had unpacked and taken the master bedroom. They had never owned even half a house before. They'd raised their daughter, Anna, in an apartment near the Ala Wai canal. The balcony there was big enough only for two chairs and Anna's bicycle. The kitchen appliances in that apartment were the color people called avocado. It was really more the color of guacamole left in the refrigerator, or the tint of canned asparagus.

∾◠∾

Evelyn began to come home from work earlier, gradually, almost imperceptibly—a few minutes earlier each day. With a pounding heart she turned her key in the lock. As softly as she could, she pushed open the swollen front door. There was always a cracking sound as the door swung open, no matter what she did. But she slipped off her sandals and hurried in, half expecting to see Lily on the stairs or catch sight of her in the kitchen. She listened for footsteps; her eyes darted over the living room. She hoped to see her sister downstairs, but the hope was mixed up now with a kind of fear because she hadn't seen her for so long.

She imagined Lily cutting open the papayas Stan kept on the counter. Or watching television five hours at a time, curled up in the leaky bean-bag chair that was Anna's before she went to college. Walking through the house in her little tabbies. Lily was small, like Evelyn. They both had size-5 feet. She even imagined Lily instructing yoga classes in the living room. That had been her profession years ago. She would bend, and breathe, and walk around the room, watching her students. Tense shoulders would dissolve at her touch. Clenched muscles would melt. She imagined Lily sitting down at the piano, a lovely Yamaha ruined by the humidity, and playing Chopin in her own curious way, as if she had serious reservations about where the music was going. Lily had soloed with the Honolulu Symphony in 1950, when she was nine, a great event for the family. Evelyn watched as Lily received a three-strand *ilima* lei from Tutu and a money lei from Auntie Maude, dollar bills folded into flowers and strung into a beautiful green mass. Evelyn got a crisp

two-strand *pikake* lei that hung like a long pearl necklace.
After an hour the lei was limp on her neck. It smelled so
sweet the fragrance seemed to wring out and exhaust the
flowers. She got that lei after Lily's performance, because
she was the sister.

But where was Lily now? Maybe in the mornings she
snuck out of the house altogether, slipped down the
street, and took the bus. She could get all the way around
the island if she transferred in Waikiki. All the way
around, or almost, for seventy-five cents. They used to
take the two-hour trip in rattling buses from the YMCA
summer camp. Every summer they went on that field
trip. Lily and Evelyn were on different buses, of course,
with their age groups. In swimming class Evelyn was a
Polliwog, while Lily had already passed her Fish test.
Evelyn was waiting to become a Fish. She was waiting to
get to the blue piano book and the green reading level,
and backflips.

✑

Evelyn began to make mistakes at work. She nearly
scalded herself with hot oil at the deep fryers. She cut her
finger slicing sweet potato and forgot the extra crackle
batter for the tempura. She got behind on the orders,
because all the time she was wondering, Was Lily eating
pistachios on the living-room floor? Shelling them into
the wastebasket? Was she taking a long bath—washing
her hair, leaning back in the tub?

"What's wrong wit' you?" her boss asked her. He was
a young kid just graduated from UH.

"My sister's moved into the closet." Evelyn sighed.

"The closet? How come?"

"I don't know," Evelyn said.

"Whoa," her boss said. "She came out of the closet, and then she went back in?"

On her way to the bus stop each morning, Evelyn began walking back to the house, as if she'd forgotten something. Then she started rushing home in the middle of the day. She thought somehow she could get home when Lily wouldn't expect it. She would meet her on the stairs; she would sit down next to her at the kitchen table, and they would talk. It had to happen, sooner or later. Evelyn left work early; she came late. Every day she tried her luck, testing the odds like a gambler. In the end, she lost her job.

The day her boss fired her, Evelyn stood in her mother's kitchen and brewed a pot of green popcorn tea. This was a strange but soothing drink: green tea with tiny bits of popcorn floating in it. The tea came from a Chinese store in Kaimuki, where her family often had dinner at the King's Garden. They would walk home in the warm twilight past Harry's Music Store, where Lily's music came from—the hardest kind, in manila covers and with black printing, whole chains of tiny black notes, whole archipelagoes.

"I never liked that job," Evelyn explained to Stan when he got home. "I've been thinking about it for a long time. I want to go back and finish my degree. I've just got one more year, and there's a real shortage of chiropractors right now; there's a real need."

"I've got a real need for your sister to get out of that closet," Stan said.

Evelyn gave Stan a back rub. She lay him down on the living-room floor and rolled him out on his back and massaged his ankles. She poked the soles of his feet with the eraser end of a pencil. She knew Stan was thinking about money. She knew he was worrying about the termites. The exterminators were on hold until Lily came down. And no one but Lily knew when that would be. It wasn't a question of asking Lily or reasoning with her. It was one of those things you couldn't change. Like fate. Like the weather. Of course, Stan knew all about the weather; he was a meteorologist. But he hadn't wanted to be one.

At night, in bed, Evelyn could almost hear the bugs chewing the house away. She could hear the soft thuds of the cockroaches flying in the kitchen, batting against the walls. Mold and damp crept over the bathroom tiles. She and Lily had inherited a house dissolving like a white sugar cube into the tropical soil, a succulent white house. Long ago the termites had begun colonizing the cabinets; the ants wove in and out, exploring. For years ferns had been growing on the garage roof. A lush canopy of ferns and deep-green moss. The house had a life of its own. Tenting the whole place would be a custom job. The tent would be rolled out and clipped right onto the house, over the tall roof, around all the corners. The house would have to be wrapped up like a Christmas present for the fumigators, sealed up so none of the bugs and poison would escape. It would cost four thousand dollars, plus their hotel bills while the house was sealed away. They didn't have that kind of money. It wasn't just Lily holding them up.

She lay in bed and imagined Lily curled up in the dark closet like the curled-up frond of a tree fern furled into its tight, secret knot. She imagined Lily gliding up and down the stairs, opening the cupboards, her hair swinging behind her, batting softly against the walls.

᠀ᡇ᠀

The kids came home for winter break and ran through the house like giants. The kids were Anna, their daughter, and her boyfriend, Mike. They were both music-education majors at the University of Puget Sound, and they sang together and banged on the piano. Clouds of dust rose wherever they walked.

Anna sat in the kitchen and caught the flying cockroaches in her bare hands and threw them out the door. Anna was big, like Stan. Almost six feet. She had hazel eyes and hair so thick and long it stood out like a brown cloud around her shoulders. When she braided it down, it bounced back up. She'd inherited the hair from the Hawaiian side of Evelyn's family.

With the kids around, Stan moved differently. His shoulders weren't tight, and he didn't tense up in his neck. Anna was his baby. He'd set out to raise her without the pressure he'd had as a child. Stan had always told Anna—ever since she was three years old—"Listen, no one's telling you what to do, where to go, what kind of person to be." Anna didn't understand all this when she was three, but she did grow up extremely calm. They had raised her without a bedtime and without a curfew, and she was tall and mellow, as some girls are when they grow up with lots of boyfriends and few rules. Anna and Mike spent their days out at the beach. Fine sand spread over the kitchen floorboards and in between the cushions of the couch.

When Evelyn left dinner for Lily by the closet door, Anna came upstairs with her. "Hi, Auntie," she called through the door, "Come out soon. We miss you. The piano is lonely."

"Anna," Stan said at dinner. "It's no joke. Auntie has got Mom waiting on her hand and foot."

"I guess she likes it in there," Anna said. At her side, Mike ate steadily.

Evelyn dreamed that night that she was inside the closet. She'd forgotten how big it was. There was an antique sofa and a phonograph, a pair of tap shoes, and a stack of books up to the round porthole window. *Little Women* and *Doctor Doolittle*, twelve Oz books and algebra texts. Lily sat in a wicker rocking chair in there, crocheting.

A scream woke Evelyn. It took her breath away. Lily! she thought. Stan sprang up. They rushed downstairs and nearly collided with Lily, wide-eyed in the pale light of the open refrigerator. Mike stood naked at the kitchen door.

Mike looked around bewildered, sunburned and hairy. "I was hungry," he said.

"Lily!" Evelyn said. "Please. I want to talk to you." But Lily had already started to run.

"Lily! Lily!" Stan yelled, and he scrambled after her up the stairs. He caught at her wrist, but she pulled away so hard he lost his balance and fell. Lily rushed up the stairs and out of sight.

"Stan, you scared her!" Evelyn said. She looked at Stan and Mike. "You scared her. Both of you."

Mike was still standing there naked. What was wrong with him? Why didn't he put something on? Where was Anna?

Anna had slept through the whole thing.

❧

Stan took off from work and made phone calls. He stayed home the next day too, so that he and Evelyn could talk with Roselva, the social worker.

Roselva came and embraced them both. She wore a red muumuu and carried Lily's files in a canvas Honolulu Academy of Arts tote bag.

They sat down together in the living room.

"Do you think she's in danger?" Roselva asked.

"In danger? Of course not," Stan said. "She's not exactly starving. She comes down, we think, to use the facilities. But not when we're around."

Roselva took some notes. "Do you think she's afraid of something?"

"No," Evelyn said.

"Well, I'll go and try to talk to her," said Roselva. Stan got up, but she shook her head. "I think she'll want to speak to me privately," she said, and she walked up the stairs.

Stan and Evelyn sat in the living room and strained their ears. They heard the creak of the stairs and the squeak of the second-floor landing. "You think she's really going to come out and talk to her?" Evelyn asked Stan.

"Not a chance," Stan said.

But half an hour passed. Evelyn stood by the front window and watched the light rain drift in a mist down the street. Birds splashed in pools of water between the roots of the macadamia-nut tree. In the winter she and Lily used to go mud-sliding near Paradise Park, up at Jackass Ginger. They took torn cardboard boxes and hiked up, ankle deep in mud. They grasped the slick stems of the giant philodendrons, they ducked under the twisting vines. Invisible birds flew overhead among the leaves. There was a trickle of water, a hum of mosquitoes. When they got to the top they flung themselves down on the flattened boxes. Covered with mud, they trudged back up again, scratched their mosquito bites, slicked their hair back in muddy waves. Hidden beyond the trees was the cool pure reservoir, deep, clear, and forbidden.

"Well," Roselva said. She startled Evelyn and Stan as she came back into the living room.

"She came out?" Stan asked.

"She came out," said Roselva.

"What did she say?" Evelyn asked. "What does she want?"

"She wants to stay where she is." Roselva shut her notebook. "I know this is very hard for you."

"Isn't there something you can do?" Stan asked.

"Well," Roselva said. "The state can't just go up there and police her lifestyle."

"Lifestyle! But she's sick," Stan said.

"Yes, she is ill, but she does have rights," Roselva said.

"So my wife has to spend her nights cooking for this woman? This is a manipulative recluse we have up there," Stan said. "This is a woman with a bunker mentality. What if she goes berserk one night? What if she decides to burn the house down?"

"There are groups—for families," Roselva said. "There are resources. I know this is a big adjustment to make."

"We can't adjust to this," Stan said. "We can't live like this."

"But the fact is," Roselva said, "she's in no danger, either to herself or to the family. There is no sign of drug abuse, sexual abuse, or alcoholism. She's not a runaway, of course."

"No!" Stan threw up his hands. "It's just the opposite!" And of course this was true. Lily was not a runaway. Somehow she had done the other thing. Somehow she had gone into internal exile. At the top of the house she had become a stowaway.

                          ⟳

Rain washed the valley green. It ran down green ridges into tiny waterfalls and rivulets and then into Manoa Stream. The ground was soft, the black streets sparkled. Anna and Mike came home that night pink with the sun from the beach in Waimanalo. "You guys should come with us tomorrow," Mike said.

"It's not raining out there," Anna told them.

"We'll see," Stan said. He glanced up at the ceiling in his aggravation, as if Lily could see them. But the next day was Saturday, so they went.

Early in the morning, Evelyn packed a cooler with tofu sandwiches, carrot and celery sticks, grapes, bottled water, tangerines, and Maui potato chips. She took a bottle of meat tenderizer as well—to rub on in case someone was stung by jellyfish. Then, at the last minute, she ran up the stairs to the closet door. "Lily, do you want to come to the beach?" she asked. "I think it would be good for you to get out of the house. Get some exercise."

She waited, but there was no response. "I'm leaving you some fruit," she said. She left a little pyramid of tangerines by the door.

They drove out to the other side of the island, and

the sea spread out green before them, violet blue in the distance. The sky was dry and distant, as if rain had never existed.

When they unfurled their tatami mats, the white sand whipped up and sent tiny, almost transparent crabs scurrying into new holes. Anna and Mike plunged into the surf, bobbing and paddling out into the waves. The wet sand sucked up their leaping footprints. Evelyn followed them slowly. She stood where the waves broke at her waist. The air was sweet and salty, like dried salted plums. Maybe they should stop and buy some on the way home. They always used to stop on the way home from the beach and finger the racks of dried seeds. There was dried lemon peel; you peeled it open and picked out the bitter seeds before you ate it, tangy and salt-dusted. There were bags of shredded ginger, wet and fibrous mango strips, juicy black rock-salt plums you sucked until the pits scraped your palate, dried kumquats, plump and tart. I should get some for Lily, she thought as she bobbed over the waves.

On shore, Stan slept, out among the sea grapes, eyes shut, zinc oxide on his nose. The kids were swimming away, paddling farther out like a pair of Irish setters. And, in between, Evelyn stood in the water. She was still thinking about Lily. She couldn't help it, even out there in the ocean. Lily lived now in her mind, with her piano and her yoga mats and her lunchbox from school, her books, her tap shoes—she'd set up housekeeping. When Evelyn swam, Lily was swimming. When she dreamed, Lily was dreaming. Always her sister was with her. The memory of her filled Evelyn. Every tiny eyelash of her. The touch of her dog-eared piano music, paper worn soft as cloth, the origami boxes that she had made, the school uniforms, Black Watch plaid and white short-sleeved shirts and sandals. The firecrackers on New Year's at the splintering old temple with its litchi tree, the ground carpeted with red wrappers and litchis. They were all there inside Evelyn. They filled her to the brim, the tiniest details of her sister. No matter how she tried, she could not stop thinking about Lily. It was because she would never get her back.

No one but Evelyn knew anymore what Lily used to be. No one else knew the record and the history of her brilliant life—all her accomplishments, playing the piano and swimming, all her days. They lasted only in Evelyn's memory. No one else could picture them. That was the worst thing for Evelyn—that somehow she was the last of her sister's family and friends, the last of the listeners from those old recitals and the Young People's Concert with the symphony, when Lily played in her muumuu with her tiny perfect fingers, her hair braided in two glossy braids. Her sound was big and serene. She was like a jockey riding that black concert-grand piano. Now all the applause was gone, and all that hope; and that old Lily, the one Evelyn so looked up to, now lived in Evelyn's head.

Evelyn stood waist deep in the ocean, and she jumped over the crests of the incoming waves. She kicked her feet at the smooth sand under her. "Get out of my head," she called into the wind. And she thought, Stay in the closet but get out of my head. She didn't mind bringing dinner to the closet door, or taking away the dirty plates; she didn't mind, even if Lily came downstairs while they were asleep. None of that mattered. It was the old thoughts and feelings that welled up inside her. The memories that rose up. That was what was hard to bear. She watched the kids bobbing in the distance. She took a deep breath and let it out slowly. She breathed out, as if she could blow Lily back into the world. Lily believed in breathing. It was the center of yoga. Breathing was the most important thing.

Shivering, Evelyn walked in onto the beach, and the white foam licked her heels. The ocean rose up behind her. Big, but not big enough.

✿

Tight-wrapped lumpia boiled up to the top of the bubbling oil, and Evelyn skimmed them out with her open wire ladle. The kids were already sitting at the table. Evelyn set aside four lumpia on a paper towel for Lily and took them upstairs with a little dish of sauce. "It's ridiculous," Stan was telling the kids downstairs. "Ridiculous." Evelyn knelt down and put the plate of lumpia by the door. She didn't feel ridiculous. That wasn't the word. She was exhausted and trembling, hot with sunburn between her shoulders. She was aching. But they ate dinner as usual, watched the news on television. The kids went out to a movie. Stan said the sun had done him good.

At night, when she was falling asleep, Evelyn felt the rise and fall of the waves against her body. It had always been that way when they spent the day at the beach. The rhythm of the waves stayed with her, washed over her. She dreamed she was jumping waves with Lily. She dreamed of the nights after those long jumps over waves. How she and Lily would fall asleep with the waves still rushing against them. And the waves rose up in their beds, and the two of them kept on leaping, kicking up the sand, and springing over the white water, heads up over the tangled crests of the waves.

Glossary of Hebrew, Yiddish, and Hawaiian Words

ALEPH BES   Hebrew alphabet

ALIYAH; plural, ALIYOT   the honor of saying a blessing before and after a segment of the Torah reading

ARK   the curtained alcove or cabinet where the Torah scrolls are kept

ASHKENAZIC   Jews and Jewish traditions of Eastern European origin

BAAL KOREH   the reader of the Torah

BAAL TSHUVAH   a returnee or penitent; a person who becomes more observant or pious

BARUCH HASHEM   blessed be His (God's) name—often said in gratitude

BEGED ISH   men's clothing. Biblical law forbids crossdressing.

BET KNESSET   house of assembly; the Hebrew term for synagogue

BIMAH   the synagogue dais

BROCHA   a blessing

CHALLAH; plural, CHALLOT braided loaves of bread eaten on the Sabbath

DAVEN to pray out loud or in an undertone

FRUM pious or devout, said of a ritually observant Jew

GABBAI the congregant member who assigns honors such as *aliyot* and the leading of different parts of the service

GAN a preschool; short for *gan yeladim*, the Hebrew translation of kindergarten

GRINA CUSINA the "greenhorn cousin"; a phrase given currency by a popular Yiddish song of that title

HAGGADAH the book used at the Passover seder table; it narrates the Exodus from Egypt and embodies the prescribed ritual for commemorating the flight and redemption

HAKU LEI a special woven lei worn on the head; the maker weaves in tiny orchids, rosebuds, and ferns, for example, binding the stems together with raffia into a circlet

HALAKHAH; HALAKHIC Jewish law as elaborated in the Talmud and legal codes founded ultimately on biblical law

HANA short for *hana okolele*, a children's taunt; in Hawaiian *Hana* means "work"; *okolele* is the diminutive of *okole*, which means *tuchas*. *Hana okolele* means "they're going to work your backside."

HAOLE in Hawaiian, literally an outsider or interloper; the word is often used to describe Caucasians. (*See also* mainland haole.)

HASHEM word used to refer to God; literally, the Name—substituted to avoid using God's name in vain

HASIDIC   pertaining to the Pietist movement founded by the Baal Shem Tov c. 1735

HILLEL   Hillel organizations are Jewish student centers established by B'nai Brith at universities. The centers are named after the great Rabbi Hillel.

HURBAN   a tragedy, a catastrophe; the Yiddish word used to describe the destruction of the Temple

ILIMA   a small orange flower strung together in tightly packed ropes for leis; considered precious in Hawaii and priced accordingly

IMA   Mommy

IM YIRTZEH HASHEM   God willing

KABBALAH, KABBALISTIC   literally, the tradition; Jewish mysticism

KADDISH   the Aramaic prayer recited to close each part of a Jewish service; also read or chanted by mourners

KETUBAH   the Jewish marriage contract that spells out the rights and responsibilities of husband and wife, written in large part to safeguard the wife

KIDDUSH   a blessing over the wine recited before a festive meal: also refreshments served with wine after the blessing

KIPAH; plural, KIPOT   the skullcap worn by traditional Jews

KITTEL   the white shroud worn as a memento mori by the person leading Rosh Hashanah or Yom Kippur services and sometimes by some congregants as well

KOA   an increasingly rare Hawaiian hardwood with a rich brown tone

KOL NIDRE   the solemn prayer recited three times at the first evening service for Yom Kippur

KUGEL   pudding usually made of noodles in a casserole

LAIIN   to read with proper cantillation from the Torah; a skill requiring knowledge of the melodic pattern assigned to each word in the text and an ability to read the ornamented and unvoweled script of the scrolls

LANAI   the Hawaiian word for patio, or in older homes, verandah

LAU LAU   meat or fish wrapped in ti leaves and then steamed

LUBAVITCHERS   members of an activist Hasidic sect, Chabad, most recently led by Rabbi Menachem Schneerson; the sect works to return Jews to ritual observance

MACHZOR   the prayer book used on the High Holidays

MAILE LEI   an open lei made of the long, green maile vine

MAINLAND HAOLE   a Caucasian from the continental United States—less well thought of than the haole who was born and raised in Hawaii

ME'AH SHE'ARIM   the neighborhood in Jersulam where particularly observant Jews live and work

MECHITZAH   the partition separating the men's and women's sections in an Orthodox synagogue

MESHIACH   the Messiah

MEZUZAH   a capsule affixed to the doorpost of a house; it contains the scriptural reminder that God is one

MIKVEH   a bath used for ritual purification

MINHAG   tradition, custom; often without the full force of *halakhah* and subject to regional variation

MINYAN   the quorum of ten men traditionally required for a Jewish service

MITZVAH   a good deed; fulfillment of a divine commandment

MUSAF   the additional service following the Torah read-

ing; it replaces the additional sacrifice prescribed for
Sabbath and holidays

NEBBISHEH   wimpy, pathetic

NEFESH   soul

NIGGUN   melody

PAREVE   neither dairy nor meat

PEKLACH   little bundles

PIKAKE   a small white jasmine blossom used for leis

POI DOG   a mongrel dog; the name of Rap Replinger's
comedy record, popular in Hawaii in the 1970s

POSK (POSKEN)   to render a ruling in Jewish law

PUPIK   navel

THE REBBE   a title of respect and endearment given by
Hasidim to their leader, Schneerson; other sects also
refer to their respective leaders as the Rebbe

REBBETZIN   wife of a rabbi

SCHVARTZE   Black

SEPHARDIC   Jews and Jewish traditions of Spanish origin

SHABBATON   a Shabbat weekend get-together for praying, singing, socializing, and discussion of the
weekly Torah portion

SHABBAT TSHUVAH   the Sabbath of Repentence, between Rosh Hashanah and Yom Kippur

SHABBES, SHABBOS; also SHABBAT   the Sabbath

SHACHARIT   the morning service

SHEHECHIYANU   a blessing to celebrate a milestone

SHELIACH   an emissary

SHIKSA   non-Jewish woman

SHMATAS   rags

SHOMER SHABBOS   Sabbath observer

SHTICKL   little bit

SHTIEBLE   a tiny synagogue

SHUL   a synagogue

SIDDUR   a prayer book

SUCCAH   a light-roofed temporary booth commemorating Israel's wanderings in the desert; traditionally decorated with harvest fruits and vegetables.

SUCCOTH   the autumn feast of Tabernacles, or booths

TAKEH   an exclamation: really!

TALLIS   a fringed prayer shawl

TALMUD   the principal work of rabbinic literature comprising the Mishnah, or ancient code of Jewish law, and the extensive, discursive commentary of the Gemarah, a rich collection of rabbinic homilies, legal opinions, obiter dicta, legends, and lore

TANACH   the Hebrew Bible, comprising the five books of Moses, the Prophets, and the Sacred Scriptures

TANYA   the mystical book written by Schneur Zalman of Liadi in 1798; studied daily and revered by Hasidim

TAPA   papery cloth made by pounding bark

TEFILLIN   an appliance for morning prayer, composed of leather straps and two boxes containing parchment manuscript selections of scripture; observant male Jews put them on each morning for their daily prayers in order to fulfill the commandment to the faithful that they should "bind them for a sign upon thy hands and they shall be as frontlets between thy eyes"

TIKKUN   a book designed for preparing the public reading of the Torah; contains two columns, one a fully pointed, punctuated and cantillated text for study, and the other a parallel lithographic facsimile of the consonantal text as it appears in the Torah scroll

TREIFE   nonkosher

TSNUISTIC   modest

Tu Bishevat   spring holiday celebrating the first flow of
   sap

Ulua   a jackfish inhabiting Hawaiian waters; adult speci-
   mens can weigh up to two hundred pounds

Yashar Koach   congratulations; may your strength in-
   crease

Yeshivah   a school for Talmud study

Yichus   good connections, good relations, or prestige,
   particularly family pride; also used to mean big deal,
   big wheel

Yiddishkeit   Jewish ways and values

Yizkor   memorial service for the dead

Yontif   holiday

Zeidah, Zeide   Grandpa